IF AT FAUST
YOU DON'T
SUCCEED

IF AT FAUST YOU DON'T SUCCEED

Roger Zelazny &
Robert Sheckley

SPECTRA™

BANTAM BOOKS
NEW YORK • TORONTO • LONDON • SYDNEY • AUCKLAND

IF AT FAUST YOU DON'T SUCCEED
A Bantam Spectra Book / March 1993

SPECTRA and the portrayal of a boxed "s" are trademarks of
Bantam Books, a division of Bantam Doubleday Dell
Publishing Group, Inc.

Library of Congress Cataloging-in-Publication Data
Zelazny, Roger.
If at Faust you don't succeed / Roger Zelazny and Robert Sheckley.
p. cm.
ISBN 0-553-37141-X
1. Faust, d. ca. 1540 — Fiction.   I. Sheckley, Robert, 1928-
II. Title.
PS3576.E43138   1993
813'.54 — dc20   92-30541
CIP

Published simultaneously in the United States and Canada

Bantam Books are published by Bantam Books, a division of Bantam
Doubleday Dell Publishing Group, Inc. Its trademark, consisting of
the words "Bantam Books" and the portrayal of a rooster, is Registered
in U.S. Patent and Trademark Office and in other countries.
Marca Registrada. Bantam Books, 666 Fifth Avenue, New York,
New York 10103.

PRINTED IN THE UNITED STATES OF AMERICA

FFG   0 9 8 7 6 5 4 3 2 1

Acknowledgment

We would like to thank all those who suggested titles for this book — Willie Siros, Scott A. Cupp, Kathi Kimbriel, Jane Lindskold, Walter Jon Williams, and Thorarinn Gunnarson. And yes, *A Faustful of Talers* did have a certain ring to it.

IF AT FAUST
YOU DON'T
SUCCEED

THE CONTEST

Chapter 1

The two representatives of Dark and Light had agreed to meet at the Halfway Tavern in Limbo, there to set in motion the Contest that had been agreed between them.

Limbo was a gray sort of place with very even lighting. It existed between the Abode of Light and the Abode of Dark, a nebulous waiting-room sort of a place, vague at the best of times, but not entirely devoid of qualities.

There was the Halfway Tavern, for example, situated right in the middle of Limbo. The tavern was a queer, rickety old wooden building with a crazy tilted roof. It had been built on the line that separates the part of Limbo nearest Heaven from the part nearest Hell. This place didn't get much business, but it was supported by equal contributions from Light and Dark. It was maintained for the succor of those spirits who happened to find themselves passing through on their way to somewhere else.

"So this is the famous Halfway Tavern!" said the Archangel Michael. "I've never been here before. Do they have a decent sort of a kitchen?"

"It is reputed to be quite good," said Mephistopheles. "But half an hour later, you don't know that you've eaten anything. Persuasive but insubstantial, like the rest of Limbo."

"What's that region down there?" Michael asked, pointing.

Mephistopheles peered. "Oh, that's the waiting area. In the old days, that's where they sent virtuous pagans and unbaptized babies, to wait until something could be done with them. That's not important nowadays, but a lot of people still find their way there for one reason or another."

"I wonder if this is the best place for our meeting," Michael said, for he didn't like the look of some of the things he could see going on in the waiting area.

"It was agreed beforehand between your people and mine," Mephistopheles said. "Limbo is neutral territory, neither fish nor fowl, and certainly not good red meat. What better place for us to meet and begin the contest? Come, shall we go in?"

Michael nodded a little reluctantly, but proceeded into the tavern.

Michael was tall even for an archangel, and well made, since heavenly bodies tended toward athleticism. He had black kinky hair and a hooked nose and olive skin, souvenirs of his Semitic and Persian ancestors. In the old days, Michael had been the guardian angel of Israel, back when there were still local deities who had not been subsumed into the One God system that had proven so popular on Earth. Michael could have had divine cosmetic surgery, since in Heaven you can look any way you want, as long as you don't use your looks for your personal advantage, but he kept his features in memory of the old time, even though he could have been a blue-eyed blond like the other archangels. He thought wiry black hair and aquiline features lent him an air of distinction.

"It's chilly out there," Mephistopheles said, rubbing his hands together briskly. He was of average height for a high officer in the ranks of Darkness, lean, with a long, narrow face, long-fingered hands, and small, shapely feet that he kept in patent-leather pumps. His hair was jet black, sleeked straight back, with a natural part in the middle. He wore a small moustache and a pointed beard of the type known as an imperial because he had been told it made him look untrustworthy.

"But how could it be cold?" Michael asked. "In Limbo there is neither hot nor cold."

"People say that," Mephistopheles said, "but it's not true.

That stuff about Limbo having no qualities is patently false. There's enough light to see by, isn't there? And if you can have light, why not cold?"

"In Limbo," Michael said, somewhat pompously, "one sees by the inner vision."

"And shivers with the internal cold, I suppose," Mephistopheles said. "No, you're wrong about this one, Michael. The wind that blows through Limbo can sometimes be exceedingly biting, blowing as it does from the direction of Despair."

"I'm not wrong," Michael said. "But I suppose it's part of the scheme of things that you and I should disagree, representing, as we do, two glorious but opposed viewpoints. And that is how it should be, of course."

"I think that's my line," Mephistopheles said cheerfully, sitting down in the booth opposite Michael and drawing off his gray silk gloves. "I suppose we can agree that we disagree on almost everything."

"Especially on the matter of cities versus country."

"Yes. Our last contest left that inconclusive, didn't it?"

Mephistopheles was referring to the recent great Millennial contest in which the forces of Dark and Light had contested for control of mankind's destiny for the next thousand years. That contest had centered on the conceit proposed by a young demon named Azzie, who had reenacted the Prince Charming legend, intending to bring it this time to a dolorous conclusion, and to do so through no machinations of his own, but solely through the spirit of Failure expressing itself through Prince Charming's concocted body. Good had gone for the bet, although the contest appeared to be biased in favor of Dark. But Good always enters such contests, assuming that the pull of Good is so great among mankind, a sentimental lot, that someone has to weigh the scales in favor of Evil for there to be anything of an agonal nature going on at all.

The Dark side, for its part, delighted in putting forth schemes of an involved nature, since the Dark side of things feels at home only in complications. Light, being simple, albeit in a doctrinaire way, was pleased to confront the dubious inventions of Dark, oftentimes losing because you can only weight a scale so far before it comes crashing down on one side, which is then considered preordained.

The proprietor of the tavern came over. He was an indistinct fellow, as are all who stay for any length of time in Limbo, and the only definite things about him were the cast in one eye and his large and clumsy feet.

"Yes, my lord," he said to Mephistopheles, louting low. "What can I bring you?"

"An ichor daiquiri will do very nicely," Mephistopheles said.

"Yes, lord. And could I interest you in a slice of devil's food cake? Fresh today!"

"All right. And what else have you got?"

"The ham is very nice today. We have a place in Purgatory that devils it for us especially."

"No blood sausages?"

"That's only on Thursdays."

"Well, bring along the deviled ham," Mephistopheles said. To Michael he remarked, "Can't let the side down, can we?"

"Certainly not. But isn't it time we got down to business?"

"I'm ready," Mephistopheles said. "Did you bring along an agenda?"

"No need," Michael said. "It's all in my head. It has fallen to our lot to decide upon the next Millennial contest. Hopefully, also, we will settle the question of the Goodness or Badness of cities this time around."

"How quickly time passes when you're immortal!" said Mephistopheles. "Being a master of one-pointed concentration has something to do with it too, of course. Well then, let the cities rise like mushrooms."

"Like flowers is an apter image," Michael said.

"Which is the truer image remains to be seen," Mephistopheles said. "So, trot out one of your urban saints and my merry crew of demons and I will have him forswearing Good in no time."

"No, he needn't be a saint," Michael said, demonstrating again Good's irresistible tendency to give up advantages. "And anyhow, we have something more elaborate in mind. Something with a bit of sweep and grandeur to it to be held in a variety of times and places throughout the new millennium. But I'll tell you about that later. For now, are you acquainted with our servant Faust?"

"Of course," Mephistopheles said, though here he committed a typical error of the Dark side, pretending to knowledge that he didn't have. "You mean Johann Faust, of course, the well-known magician and mountebank who resides in—where was it now?—Koenigsberg?"

"Whether or not Faust is a mountebank is still under discussion," Michael said. "But he's not in Koenigsberg. You'll find him in Cracow."

"Of course, I knew that all along," Mephistopheles said. "He's got a little place near the Jagiellonian University, does he not?"

"Not at all," Michael said. "He resides in chambers in Little Casimir Street near the Florian Gate."

"It was on the tip of my tongue," Mephistopheles said. "I'll go to him at once and put the scheme to him. What *is* the scheme, by the way?"

"Here comes your deviled ham," Michael said. "While you eat it, I'll explain."

Chapter
2

Johann Faust was alone in his chambers in Cracow, that city in distant Poland where his peripatetic scholar's path had taken him. The officials of the Jagiellonian University had been glad to have him, for Faust was a considerable scholar who had by heart the most important writings in the world — those of Paracelsus, and Cornelius Agrippa before him, and, before him, the secret writings of Virgil, supreme magician of the Roman days. Faust's chambers were simple — a bare wooden-planked floor, swept clean each morning by the serving girl, who muttered a prayer each time she entered Faust's oval-headed door, and spit between her fingers for good luck, because you need all your luck when you clean up after a man as uncanny as Faust. She had crossed herself when she saw, there on the floor, the pentagram, chalked afresh each morning, with its spaces filled with wriggly Hebrew letters, and with symbols that not even the Masons understood.

The furnishings of the room never changed. In a corner was Faust's alembic. The coal fire in the small fireplace burned faintly but hotly; Faust kept it stoked up night and day, summer and winter, for he suffered from chilblains that never entirely went away. There was a window, but heavy velvet drapes generally kept out the light of the day. Faust liked an even lighting, and his eyes were accustomed to the flicker of the fire and the yellow flames of the candles burning in pewter holders in a dozen places around the room. They were tall candles of good

beeswax that common citizens could not afford. But some of
the wealthy citizens of Cracow kept Faust supplied with these
tapers, which were finer than any seen anywhere but the ca-
thedral. They were scented, these candles, with balsam and
myrrh, and with rare floral essences distilled from the brilliant
flowers of spring. Their odors in part overcame the vapors of
mercury and gold and other metals, whose fumes rendered the
closed chamber unfit for any but an alchemist long practiced
in his art.

Faust was walking up and down his chamber, ten paces in one
direction to the wall with its portrait of Agrippa, ten paces to
the cabinet with its marble bust of Virgil. His long gray scholar's
gown flapped around his spindly legs as he marched, the candles
wavering in the slight breeze of his passing. As he walked he
talked to himself aloud, because long familiarity with that inner
solitude that only the learned know had accustomed him to this
form of social intercourse.

"Learning! Wisdom! Knowledge! The music of the spheres!
The knowledge of what lies at the bottom of the uttermost seas,
the certainty of being able to say what the great cham of China
eats for his breakfast, and what the emperor of the Franks says
to his mistress in the stygian dark of the night! These are fine
things, no doubt! Yet what do they mean to me?"

The blank-eyed bust of Virgil seemed to watch him as he
paced, and on the Roman's thin, pale lips a slight expression
of surprise might have been noticed, because this discourse by
the learned doctor was unlike any that had come from his lips
heretofore.

"Yes, of course," Faust went on, "I know these things, and
many others besides." He chuckled ironically. "I can detect the
harmony of the divine spheres that Pythagoras knew. In my
investigations I have found that still point from which Ar-
chimedes claimed the ability to move the terrestrial globe itself.

And I know that the lever is the self, extended to infinity, and the fulcrum is the esoteric knowledge that it has been my lifetime task to learn. And yet, what does it mean to me, this confabulation of miracles to which I have given countless hours of study? Do I live any better than the most ignorant village swain, who seeks his love among the haystacks? True, I have honor among the old men of the cities, and am renowned among the so-called wise ones, of this country and many others. The king of Czechoslovakia has put a golden circlet on my forehead and declared me peerless among men. Does this cause my ague to diminish when I awaken on a chilly morning? Do the fawning ministrations of the king of France, resplendent in his lynx ruff and soft boots of Spanish leather, with the circlet of Clovis on his narrow head, bring any relief to my dyspepsia, my morning sweats, my evening despair? What have I in fact achieved in my attempts to encompass the ever-expanding sphere of knowledge? What is knowledge to me, what is power, when my body shrivels daily, and my skin draws tight around my features, presaging the skull beneath the mottled flesh, which must in time come out?"

There was a sound outside, but at first Faust heeded it not, so full of his lament was he.

"This pursuit of knowledge is all very well. At one time, when I was a youth, ages, decades ago, I thought that all my heart's yearnings would be satisfied if I could capture that divine essence and distillation of knowledge that only the angels know. Yet how satisfying is knowledge, really? What would I not give for a sound digestion? I sit here and eat my daily gruel, since it is all my stomach can digest, while outside the rude red world bustles on, sweaty and unthinking! What is it to me, this piling up of knowledge upon knowledge, amassing a dungheap of wisdom in which I burrow like a beetle? Is this all there is? Would a man not be better off ending it all? With this slender dagger, for example?"

And so saying he took up a thin-bladed, keenly pointed stiletto that had been presented to him by a student of the great Nicolas Flamel, who was now buried in Paris at the church of Saint-Jacques-la-Boucherie. Faust held it up to the flickering candlelight and watched the reflections play up and down its narrow blade. Turning it this way and that, he said, "Is it in vain, then, that I have learned the several arts of calcination, sublimation, condensation, and crystallization? What good now does my understanding of albification and solidification do for me, when the inner man, Faust the homunculus, the ageless spirit of myself who resides within this aging flesh, is sorrowful and confused, purposeless and adrift? Might it not be better to end it all with this well-made bodkin, inserting it into the pit of my stomach, for example, and ripping upwards, as I have seen the gorgeously costumed Orientals of a distant eastern island do in my visions?"

He turned the stiletto again and again, fascinated by the play of light upon the blade, and the wavering candles seemed to cast a disapproving expression across the white face of Virgil. And there came again that sound that had barely ruffled the surface of his attention: it was the sound of church bells, and Faust remembered belatedly that this was Easter Sunday.

Suddenly, as quickly as it had arisen, his black mood began to dissipate. He moved to the window and opened the drapes.

"I've been breathing too deeply of the fumes of mercury," he said to himself. "I must remember, the Great Work is dangerous to the practitioner, and carries with it on one side the danger of failure, on the other, success and the risk of premature despair. Better for me to go out into the air this fine morning, walk about on the newly sprung grass, even take for myself a glass of beer at the corner tavern, aye, and perhaps a toasted sausage, too, for my digestion feels better this morning. The vapors from the alembic have their counterpart in the vapors of the mind. I'll go forth this instant to dispel them."

And so saying, Faust slipped into his cloak with the ermine trim, a cloak that an emperor might not have scorned, and, making sure he had his wallet, though his credit was high, left his chamber, heading out the front door into the bright sunshine and uncertainties of the new day, uncertainties that even the most skilled of alchemists might not foresee.

Chapter 3

The bells from the many churches of Cracow were sounding their Te Deums as Faust walked along Little Casimir Street, away from the Florian Gate, in the direction of Drapers' Hall in the big market square. He could tell each church's bells by their sound: the high and heavenly carillon from the convent of Mogila, the brilliant steely middle tones of St. Wenceslas, the great rolling voice of St. Stanislaw, and, dominating all, the thrilling bass from the deep bells of the great Church of Our Lady at the corner of the market square. It was a brilliant Easter Sunday, and the sun's golden light seemed to penetrate into every corner of the steep-roofed old city. The sky overhead was a bright blue, and there were soft-edged, puffy little white clouds of the sort painters like to depict as fitting resting-places for cherubs and allegorical figures. So fine a day could not help but cheer Faust's spirits, and so he took the shortcut to the market square along the noisome little alley called the Devil's Walk. Here the buildings bulged out like fat-bellied men in a steam bath, and there was not room for two people to walk abreast. The alley, with the steep overhanging roofs blocking the light, was a place of deep shadow on even the finest day. Faust had not gone ten yards before he began to regret his decision. Should he not have taken the high street, even if it would take a few minutes longer? After all, what did time matter to an alchemist and a philosopher?

He almost turned back, but some stubbornness in his nature decided him to persevere. The final turning of the alley was just ahead, and after that it would give out to the noisy bustle of the market square.

He approached the corner, walking more rapidly now, his scholar's gown rustling as he urged his thin shanks to greater speed. He went by a darkened doorway on his right and another on his left. There was light ahead.

And then there was a voice at his shoulder, saying, "Excuse me, sir, a moment of your time . . ."

Faust stopped and turned, prepared to chastise the importunate wretch who had the temerity to delay him. He looked into the doorway but could see no person. He was about to go on when he heard a whirring sound in the air. His rapid brain told him that something was amiss; but the insight came to him almost simultaneous with the crashing of a blunt object of considerable hardness against his temple. He saw stars for a moment, and great shooting comets, and then knew nothing as black Unconsciousness gathered him into her dark mantle.

Chapter
4

While this was going on, in another part of town, at the little tavern called the Pied Cow, a tall, yellow-haired jackanapes of a fellow was having a morning bowl of borscht at one of the rustic tables set outside. He was a tall, thin fellow, cleanshaven in the new Italian fashion, his clothing a gentleman's cast-offs, his head o'ertopped by a mass of unruly curls. He sat now, thin features intent, red lips pursed as he surveyed the street.

The tavern was situated across the street from Faust's chambers. The Pied Cow was a homely place of no great pretensions, an abode favored by sturdy vagabonds from the four corners of Europe, who had come to Cracow in these years of its prosperity, in that brief golden time between the Hunnish invasions and the ferocious onslaught of the Hungarians, when the city was noted far and wide, not just for its learning, which had attracted Dr. Faust, but also for the prosperity of its citizenry, and for the great merchants who journeyed to this place from Germany and Italy with precious wares.

This jackanapes, whose name was Mack, and whose sobriquet was the Club, a reference to the instrument that he carried in his belt, and used more often than an honest man would, had come to Cracow, some say from Troyes in Frankland, others from the stews of Londontown in distant England, to seek his fortune. Mack the Club was not prepared to let his fortune wait its own sweet time to call. He was an enterprising rogue, quick-witted and not unintelligent, who had spent a year in a monastery learning the scrivener's trade before deciding to follow more direct methods of making his fortune.

Hearing of Faust, he had spied upon the learned doctor, well aware of Faust's reputation as a necromancer who had won great wealth in this world in the form of precious metals used in his alchemical pursuits, and gifts and souvenirs from grateful kings who had found the doctor's remedies efficacious in the treatment of their myriad woes.

Mack had devised a scheme to rob the prominent doctor, figuring that a magician like Faust who has piled up goods in Heaven has little need for the dross of this Earth. Mack had accordingly taken unto himself a confederate, a loutish Lett who had no skill but the ability to waylay passersby by knocking them over the head with his cudgel. Mack had determined that this was the very day on which he would divest Faust of his more portable worldly goods.

For a week Mack and the Lett had scouted out the territory and noted the movements of the good doctor. Faust was a moody sort and not given to those regularities of habit that make honest men so easy to steal from. For one thing, he stayed indoors a lot, pursuing his magical experiments. But even Faust had to come out occasionally, and when he did, his footsteps always moved in a preordained direction, down Little Casimir Street and into the Devil's Walk, the shortcut to the great Jagiellonian University.

When at last Faust emerged on this Easter Sunday, Mack's scheme was set and all was in readiness. The Lett had been stationed in a dark doorway in the alley, and Mack took up his position at the Tavern of the Pied Cow opposite Faust's dwelling place. And now the time had come, for the Lett had agreed to rush back to the tavern to warn Mack if anything went wrong at his end.

Mack finished his borscht, laid down a copper coin for

payment, and, moving in a leisurely way that belied his inner excitement, strolled over to the doctor's residence. A glance up and down the street ascertained that the good folk of the neighborhood were away for Easter services. Under his arm Mack had a parcel of books purporting to give magical formulas. He had picked them up at no cost from a monastery library in Czvniez. If the unexpected should occur and someone should enquire as to his purpose in the doctor's house, Mack could say he was delivering these books, or offering them to the doctor for sale; for Faust was known to collect such things in his quest for the formula for the Philosopher's Stone.

Mack strolled to Faust's house. He knocked at the door for form's sake. No one responded. He had seen the landlady leave earlier for services, her wimple somewhat askew, for she was known to be a tippler, and a basket of herbs and simples on her arm, since the good woman was much given to visiting her sick aunt and plying her with country remedies.

Mack tried the door. It was latched with a big iron key of simple design. Mack had its counterpart in his pocket, and he took it out now and fitted it to the lockhole. The key at first would not budge, and Mack wiggled it back and forth, then withdrew it and greased the key from a small container of badger's fat, a sovereign remedy for sticking locks. The key turned, and he pushed the door open.

The high old house was gloomy within. Mack entered, closing the door behind him. A turn to the left brought him to the door he had long since ascertained led to the doctor's study. He pushed it. It was not locked.

It was twilight in the doctor's room, for the bright sunlight had no direct means of ingress, but rather filtered in after due reflection on the shadowy wall. Virgil's pale bust seemed to watch him as he stepped noiselessly through the room, the floorboards forbearing to creak, so light was his passage. The room still held fumes of mercury and sulphur and burnt candles and mouse droppings. The glass bottles and retorts of the doctor's alchemical equipment stood on a nearby table, stray glints of light reflected from their glassy surfaces. There in one corner was the doctor's sleeping cot, two planks laid across two low trestles, yet with an ermine mantle thrown over it that revealed the doctor's luxurious tastes.

Mack paid no attention to these. They were but the stage settings for his deed, which was to find that which was small, valuable, and—since he was in his own way a connoisseur—beautiful as well. For example, that single emerald lying carelessly by itself on the big deal table that was the doctor's work space, next to the crystal ball with the skull lying next to it. The emerald would do very nicely for openers. Mack made his way toward it. His hand, with its long fingers not too clean around the knuckles, was about to close on the object, when suddenly there was a very loud sound from within the room.

Mack was frozen in midflinch, for that sound, coming as a crash of thunder in the high mountains when the autumn storms come rushing down from the north, seemed to presage a reversal of the natural order of things, for how else explain why Nature's loud hurrah had come from within the room rather than outside where it belonged? And how explain the sudden coruscation of fire that appeared spontaneously in the middle of that dark-walled room, leaping up from the floorboards in great licking tongues of red and orange flame?

Still frozen, his mouth agape with wonder, Mack saw a figure form up, mistily at first and then with sharp definition, in the middle of the flames. It had the appearance of a man, a longheaded man with sleek black hair with a natural part in the middle, with a thin moustache and that short, pointed beard known as an imperial. He was dressed in dark clothing of somber magnificence, and bore with him a roll of parchment tied with a red ribbon.

"Greetings, Dr. Faust," said the figure, stepping out of the flames that then extinguished themselves. "I am Mephistopheles, a prince in the forces of Darkness, thrice holder of the Bad Deed of the Year award from Standard Demonics, one of our great multitemporal corporations."

Mack came unfrozen sufficiently to say, in a clumsy stutter unlike his usual glibness, "Oh. Hello. Pleased to make your acquaintance."

"You are surprised, perhaps, by my somewhat unorthodox entrance?"

"Oh, no, not at all," Mack said, for whatever else he would think when his brain unfroze sufficiently to permit cerebration, he knew it would not be well to offend this being. "I mean, whatever seems suitable."

"I made the Little Grand Entrance — there not being room here for the Grand Grand Entrance, involving as it does timed explosions of rockets and barrels of gunpowder — to offer, in a moment and in a compact metaphor, my bona fides. I am indeed Mephistopheles, a prince of demons, and I do indeed come from The Other Side with an offer I think you'll be unable to turn down."

Mack had by now recovered his sangfroid, for he had grown accustomed, in his way of life, to sudden changes of fortune. True, he had never encountered a devil before, but this sort of thing was only to be expected in that day and age when miracles took place daily from one end of Europe to another, and the effects of witchcraft were a matter for continual comment.

"Now tell me, Dr. Faust," Mephistopheles said, "would you care to listen to my proposition?"

Mack was aware, of course, that this great demon Mephistopheles had made a mistake, thinking he was the learned doctor Faust. So even demons could be in the wrong! But he wasn't about to correct him. For one thing, it probably wouldn't be safe, not after Mephistopheles had gone to all the trouble of staging a Little Grand Entrance; and for another, it sounded as if some profit might be gleaned from this fortuitous encounter.

"I'd very much like to hear your offer," Mack said. "Do take a seat — that trestle chair should serve you well enough if you don't burn through it — and tell me what you had in mind."

"I thank you for your courtesy," said Mephistopheles, sweeping back his coattails as he sat, and causing the tallow candle in its charred oaken container to burst spontaneously into flame. Several more candles followed suit. At last getting the lighting as he wanted it, so that it cast long, sinister shadows across his face, Mephistopheles said, "How would you like, for openers, wealth of an extent and a greatness undreamed of since the days when Fabius Cunctator sacked Carthage? This wealth would be in the form of many well-made caskets full of gold coins of a purity undreamed of in earthly coinages. And it would be accompanied by barrels of the most precious stones, pearls the size of hens' eggs, diamonds as large as pomegranates, and an emerald large enough to form a dining table for six persons. And there would also be a perfect set of ten matched rubies of deepest fire, each the size of a horse's turd. And there would be much more besides, the detailing of which would tax even supernatural vocal cords and which may well be left to the imagination."

"I get the idea," Mack said. "That sounds very good indeed. It would be churlish of me to ask you to specify the exact number of barrels of gems and caskets of gold. Even if it were only one of each it would be a most excellent present."

"These are not presents," Mephistopheles said. "They may be considered payment for a service I shall require of you, and for one thing more."

"It's that one thing more I'm afraid of," Mack said. "No offense meant, of course."

"None taken. It is a pleasure to be able to speak frankly. But there is no trick here, Faust. Do you think the Dark Powers would go to all the trouble of hiring my services and staging a Little Grand Entrance all for the purpose of duping you? Your credulity might be tested at far less expense!"

"Hey, don't get me wrong, the wealth thing sounds very good. But was there anything else? Like, who am I supposed to enjoy this wealth with?"

"As for that," said Mephistopheles, his eyes sparkling as the thought of concupiscence entered his mind, "we will also provide you with a bevy, or even two bevies, of such beauteous maidens as the world has seen only in its fevered dreams of hopeless longing. These young ladies, Faust, each of them fit for a potentate, come in a variety of delectable shapes and colors, with hairstyles to suit every mood. In addition to their pulchritude, they also excel in the arts of love, possessing deliciously soothing skills as well as intoxicatingly exciting ones. Some of these ladies can give you intellectual companionship, Faust, while others will suit your brutish or childish moods, while still others will just be around to bring you your morning borscht. They also have the advantage of loving, next to you, nothing so well as lying in a cool chamber in a cataleptic sleep until their services are required again. And not only are they a practically inexhaustible gift of sensuality in themselves, they all have best friends, sisters, and mothers, who can provide piquancy by standing by to be seduced."

"That is indeed wonderful," Mack said. "I am in awe of the way you have solved one of mankind's oldest dilemmas." He wanted to add, Mephistopheles, you have convinced me, go bring on the dancing girls, just tell me who you want me to kill. But native caution rose again in him and he said, "And where am I to enjoy my new lifestyle with unlimited wealth and boundless women?"

"Why, where you please," Mephistopheles said. "But if none of the present divisions of the world please you, we can

take you elsewhere in time, to any moment in any place anywhere, even the ones that do not yet exist, because there is a
law that says that that which is conceived must exist from the
moment of its conception. And we can set you up in such a
place as a great doctor of learning, or a prince of your own
state, or a wealthy churchman, or what you please. We like to
think of ourselves as occupational therapists, too, so you may
do what you will in this new place, and if the job does not exist,
we create it for you. We can find you a purpose in life that will
suit you down to a T, no matter what kind of a T you are. And,
with potions and simples that we supply free with our offer,
we ensure you a long, happy life and a decline so gradual that
you don't even notice it."

"Until the end, of course," Mack said.

"Of course. You could hardly miss noticing that."

Mack considered for a moment and then said, "You don't
by any chance offer immortality, do you?"

"You drive a hard bargain, Faust! No, we don't offer
immortality. Why should we? This new enhanced package of
ours, limited as it may be in terms of what is possible to the
imagination, is still enough to buy a trillion like you for the
least part of it."

"How well you know us!" said Mack. "How wise you
are!" But actually he thought that Mephistopheles was pomp-
ous, stuck-up, and more than a little silly. Mack felt he could
handle this spirit, not knowing, of course, that he was falling
for one of Hell's subtlest delusions.

"I just thought, if you had some immortality left over — I
gather you don't need it yourself — how nice that must be —
well, that you could throw some my way."

"But that would defeat the whole purpose of my making
you an offer. What profit is there for me unless I get your soul
in the end?"

"You're right, of course, looking at it that way. Longevity
is plenty good enough."

"That we offer, and rejuvenation as well."

"There *is* the matter of my soul."

"Bear in mind, the soul clause is a contingency deal. It comes into effect only if I fail to satisfy you completely over the course of our working together. Then you keep your soul, we shake hands, and go away friends. Can't say fairer than that, can I?"

"Hey, I'm not arguing," Mack said. "Now, what is it you want me to do?"

"We want you to play a part in a little contest my friends and I have devised."

"What sort of a contest is it?"

"One of the temporal-moral variety. We will put you into a series of situations in which you will play a part. Each episode will take place in its own distinct time and place. We will move to past or future, as the dictates of the game require. You will play a part in each episode. You will have a choice in each episode. How you make your choice, for what reasons, and with what end in mind, will be watched and judged. We will judge you, Faust, but not as you yourself, rather as a champion and exemplar of mankind, the one chosen by both of us to provide a reading on human morality, ethics, and other near-imponderable subjects. I say this very clearly to you, Faust, because I expect you to understand it before we begin. But once we start, you will not think much of the underlying awesomeness of the premises upon which this operates, for you will be too busy trying to watch out for your own skin."

"I see," said Mack, trying to grasp it.

"That is the bargain, Faust. The cast is ready, the scene is set behind the curtain, the players are all frozen into place, and the play is about to begin. We only wait for you to say the word."

He really is a long-winded devil, Mack thought. And Mephistopheles seemed something of an idealist despite his pretensions to cynicism. But there was no doubting the genuineness of the offer, nor was there any sense procrastinating with the dictates of his soul.

"I'm your man," he said. "Let's begin."

"Sign right here," Mephistopheles said, unrolling the slightly scorched parchment that he carried, proffering a quill and pointing his long sharpened fingernail at a vein in Mack's forearm.

Chapter
5

The protagonists of the drama in Faust's chambers might, had they not been so involved in their own situation, have noticed a face that appeared momentarily at the one uncovered chamber window, then ducked down out of sight. It was Faust himself.

He had picked himself up in the Devil's Walk, his scalp bleeding from the Lett's powerful but clumsily directed blow. He had tottered for a moment, then sat down upon a curbstone to regain his senses. The Lett came out of the doorway then, and had raised his oaken cudgel to ensure a really deep unconsciousness, or perhaps death—whatever. A man couldn't be too finicky about these things, not in this day and age, not with the plague, ghastly in its gray cerements, raging in the south of Europe, not with Moslem warriors, bearing curved swords and imbued with an inexhaustible fanaticism, boiling up from Andalusia and threatening to break out again through the Pyrenees as in the days of Charlemagne, to wreak havoc on the soft cities of Languedoc and Aquitaine. These matters concerned the Lett not at all. But before he had a chance to strike again there was a sound of full-throated men's voices lifted in lively dispute, and he knew it was university students, natural enemies to the caste that the Lett, all unknowingly, represented. They spotted him and raised the cry. The Lett took to his heels and raced away, to live to hit people over the head

another day, and continued running until he was well clear of
Cracow, at which time, seeing that he was on the road to
Bohemia, he continued to the south, and so moved out of our
story forever.

Faust was lifted to his feet by the students and brushed
clean of the dirt and chicken entrails he had fallen into. Sewers
in those days were no more than the dream-children of the most
impractical of those architects who created our dark, cramped,
smelly but friendly cities of the Dark Ages.

As soon as he could walk, Faust shook himself free of the
students and, head still reeling, hurried home. He saw that his
front door was ajar. Approaching cautiously, he went around
to the side, where his unshrouded window was, peered in, and
was astounded to see two figures, one of them quite plainly
Mephistopheles, whom Faust had seen many times in the pictures in the grimoires that were the chemistry books of the time,
but never in person. He ducked his head and listened.

The voices wafted out the window, and insinuated themselves into Faust's ear.

It was at the point where Mack was about to sign his name
in blood to the parchment Mephistopheles had brought that
Faust came unglued. There was an impostor in his house! The
devil was tempting the wrong man!

Faust turned from the window and raced around the house
to the front. He entered, throwing back the heavy oak door so
that it banged against the wall. Faust raced down the hallway,
braked at his door, and threw it open.

He was just in time to catch Mack's final flourish as he
signed the parchment. Then the devil rolled up the parchment,
saying, "Now, my dear doctor, we will proceed to the Witches'
Kitchen, where our expert cosmeticians will put you into condition for the adventures that lie ahead."

And then Mephistopheles raised his hands, flames sprang
up, bright iris and violet flames, tinged here and there with

sinister heliotrope, and flared in glory around the two figures. When they subsided the figures were gone.

"Damn!" Faust cried, running into the room, stopping, and pounding his fist into his palm. "One minute too late!"

Chapter
6

Faust glared around into the gloom-shaded corners of his room. For a moment he thought he detected a presence among the bat-winged shapes in the ceiling. No, there was no one here. They had gone, the two of them, the impostor and Mephistopheles. Nothing remained but a faint smell of brimstone.

It was apparent to him what had happened. Through some miserable concatenation of circumstances, a stranger had broken into his chambers. It was that tall, yellow-haired zany whom he had glimpsed through the window. And Mephistopheles, that silly demon with the grandiose name, had somehow mistaken the fellow for him.

He frowned and shook his head. Faust had overheard enough to know that Mephistopheles had proposed some fine adventure, and was even now carrying the impostor away to it, and to rewards that belonged by right to Faust. And Faust was left alone in this dreary room, in this mundane city of Cracow, where he was supposed to carry on his life as though nothing had happened.

Well, damn it, he wasn't going to have it! He would go after them, if necessary to the nethermost realms of space and time, find Mephistopheles, expose the stranger for the impostor that he was, and take his rightful place in the glorious unfolding of things.

Faust flung himself into a chair. His brain was exploding

with ideas. First he had to go to where Mephistopheles and the impostor were. They had vanished in a flash of flame and fire. That argued that they were not on the Earth. This meant that he would have to conjure himself past Earth and its mundane provenance, into the aethereal realm where spirits hold sway, where the dead perform their mournful revels, where the elves, pixies, kobolds, dwarves, and other creatures from the pagan past have their true home.

But then he considered for a moment. Was he ready for this? It would be a supreme test for any magician. And Faust, though he counted himself among the first rank in the controlling of the magical arts and the acquisition of esoteric knowledge, was not in his first youth. It might be beyond his powers. He might get himself killed. . . .

And then he remembered that only hours ago he had been considering killing himself! And why? Because nothing had seemed very interesting to him anymore. Life had stretched ahead of him in its tedious regularity, scarce in pleasures, replete with pain, devoid of meaningful accomplishment. Now he was interested again, to put it mildly! The adventure that was his by right of fame and accomplishment had been taken from him. That he would not countenance. If it must, let this adventure kill him. Nobody was going to steal his offer from the devil!

He rose and kicked up the fire, which had burned down to glowing embers. He added wood and got a nice blaze going. He washed his face in the basin of almost fresh water the servant had left just two days ago. He found a piece of dried smoked beef, and washed it down with a tumbler of barley ale. And all the time he was planning out his next steps.

He would need a really strong spell to transport him where he needed to go. It would have to combine the potency of a Sending with the puissance of a Visitation. Transportation Spells were notoriously difficult, involving, as they did, the sending forth of a corporeal substance, in this case himself, to regions where creatures usually walked around in subtler bodies. The sheer amount of spiritual energy required for this was daunting.

He went to his bookcase and rummaged through his grimoires. He found a formula in Hermes Trismegistus' *Surefire Travel to the Stars*. But it was too complicated, calling for ingredients difficult to obtain, such as a Chinaman's left great toe, which was an item almost impossible to procure in Eastern Europe at that time, though in Venice they had a goodly supply of them. He searched on. In his *Concordance to the Malleus Mallificarum* he found a simpler formula with fewer ingredients. He set to making it.

Batwort . . . He had a whole vial of that around somewhere. And the recipe called for toad's stools, four of them entire, but luckily he had some, nicely dried and stored in a thimble. Hellebore was never any problem, white willow was common, mercury he had on hand, he was out of blackened wormwood but could pick up some more at his neighborhood pharmacy. But what was this? "Will not work without a fragment of the True Cross"!

Damnation! He had used up his last fragment last month!

Wasting no time, Faust picked up his wallet, put his emerald into it for unexpected emergencies, and went out into the street.

The corner pharmacy was closed for Easter Sunday, but by pounding on the shutters he managed to bring forth the pharmacist, who, grumbling, told him he had no True Cross in stock, and didn't know when the next shipment would arrive from Rome. He did, however, have a supply of blackened wormwood, which Faust purchased.

He slammed out of the place then and proceeded as fast as his thin shanks would take him to the bishop's palace on Paternoster Row. The servants let Faust in, for he and the bishop were old cronies and often exchanged learned quips late into the night over a bowl of porridge (because the bishop's stomach was, like Faust's, not what it should have been).

The bishop, lounging back in his great armchair in comfortable corpulence, shook his head uncertainly.

"I am so sorry, my dear Faust. The most recent Advice from Rome is that we are not to permit bits of the True Cross to be used for idolatrous purposes."

"Who's talking idolatry?" Faust demanded. "This is the science of alchemy we're talking about here."

"But to what end do you want to use it, my son? To gain great treasures, for example?"

"Not at all! I want it to right a great injustice!"

"Well, I guess that's all right," the bishop said. "But I warn you in advance, True Cross has gone up in price, which is only to be expected since it *is* a substance in limited supply."

"All I need is a fingernail-sized fragment. Charge it to my account."

The bishop took out a small japanned box containing True Cross fragments. "I was meaning to speak to you about your account."

Faust reached into his wallet and set down the emerald. "There's my down payment!" He wrapped the fragment of True Cross in birchbark and then rolled it into an old altar cloth while the bishop admired the shine of the emerald.

With the fragment wrapped securely, Faust hurried home. He started up a coal fire beneath his alchemist's furnace, and pumped the groaning leather bellows until the fire glowed red and white and gave off streams of tiny diamond sparks. Then he gathered the ingredients together. He put the jug of aqua ardens on a table near him, taking care not to spill it, since it could eat through anything not coated with aqua ardens repellent, powdered the sublimated antimony in a little brass bowl, laid out floral essences on one side, and, on the other, the toad turds, the calcified bat dung, the crystallized woodchuck's piss, and the fortified graveyard mold. He took care to keep them separate. It wouldn't do to mix them prematurely! Over here were his tartar, alum, and yeast. Here was the nigredo, which he had made just last week. He hated to sacrifice it, for with the right process it could produce a phoenix, and the phoenix was the loveliest of allegorical birds. But there was no time for aesthetics now! He was ready to begin.

And there came a knock at the door. Faust tried to ignore it, but it was repeated, and then repeated again, and behind it he could hear a babble of voices. In a very bad humor he stomped to the door and opened it.

Standing outside were four or five young men — it was hard to be sure of their exact number because they bobbled around so.

"Dr. Faust, sir! Don't you recognize us? We are students from your class in Origins of Alchemy 1b at the University. We need some advice on why the feminine anima image is always found in the changeable hermaphroditic body of Mercurius. They're bound to ask it at finals, sir, and we can't find a thing about it in our Introduction to Alchemy textbooks."

"Why, damn it," Faust said, "the entire subject of hermaphroditism and the sexual imagery of alchemy is covered in *New Directions in an Old Science*, by Nicholas Flamel, which I assigned you at the beginning of the year."

"But it's written in French, sir!"

"You are supposed to know French!"

"But it makes no sense, sir, because if the principle of hermaphroditism according to Aristotle can be subsumed — "

Faust held up his hand, commanding silence. "Students," he said, "I am embarking on a difficult and complex experiment that will probably go down as a landmark in the annals of alchemy. I cannot permit the slightest interruption. Go to one of the other professors. Or go to the devil! Just get away from here now!"

The students left. Faust gave another bellowsing to the

fire, checked to make sure his descensories, with their hair-thin crosslets, were clean and in working order. The alembics were already heated and ready to go, the sublimatory was in satisfactory condition, and the cucurbit was finally balanced to his satisfaction. He began.

As the elements entered the crucible they changed colors in a satisfying manner. Reds and greens swirled in the gleaming liquid, layers of vapor were let out and condensed into a mist that rose to the ceiling and hung there like a transparent gray serpent. Faust put in the True Cross fragment. The substance lighted up for a moment and then turned black.

It is very bad when an alchemical reaction turns black. Luckily, Faust had noted the double flash of silver that occurred just before the blackening. He turned to his *Alchemist's Trouble-Shooting Manual,* produced by the wizards of Cairo University and translated by Moses Maimonides, and looked up the reaction. He read: "A double silver flash before the materia confusa goes to black means that the fragment of Cross used in the reaction was not True Cross. Check it with your religious assayer before going any further."

Damn it! Stymied again! And this time there seemed no way out. Unless there was a substitute for True Cross? He raced to his library again, but found nothing of use on its groaning shelves. He felt like screaming, so deep was his frustration. And then his gaze fell upon the parcel of books brought by the man who had entered his apartments.

He looked through them and his lip curled with contempt. They were nothing but trumpery imitations of the real thing, fairground playthings to be sold to the ignorant. But here among them was one title he recognized, though he had never been able to obtain it. It was *The Marrow of Alchemy,* and was a German translation of certain key texts from Eirenaeus. How had that gotten in here?

He flipped through it and came upon the following statement: "True Cross is in appearance almost indistinguishable from Almost True Cross. Unfortunately, it will not work in formulas of alchemy. However, Almost True Cross can be boosted in its power and so serve for the real thing by adding equal amounts of potassium and common lampblack."

Faust had his vial of potassium right to hand. He had no lampblack, but if, as he suspected, the serving girl hadn't cleaned the lamps recently . . . Yes, he was right, plenty of lampblack!

After the lampblack and potassium were added there were various changes of light and color in the mass in the alchemist's furnace. A dense gray vapor arose and for a moment clouded Faust and his equipment. When the vapor had dissipated, Faust was no longer in the room, nor, for that matter, was he in Cracow.

Chapter 7

Faust's first impression was of a pearly grayness that suffused everything. That persisted only for a moment, however, as Spiritual Space accommodated itself to the novelty of having an earthly observer within it by expanding outwards on all sides. After that, Faust saw that he was standing just on the outskirts of a small city, very like in appearance to cities he had seen in his travels around Europe, though by no means identical.

He had certainly gotten to this place very quickly. But that stood to reason, since the Spiritual Realm, having no substance except for that imposed by the temporary rules of Solidification, can be shrunk down to a tiny compass by Nature, which abhors a vacuum and isn't about to leave a lot of unused space around, either. The learned doctors at the Jagiellonian taught that when the Spiritual Realm wasn't being used, it resided in a space no larger than a pinhead—to such an infinitesimal mass may the immaterial be reduced! The only thing that would cause it to expand was the presence of an observer. Then the space created itself, with the sort of scenery and personnel as might be expected in this place and at this time.

Faust entered the city and saw a row of storefronts. Above each was a sign. Faust could not decipher the lettering on them, by which he knew they were not for him to enter. At last he saw one sign that read, THE WITCHES' KITCHEN. And he knew that was the place he was to go to. (So much is inherent in the Transportation Spell, which takes you unerringly to the threshold of your next adventure, though you're on your own after that.)

Faust approached the Witches' Kitchen. He walked up to the door and touched it with a gingerly gesture. He had been afraid that his hand would pass through it, since only spirit is supposed to exist in such a place, and spirit is well known for its ability to pass through other spirits. But the door felt solid and a moment's reflection told him that even if a body in this place were not solid, it would have to act as though it were in order for anything to happen; for as the ancient philosophers have pointed out, there's no drama unless things can bump into each other. But how, being aethereal, had they managed to become solid? Faust decided that it must be because the entities here had taken a formal oath to maintain solidness despite the comforts of intangibility, and above all not to melt into each other.

Faust entered the Witches' Kitchen and saw a whole host of small demons of not very frightening aspect attending to a group of patrons who sat in chairs with striped sheets over their bodies. It seemed to be a beauty salon of some kind. These demons were evidently barbers, or surgeons, for not only did they cut hair, they also scalloped away fat from obese bellies, trimmed beef from sausagelike thighs, and added strands of glistening red muscle to wasted arms and shrunken calves. They scrubbed dirt off the body and sandpapered blemishes out of the skin. Under their skilled claws, faces were reconstructed, the devils utilizing gobs of all-purpose flesh that they kept in vats beside their barber chairs.

In a moment, however, it became obvious that the demons were mere assistants. Walking among them, supervising, and themselves performing the more delicate bits of reconstruction, were a dozen or so witches. They all wore the same ragged, rusty garments, and they had high peaked hats perched on their narrow heads, hats whose brims sloped uncannily over their glittering eyes. And they all had high lace-up boots around their skinny shanks, and most of them had a baleful black cat perched on a knobby shoulder.

"Well, what's this?" said a senior witch, whose rank could be told by the black crepe rose she wore pinned to her hat. "Are you the basic material package we requested? Step over here, dearie, and we'll have you dismembered in no time."

"I am nobody's package," Faust said proudly. "I am Johann Faust, a doctor of the Earth Realm."

"It seems to me we just had a person of that name passing through here," the witch said.

"Was he accompanied by a tall, skinny demon named Mephistopheles?"

"Why, yes, he was, though he wasn't skinny to *my* tastes."

"That man with him was not Faust! He was an impostor! *I* am Faust!"

The witch looked at him levelly. "I *thought* he was young to be a learned doctor! Do you have any identification?"

Faust rummaged through his wallet (which had been transported and spiritualized but otherwise was the same as back on Earth) and found an honorary sheriffship from the town of Lublin, a voter's registration shard from Paris, and a silver commemorative medal awarded to him at the Great Fair of Thaumaturgy that had taken place two years past in Prague.

"Well then, you *are* Faust," the witch said. "And that other fellow deceived me, and Mephistopheles, too, unless I miss my guess. It's too bad. We gave him such a nice rejuvenation. You would have wept to see how beautiful we made him."

"It was wrongly done!" Faust cried, gnashing his teeth. "Now you must do the same for me!"

"That will not be possible," the witch said. "We already used up most of the allotment for that rejuvenation. Still, let's see what we can do."

She guided Faust to a chair. There she called over one of her demon assistants, and the two conferred in low voices.

"The trouble is," the demon said, "we used up almost all the longevity serum on the other fellow."

"Strain out the dregs and use them. They're better than nothing."

"But his features!" The demon tilted Faust's head to one side and then to the other. His eyes, hard as agates, studied Faust's features and showed no sign of being impressed. "Lacking a beauty pack, what can I do with this gross, long-nosed, sunken-cheeked, thin-lipped, and ill-formed visage?"

"Hey!" Faust cried. "I didn't come here to be insulted!"

"Shut up," said the demon. "I'm the doctor here, not you." Turning to the witch, he said, "We could build up his physique, not to superhuman powers, of course, since that preparation hasn't come through, but to a respectable degree."

"Do what you can," said the witch.

The demon worked swiftly and with an élan that frightened Faust until he perceived that the demon's ministrations didn't hurt. Then he relaxed in the chair while the demon, humming monotonously to himself, plucked away some of the more pendulous portions of Faust's anatomy and molded fresh flesh in their place, holding the strips of dripping skin in place until they had hardened to the bone. Lastly he ran strands of nerve and muscle and sinew into the appropriate places so that Faust could smile or grimace or move his limbs, and fixed them in place with small applications of Universal Fastener.

He finished, trimmed off the final odds and ends, stepped back to study the result, and nodded sagely to himself, saying, "Better than I expected, given the materials I had to work with." Then he brushed Faust off, whisked off the striped sheet, and bade him look at himself in one of the tall wall mirrors.

Faust beheld in the glass a man rather more robust than he remembered himself. His skin had lost the waxy whiteness of old age and had taken on the ruddy hue of the middle years. His eyesight was improved, too, as well as his hearing. His features were still recognizably his own, but the demon had fined down his rather peremptory nose, brought out his chin a bit, and taken away his dewlaps. All in all he was a better-looking man than before, though he was still not likely to win one of the male beauty contests that were held secretly in some parts of Italy.

"It's better," Faust admitted, studying himself in the mirror, "but it's still not good enough. It is my right to have the full rejuvenation treatment!"

The demon shrugged and turned away. The witch said, "Let us not speak of rights. We gave you this much out of the goodness of our hearts. Never say that witches are all bad! For the full works, you will have to get a requisition slip signed by Mephistopheles himself, or one of the other great princes of Light or Dark. Only then can we requisition the materials from Central Supply."

"I'll get that," Faust said, "and a lot else besides. Where did Mephistopheles say he was going next?"

"He didn't mention it to us."

"In what direction did he decamp?"

"Straight up in the air, in a cloud of fire and smoke, as is his wont."

Faust knew that he could not do that. His Transportation Spell was too limited. It had brought him to this place, but it had not the power to carry him further. He would have to return to Earth and make his plans.

Chapter 8

It was a disconsolate Faust who rematerialized inside the pentagram chalked on the floor of his chambers. Coming from the workmanlike bustle of the Witches' Kitchen, his own quarters struck him as unbearably shabby and forlorn. That damned servant girl hadn't even dusted his skeleton! And his cloaks were still mud-caked from the spring rains. There were going to be some changes around here, he decided. He gnashed his teeth.

This was what came of being nice to people: impostors without even a casual knowledge of alchemy thought they could come in and steal your long-awaited pact with the devil. Like hell they could! He'd show them!

Meanwhile, there was his rejuvenation to consider. He noticed that he seemed to have a lot more energy than before. His irascible nature, which had begun to soften with age, returned now with a rush. Damn it, he was Faust! He was strong! And he was hungry!

He turned to his pantry. There on the top shelf was his bowl of porridge, a goodly lot of it left over from last night's cooking. He stirred it with his long spoon. It had lumps in it, and was the color of corpse fat. His newly rejuvenated digestion told him he couldn't tolerate that stuff any longer. Especially now that the witch at the Witches' Kitchen had thoughtfully given him a fine set of teeth, as good as new except for a chip in the left incisor. He didn't want porridge! He wanted meat! And revenge, revenge!

Without further ado he left his room, went down the stairs, and out into the street. It was evening now, a blue and delightful evening, fit consort of the fabulous Easter day. Faust paid it no heed. He had better things to do than sing strophes to the weather! He crossed the street and clumped into the tavern he frequented.

"Landlord!" he cried. "I'll have a slice of your roast suckling pig, and don't be stingy with the crackling!"

The landlord was surprised to see this sudden change of humor in the usually sober and morose-sounding Faust. But he merely enquired, "Barley and groats on the side, sir?"

"No groats, damn it, I'll have a full serving of Polish fried potatoes instead. And have the serving wench fetch me a pitcher of decent wine, not that wretched, thin Polack red."

"Tokay okay?"

"Yes, and Rhine's fine, too, just hurry up and bring it."

Faust took a table apart from the common customers, for he wanted to think. The tavern was shadowy, with a small fire in the big hearth. There were tallow wicks burning on a wagon wheel overhead. It rocked ever so slightly from its long chains set into the ceiling beam due to the draft that blew in through the ill-made door. A serving girl brought his wine, and Faust quaffed half a pint without looking up. The girl soon reappeared with his slice of pork on a wooden trencher, with an oily heap of Polish fried potatoes on the side, and even a little plate of spiced red cabbage. Faust's stomach would have rebelled at such fare a day ago, but now it suited him to a T. So did the serving girl, who had bent low to put down the trencher, revealing a bounteous bosom beneath her embroidered off-the-shoulder white peasant's blouse. She straightened, pushing back the lustrous chestnut hair that framed her oval face in comely waves, and cascaded along her neck and plump shoulders. Faust, who had thought such interests were long behind him, looked up and blinked, reacted, and then found his tongue.

"You must be new around here," he said. "I don't remember seeing you before, and I would if I had."

"This is my first day on the job," the girl said, smiling with sulky and provocative beauty. "My name is Marguerite, and I come from Mecklenburg where I was a goosegirl until the armies of Gustavus Adolphus and his wild Swedes came down from the north bringing fire and rapine and causing me to flee to the east to avoid what proved to be not inevitable after all."

Faust nodded, enthralled by her idle prattle, enchanted by her womanly charms — a fascination rejuvenated along with the rest of him.

"I am Dr. Johann Faust," he said. "You may have heard of me."

"Indeed I have, sir," Marguerite said. For in those days alchemists were among the star acts on the entertainment circuit and a really successful one like Faust could expect to be known far and wide. "Are you really master of those arts that call up precious stones and custom-designed clothing?"

Faust was about to reply when a voice from a nearby table called out, "Can't we get any service here? Our wine jug is empty! Rhine is fine, Tokay is okay, but just bring something in a hurry!"

"I must depart," Marguerite said, "to serve wine among swine."

"Why don't you come around to my place this evening?" Faust asked. "We'll divert ourselves by playing around with a spell or two."

"Delighted," Marguerite said. "I'm off at eight. Till then, *hasta la vista.*" Surprising him with her unexpected gift of languages, she hurried away to serve the other customers.

Chapter 9

Faust finished his meal and returned home. Before Marguerite's arrival, he took the opportunity of sprucing up his chambers. He carried to the back door the trash from the last week's experiments — dead cats that he had been trying to get to dance for him, old borscht and porridge containers from his most recent take-out meals, and a big pile of scholar's gray gowns that the servant had been supposed to wash and press. He pulled back heavy curtains all the way, opened shutters, and gave the place a good airing. Women, not being scholars themselves, cared about such things. When he had the room to his satisfaction he burned some frankincense in a copper basin, filling the air with pungent sweetness. Then he heated water and, stripping off all his clothes, scrubbed himself thoroughly. He felt a little foolish doing it, but what the hell, it was spring and he needed a cleaning anyhow after the long winter's funk. He put on a fresh gown and combed his hair, which had become wiry and unruly since his rejuvenation at the Witches' Kitchen. An unaccustomed yet familiar excitement suffused his newly young body. He couldn't remember how long it had been since he'd had a date.

Marguerite came to him shortly after eight, at the time of deep blue twilight, and her entrance into Faust's chambers seemed to be accompanied by a pink spotlight that hovered around her as she darted here and there, exclaiming over his alchemical equipment, gazing with wonder at his books and manuscripts, and, with her womanly and sweet-smelling presence, spreading an air of general well-being withal.

Faust's good spirits were tempered only by his sense of loss and outrage at the criminal carelessness of the infernal powers. Mephistopheles had apparently not even asked the impostor for any identification! He had just taken him at his word! It was outrageous.

A little later, Faust found himself telling the story of his grievances to Marguerite as they lay nicely curled together in his narrow scholar's bed, with a flagon of barley wine close to hand to stimulate merriment and amorousness. Marguerite was sympathetic to his tale, though her mind tended to race off on tangents of its own.

"What a wonder it would be," she said, "if you could regain the riches that Mephistopheles was no doubt going to offer you. For then, if you had a girlfriend, you could shower her with largesse and other fine gifts, and her appreciation of these things would bring you much pleasure."

"I suppose that's true," Faust said, "though I never before thought of it that way. But speaking of gifts, have you ever seen this one?" And he took a copper ring and spun it in the air and muttered certain words and the ring came down shining with the white fire of a diamond, though it was only a zircon in this case, the spell being a minor one. Marguerite was delighted, and although the ring was a little big for her small hand, declared that she knew a jeweler who would size it for a smile. And did Faust happen to have any other tricks like that? Faust obliged by turning a bunch of dried hollyhocks into a bouquet of roses with the dew fresh on them, and Marguerite said that was a good one, too, but did he have any more of the jewelry ones, which especially captured her fancy? Faust had several, and showered her with pins and brooches of showy workmanship but no great value, since there is a limit to what even so great a magician as Faust can do while lying in bed in a state of tumescence, with his head on a woman's soft bosom.

Still, he roused himself and, remembering a trick attributed to Albertus Magnus when he was touring the Levantine circuit, took one of the roses he had conjured, made several passes over it, muttered an Etruscan spell he had picked up in Naples, and produced a very showy bit of turquoise set in a sterling silver locket.

"That's amazing!" Marguerite cried. "How do you do that?"

Faust rippled his fingers. "It's all in the hands. And in the know-how, of course."

"If you can turn out stuff like that," Marguerite said, "you could be rich. Why do you live like this?" Her gesture embraced the chamber that, though sufficient for Faust's needs, did nothing to enhance the reputation of his interior decorator.

"I've never wanted riches," Faust told her. "My treasure was knowledge, and I sought the Philosopher's Stone, which is wisdom, not gold as the unenlightened believe."

"I understand that," Marguerite said. "But what's the payoff?"

"I beg your pardon?"

"Well, people always do one thing in order to get another. Haven't you noticed? They raise grain because they want to eat bread. They march to war because they want peace. They murder in order to save lives. It's always the other thing they're doing it for, the other thing which is the payoff."

"Bless you, my child," Faust said, "in your untutored way and all unwittingly you have raised a question of rather interesting philosophical implications. You are asking, what is the goal or purpose of my quest for wisdom?"

"You say it so well," Marguerite said.

Faust smiled. "Knowledge, wisdom, these are goals in themselves and require no 'payoff,' as you pungently but delightfully put it."

"In that case, why are you so angry at this impostor you told me about? His taking your reward doesn't hinder your pursuit of knowledge."

"Hmm," said Faust.

"What were you going to do," Marguerite asked, "when you became as wise as you needed to be?"

"Become wiser still."

"And when you had all of it you could have?"

Faust mused for a moment, then said, "When you have all the wisdom you need, then you are ready to enjoy the pleasures of the senses, those involved in eating, bathing, sleeping, going to the bathroom, making love, watching sunsets, and so on. But we philosophers hold those things to be merest dross."

"Dross or not," Marguerite said, "after you've got wisdom, what other payoff can they give you? Body and spirit, Dr. Faust. When you're through feeding the one, it's time to feed the other."

"There is religion, of course," Faust said. "It is thought highly of as an end in itself. Not for me, of course; accepting what is handed down, dogma, that which is traditional and generally accepted without question, interferes with the spirit of free enquiry that Faust stands for, and which tells him to follow his own judgment and the dictates of his reason, not what some superstitious priest may have said to him."

So intoxicated with his words was he that Faust jumped out of bed and, wrapping himself in a long cloak, proceeded to walk up and down the room, reasoning aloud.

"It is the perfection of the moment that a philosopher seeks, if truth be told. He wants to come across a moment so perfect that he would say to it, Stay a little longer, O precious moment. If someone could provide me with that, that man or demon could have my soul. It was probably some such matter that Mephistopheles came to talk to me about. He came here with some kind of offer. And it involved great things, because why else would Mephistopheles cause me, or rather, the impostor me, to be rejuvenated at the beginning of it? Damn it, he's going to show that man the wonders of the worlds, both visible and invisible, and probably give him plenty of luxury to wallow in, too, because that's the sort of thing devils do, not realizing, apparently, that it takes far less than a seductive woman to entice a man from the true path of virtue. Usually temptation is easy; you just have to make the merest suggestion and the sinner will run to his sin. But I digress. He's taken all that from me! For this was the grandeur of Faust, that he knew that someday he would be discovered in a big way. Do you understand, Marguerite? It was a chance to play the big time, and it will not come again."

"You can't let them get away with that!" Marguerite cried.

"I shall not!" cried Faust, and then, in a lower voice, "But what can I do? Mephistopheles and the impostor could be anywhere!"

Just then the bells of the churches of the city began to toll for the evening service. Their great brazen tones and quivering and long-resonating reverberations and their little rippling evanescent overtones vibrated in the deep labyrinths of Faust's ear, bearing with them a message of import, if only he could decipher it. . . .

Easter services. Celebrated on Earth and in Heaven. And among the Powers of Darkness, it was the time of the great anti-Easter Sabbat. . . .

And that, of course, was where he'd find them, Mephistopheles and the impostor!

"I know where they must be!" Faust cried. "I shall go after them and pursue my destiny!"

"How wonderful!" Marguerite said. "Ah, if only I could share some tiny part of that destiny with you!"

"And so you shall!" Faust cried. "You, Marguerite, shall accompany me and help me on this mission, and share in my reward!"

"That's just what I'd like," Marguerite said. "But alas, sir, I am but a goosegirl who was only recently made serving wench. I know no alchemy."

"You don't need alchemy to run my errands to the pharmacy," Faust said. He pulled on his scholar's gown. "Come, get dressed, let's begin!"

Chapter 10

A nd so Faust embarked on a frenzy of preparation. First he needed a list. Sitting down at his desk, and dipping his quill in the inkwell, he wrote down all the items he would need to produce a really first-rate Traveling Spell. Then he sat back in dismay. It would take him months, years, to assemble the ingredients he required for a spell of sufficient power to take him to the Witches' Sabbat and wherever else he might want to go after that. He had to take Marguerite into consideration, too, for he meant to take her along. The trouble was, there was no time to acquire this stuff by legal means. But he had to have it, else the Faust story, the great story of human ability and creativity against Otherworldly machinations, would never be told.

It seemed to Faust that if he wanted to win his point, it was time to consider desperate expedients, even if they were not entirely legal. If, in the long history of argumentation, the ends have ever justified the means, this was one of those times.

Then, abruptly, he knew what he had to do. He rose and picked up a packet of alchemist's tools that sometimes came in handy when Unlocking Spells weren't working. He also took a sack of Spanish wine, for he might need some fortifying before the end of *this* enterprise.

"Come," he said to Marguerite, "we've got work to do."

The Jagiellonian Museum, a great mass of gray stone set by itself in the Parque of the Belvedere just to the right of St.

Rudolph's Gate stood dark and deserted. Marguerite stood by as Faust muttered an Unlocking Spell at the tall bronze doors of the front entrance. As he had feared, something was off tonight. Sometimes a wrong intonation will throw off a spell entirely, to the extent that wizards and magicians with head colds frequently have to desist lest they call up their own destruction through the production of a snuffling sound in the wrong place. Whatever was wrong, it didn't matter, for Faust had come prepared. Taking out his packet of little instruments, Faust made short work of the lock, and, taking a swig of wine for courage, pushed open the door enough to let him and Marguerite slip through.

They were in the museum's great central hall, but the exhibits were swathed in gloom. The darkness was relieved only to a minor extent by the great windows set slantwise in the sloping roof that permitted errant rays of moonlight to enter. But he knew this place well enough to pull Marguerite along — she was gawking at the tableaux of ancient Polish kings — until the corridor ended in a stone wall.

"What now?" she asked.

"Watch. I'll show you something about the Jagiellonian most people don't know."

He felt along the wall until his fingers encountered a familiar indentation. He pressed it in a certain way. With a low rumble a section of wall rolled back on well-balanced hinges, revealing a narrow passage ahead.

"Where does this lead?" Marguerite asked.

"To the Closed Chamber, the museum's Unholy of Unholies, long proscribed by the Church, the secret museum of mystical objects from earliest times."

He led her down the passageway. It took them to a lofty room crowded with exhibit tables. In this place even Faust was in awe, for it was said that this chamber had existed long before Europe had reached its present state of civilization. Faust and Marguerite tiptoed down the aisles, and saw mystical copper rings from Ur of the Chaldeans, bronze divining rings from Tyre, sacrificial flint knives from Judaea, multiuse Egyptian wish-granting scarabs, sickle-bladed sacrificial knives of the rainbow-worshiping Celts, and more modern objects, such as the brazen head of Roger Bacon, Raymond Lull's machine of universal knowledge said to be useful for converting the heathen, several of Giovanni Battista Vico's Seals and Shadows in easy-to-interpret form, and much else besides.

"This is more like it," Faust said. Already his arms were full of magical objects.

"They'll hang you for this!" Marguerite said.

"They'll have to catch me first," Faust replied. "That's the original Mantle of Turin over there. I wonder if we should take it."

"I've got a bad feeling about this," Marguerite said, draping it over her shoulders nonetheless.

Just then there was a clang of metal from the door by which they had entered, and there was the loud stomping noise of metal-toed shoes of the sort guards wear to prevent enraged criminals from stamping on their toes.

"They have us!" Marguerite cried. "There's no way out!"

"Watch this," Faust said, and put the objects he had taken in a certain order. He waved his hands, words issued from his lips, words which must never be repeated lest they upset the natural order of things. Marguerite's lips parted in wonder as she saw a nimbus of glory arise from the objects and engulf first Faust, still holding his sack of wine, and then herself.

And so, when the guard arrived, out of breath and with pikes at the ready, trotting into the Closed Chamber, there was no one to arrest.

Chapter
11

Faust and Marguerite, somewhat windblown from their flight through the aether, arrived at the dank meadow outside of Rome where the great Witches' Sabbat was customarily held. The meadow lay between two mountains with heads like gargoyles. One rim of the great swollen red setting sun revealed that quite a celebration had been held here not very long ago. But now the party was definitely over. Empty wine sacks and paper hats were strewn all over. The orchestra players were putting away their instruments and getting ready to return to Budapest. The huge raised altar at the center of the meadow was piled high with sacrifices. But the worshipers had left, and demon servitors were cutting up the meat to distribute to the evil poor, for the poor are always with us, on Earth, above, and below.

Faust and Marguerite descended to the great grassy space where the service had been held. Faust could have cried from sheer frustration. Again, too late! To have come so far, at such great labor, and for nothing! But he quickly pulled himself together and sternly advised himself not to give way to despair. Perhaps something could yet be salvaged.

He approached one of the workers, a bearded dwarf with stumpy legs cross-gartered with strips of leather, wearing a horned steel cap of Norse design, and with a spade fastened to a little knapsack at his back.

"How is it going?" Faust asked.

"Quite poorly," the dwarf said. "This demon grabbed me

and my friends to clean up after this Sabbat, but demons never pay enough, and they never leave anything to drink."

"Drink?" Faust raised the sack of Spanish wine that he had managed to cling to since leaving the Closed Chamber of the Jagiellonian. "I could perhaps offer you some drink."

"Very kind of you, sir! My name is Rognir and I am at your service." He reached for the wine sack, but Faust drew it back out of his grasp.

"Not so fast! There's something you can give me in exchange."

"I knew it was too good to be true," Rognir said. "What do you want?"

"Information," Faust said.

Rognir, whose heavy wrinkled face had been knotting into a scowl, now raised his brows and smiled. "Information, sir? Aye, you can have all the information you want. I thought you wanted jewels. Whom do you want me to betray?"

"It's nothing so dramatic," Faust said. "I merely seek to find two individuals who were here at this Sabbat. One was a tall, yellow-haired human, the other a black-haired devil named Mephistopheles."

"Yes indeed, they were here," Rognir said. "Laughing and carrying on they were. You'd think they'd never been to a Witches' Sabbat before."

"Where did they go?" Faust asked.

"That's the sort of thing no one tells a dwarf," Rognir said. "But look you, sir, I have a parchment that Mephistopheles wrote and gave to that red-haired demon over there."

The red-haired demon to whom he alluded was none other than Azzie Elbub, the dapper, fox-faced demon who had set the previous Millennial contest on behalf of Darkness, but whose creation, Prince Charming, had come to such an equivocal ending that Necessity, who had judged the contest, declared it a push. This found no favor in the eyes of the Lords of Darkness, who had looked forward to victory and the right to rule mankind's destiny for the next thousand years. And so Azzie had not been consulted in the matter this time, the choices being left solely with Mephistopheles and the Archangel Michael.

Faust asked, "This demon, he just handed you the parchment?"

"Not exactly," Rognir said. "He crumpled it up and threw it away angrily as Mephistopheles and his rejuvenated friend vanished in a cloud of smoke and fire."

"Give me the paper!"

"Give me the sack!"

They glared at each other, then cautiously exchanged objects. While Rognir was drinking, Faust looked at the parchment and saw a list of places and dates. He knew some of the places: Paris, for example. But not London or the court of the Great Khan in Peking. And the times were all different, some of them in the past, some in the future. One thing stood out, however. The first place on the list was Constantinople, and the date was 1210. Faust remembered from his history that that was the time of the ill-fated Fourth Crusade. That, obviously, would be the first of the situations he had overheard Mephistopheles mention to Mack.

While he was puzzling over this list, a voice at his left shoulder said, "You were talking about me, I believe."

Faust looked up and saw Azzie, the demon to whom Rognir had been alluding, standing beside him.

"How could you overhear me?" Faust said. "I spoke in a whisper."

"Demons always know when someone is talking about them. You're wondering about that parchment? I'll tell you. Mephistopheles has been put in charge of the Millennial games that will decide the destiny of mankind for the next thousand years. They chose him rather than me. And me a two-time winner! He and Michael have agreed that Mephistopheles will put Faust into five situations, and the choices he makes will be judged as to Goodness or Badness, outcome, and motive, by Necessity, whom we know as Ananke."

"But *I* am Faust!" Faust cried. "Mephistopheles has gotten the wrong man!"

Azzie eyed him. His bright fox eyes narrowed, and his ruddy demon's body took on a tension that a skilled observer, had one been present, might have found significant.

"*You* are the learned doctor?"

"Yes! I am! I am!" Marguerite tugged at his sleeve so insistently that Faust added, "And this is Marguerite, my friend."

Azzie acknowledged her with a nod, then turned to Faust. "This is a very interesting turn of events."

"Not for me," Faust said. "I just want to see justice done. It's me that Mephistopheles wanted in this contest. I want my rightful place! Will you help me?"

Azzie paced up and down the trodden grass of the meadow, thinking. He harnessed his usual impatience, because there were many angles to consider here, and he needed more information before he took any action at all. But unless he missed his guess, this could be a time of opportunity for him.

"I'll get back to you later on that," Azzie said.

"Give me a piece of advice, at least! Tell me where to go next to find them."

"All right," Azzie said. "My advice is that if you intend to pursue Mephistopheles and the impostor, you will need to travel in time, and to do that, you must visit Charon and make arrangements for passage on his boat."

"Thanks!" Faust cried. And picking up the chestnut-haired girl and invoking the second part of the spell which he had concocted in the Closed Chamber of the Jagiellonian, Faust vanished into the air.

Chapter 12

Azzie watched Faust leave, noting how well the human did his vanishing. It was a crisp and definite disappearance, here one moment, gone the next, no sloppy edges or bleeding colors as less skilled enchanters were wont to leave. The fellow handled magic well for a mortal. Of course, he was Faust, and that made a difference. Even Azzie had heard of Faust.

It was just past midnight. The cleanup crews had finished with the meadow where the Sabbat had taken place. The sanitation team was just sterilizing the places where unclean beasts had burrowed. Spiritual ecologists were repairing the damage done to trees by lightning and hellfire, planting new grass on the trampled sward, and purifying the soil of the baleful elements that had been spilled on it during the night's merriment.

"That's the lot of it," the dwarf foreman, Rognir, said. "More swill than last year."

"Yes, it was pretty good," Azzie said, his eyes indicating distance and absorption.

"Can we go now?" asked Rognir. He was annoyed. He really hadn't wanted this job. Before running into Azzie, he had been walking along one of the dwarves' underground paths, humming to himself, intent on getting to the Uppsala Dwarveria Jamboree, which was being held under Montpellier this year. It was the greatest holiday of the dwarf year, a chance to show off minor variations in the ancient dances and sing new accompaniments to old songs, for the dwarves like their arts traditional. Dwarves didn't much like new things, because they figured they wouldn't last. They liked to revamp old things, adding a word here or a step there. Rognir had been practicing with some members of his klutch for several months on a variation on the tarantella. (A klutch of dwarves is a friendship group of between five and seventeen individuals. For dwarves, the klutch takes the place of family, and ensures that everyone takes a turn buying the drinks.) Rognir had planned to meet the rest of his klutch under Montpellier. He had been hurrying along, late as usual, when suddenly Azzie had come stamping through the tunnel and had spotted him.

"Hello!" Azzie had said. "I know you, don't I?"

"We met once before," Rognir said, recognizing the demon. "You were going to invest my treasure. Where *is* my treasure, by the way?"

"Out earning money for you," Azzie said. "Don't worry about it, you've already gotten the profit, remember?" He put an arm around Rognir's shoulder in what passed for a friendly manner. "You aren't doing anything right now, are you?"

"I've got an appointment," Rognir had said.

"It can wait," Azzie said. "I need you to clean up after this Witches' Sabbat. It won't take you long."

"Why don't you do it yourself?"

"I've been appointed overseer, not laborer," Azzie said. "Come on now, be a good fellow."

Rognir was going to refuse, but it is difficult to refuse a demon in a face-to-face confrontation. Demons are far more fearsome than dwarves, who aren't fearsome at all, though they can scowl terribly.

The antagonism between dwarves and demons goes far back in history, because from time immemorial demons and dwarves have shared the same underground territory, but never as equals. The demons have always set themselves up as rulers. It has never occurred to them that they should be anything else but. The dwarves found that they were always being ruled by demons. They couldn't impose their own leaders on anyone, for not even a dwarf is willing much of the time to follow another dwarf. They thought of rebelling but finally obeyed because dwarves are great sticklers for tradition, even in matters of being ruled by strangers. They love ritual, and doing everything just as it had been done before, back at some probably mythical time when people knew how to do these things better. The demons, on the other hand, were innovators. And they were maddeningly supercilious. And political. Whereas the dwarves didn't like politics. They tried to avoid the entanglements the demons seemed to thrive on. They went underground so as to stay out of everybody's way, and also because of the precious metals to be found down there. Whereas the demons like to live on the surface of the Earth, and in the Spiritual Realm. The dwarves didn't much like either. Although they knew about the Spiritual Realm, and walked in it from time to time when they needed to, they didn't like spiritual stuff. They had their own idea of what things were all about, and their idea was entirely material. It also involved only dwarves, so it couldn't really be considered a universal overview. But there they were in a universe filled with humans and demons. So they decided the hell with it and took to the underground, the last great frontier, as one of their sages put it, where they sought to live in peace, just them and their precious metals and their herds of sheep and their shaggy little ponies. But the demons could move around underground, too, and they never recognized the separate integrity of the dwarves' territories. Underground was just a big ball of dirt as far as demons were concerned, and nobody owned it.

"What about my pay?" Rognir said.

Azzie said, "Your payment in the usual form of bags of coined silver has been deposited to your account in the Hellgate Savings & Loan."

"But that's way down in Hell!" Rognir said. "We dwarves never go there!"

"You'll have to go there this time, if you want to get paid."

"When we *do* go there, they give us the runaround and ask for identification. They don't seem to realize that dwarves don't have driving licenses."

"Quit bellyaching," Azzie said in the bullying, threatening tone that was natural for him.

"And nobody gave us wine, or dinner," Rognir said in a whining voice.

"Buy your own! That's what currency is for!"

Rognir scurried away, and, assembling his fellow dwarves, all of whom were complaining to each other about the working conditions and the lack of wine, uncovered the burrow by which they had come to this place. Dwarves always traveled underground, cutting new tunnels when old ones didn't exist. It was a lot of work and sometimes it hardly seemed worth their trouble, since there were highways and byways on the surface of the world connecting everything to everything else. But dwarves are traditionalists, the old ways are best, and at least underground you know where you are. They disappeared into their hole and the last one to go set in place the grassy cover. Now the meadow had its usual mundane and somewhat bedraggled appearance and Azzie could leave as well.

Yet the fox-faced demon hesitated, still thinking about the two Fausts. What was going on? It seemed that Mephistopheles, on behalf of the Millennial Planning Committee, and with Michael's approval, had given Faust an itinerary of places where he was to influence human destiny at moments vital to the world's future history. Faust had accepted. Presumably he and Mephistopheles were going to the starting line now, so to speak, to begin the contest. But the person who would be doing all this wasn't Faust at all. He was an impostor, and Mephistopheles didn't seem to know anything about it. Curious.

Was it the sort of simple, unpredictable happenstance that can befall the most evil of us as well as the most virtuous? Or might there be a deeper plan in all this?

Azzie was in an irritated mood. Although he had a reputation as a good-natured demon, recent events had soured his usually sunny nature. Being passed over for setting up the current Millennial contest hadn't done his disposition any good. It still irked him to think that the Lords of Darkness had picked Mephistopheles, a silly devil if there ever was one, to do what Azzie had done so well before. And Mephistopheles was already parading around with the wrong man!

What results would this imposture have on the contest? Whose side would benefit from getting the real Faust out of the game? And, most important of all, who was behind all this? For the more Azzie thought about it, the more it seemed certain that someone had to be planning this. Conspiracy theories are one of the foremost intellectual achievements of Hell, and Azzie was an orthodox believer in that respect, though on other matters he had his differences from received opinion.

Yes, somebody was planning something . . . deep! And he could find out what it was and use it to advance his own cause!

As soon as he realized this, Azzie's foul mood fell away and he became positively cheerful. Because if there is one thing that makes a demon feel good, it is exposing a conspiracy plot and proving himself smarter than anyone else.

Azzie welcomed the opportunity. He had been underemployed of late. Since he'd been expecting to be chosen to set up the contest he hadn't set up anything else for himself in the way of interesting work. This would do nicely. And he had a pretty shrewd idea where to begin.

Casting a last look at the site of the Witches' Sabbat, and finding it up to standard, he rose into the air, spinning like a fiery whirligig, and then streaked off like a rocket, casting brilliant red and white spots. Let a mortal try *that* for an exit!

Chapter
13

His flight (conducted more soberly once he was in the aether) took him to the familiar regions of South Hell, where the Office of Infernal Records was located. These records were not open to the general hellish population, but Azzie knew a way by which he might get a look at them.

Avoiding the great gray Records Building with its ranks of damned souls tapping at computers, condemned to an eternity of mind-boggling boredom, but allowed an occasional cigarette break, since Dark is prepared to be lenient as long as you want to indulge in something harmful, he went to the little rustic tavern behind Records and slightly to its right. From here he telephoned Winifred Feyye, a pretty little imp of his acquaintance, who was a floor manager in the Protocols Division.

"Hey, baby, how you doin'?" Azzie inquired in the breezy style that Winnie liked.

"Azzie! It's been ages since I've heard from you!"

"You know how it is, baby. If you really want to do bad in this universe, it's a full-time job."

Now they sat in a comfortable booth in the corner and the tavern keeper served drinks, a stinger for Winnie, a devil's stirrup cup for Azzie. In that relaxing atmosphere they chatted for a while about mutual acquaintances: old Foxworthy, who was now an iron maiden repairman in the Eternal Torture Division; Miss Muggles, who was still working as a private secretary for Asmodeus; young Silver Foxxe, who was now a junior caterer for the do-bad service that supplied Dinners for the Damned. A bright fire leaped and cavorted in the fireplace, and a blind gleeman in a corner, singing the tale of Troy to the pluckings of a harp, added a note both classical and romantic.

"Oh, Azzie," Winnie said, several drinks later, "this has been such fun! I really have to go back to work now. I wish we could do this more often!"

"Me too," Azzie said. "Who knows, maybe it'll become possible? Winnie, there's a little favor you could do for me, if you wouldn't mind. I'm doing an article for the *Satanic Times* on Protocols and Agreements between Dark and Light. There's a new one that hasn't been released to general circulation yet. It has to do with the current Millennial contest."

"I know just the one you mean," Winnie said. "I filed it away only two days ago."

"I'd much appreciate a look at it."

Winnie rose to go. She was small even for an imp, and her hair, cut in a stylish pixie cut, framed her heart-shaped face and accentuated her big, dark eyes.

"I'll bring it here on my next break."

"Winnie, you're a love. Hurry back!"

The pretty little imp departed in a swirl of short skirt and a flash of thigh. Azzie sat and waited in the tavern as the slow hours passed. From time to time a worker from the Office of Infernal Affairs would come in for a quick one. The lighting here was perfectly even: both day and night it was the color of a rainy winter afternoon. A few drops of rain fell from time to time, speckling the tavern's leaded windowpanes. Azzie found a two-week-old copy of the *Infernal Internal Times*, house organ of the Office of Infernal Affairs. He read without much interest about raffles, a picnic, and the new Infernal Affairs annex. And he sipped at a succession of cafés diaboliques, laced with cocaine, which is not only legal in Hell, but is required in the sacrament to dissolution that the law requires Infernal Office workers to observe daily. And after a while, Winnie came scurrying back, her miniskirt deliciously high on her strong little thighs.

"I've got it! But I have to bring it back soon." She handed him a thick manila envelope.

"I'll just need a moment," Azzie said. He took out the roll of parchments, and, with Winnie holding down their ends, looked through them. Quickly he found the agreement between Faust and Mephistopheles.

The basic terms were laid out with a fussy exactitude that paradoxically seemed to invite quibbling. It began, "Be it herein agreed that Johann Faust, of various cities of Earth but recently believed to be in Cracow . . ." And it spelled out the terms: "The aforesaid Faust, whether of himself or such that claims his name, shall perseverantly go forth . . ."

Such that claims his name? That sounded like a loophole to Azzie, a way of excusing matters should the wrong Faust be called up. But if anyone could be in the contest, why put Faust's name on it at all?

Azzie skipped down to where the contest rules were set forth: "This Faust (which Faust? there was the ambiguity again!) will present himself for five situations, which are further set forth in the codicil. In each of these he will be given a choice of actions and, with no further coaching, will decide for himself what course to take. The judging of these events will be solely in the hands of Ananke, who will consider them from the viewpoint of Good and Bad, Light and Dark, or any other paired contraries as may express to the weighing of this contest. And it is furthermore stipulated that this Faust will act in this contest of his own free will as that term is commonly understood. . . ."

Azzie put down the parchments and asked Winnie, "Who drafted this? Surely not the Archangel Michael?"

"That's exactly who," Winnie said.

"I didn't think he was capable of such quibbling. There are ambiguities here that would delight the professors at the Institute of Advanced Prevarication."

"In fact, Michael has been studying casuistry," Winnie said. "That is the report we've heard. He claims that the inability to dissemble convincingly is a disadvantage that Good need no longer labor under."

"That's quite a fine quibble all by itself. Hmm." Azzie looked over the document again. "All this talk in here about free will . . . Do you suppose it might be a red herring? And if so, what is it intended to direct attention away from?"

"I haven't a clue," Winnie said, batting her long lashes at him.

"Perhaps not, my dear." He rolled up the parchment and returned it to her. "But I know someone who might."

Chapter 14

The person Azzie had in mind who might know was Lachesis, eldest of the Three Fates, and some say the wisest. These are the ladies who spin, measure, and cut the thread of human destiny. It is Lachesis who does all the real work, however. Clotho, who spins the thread out of the flax of undifferentiated being, is a cheerful old lady whose fingers do the work all by themselves while she lives in daydreams of a former time. Atropos, who cuts the thread, works entirely under Lachesis' directions, snip, snip, cut it here, dearie, and that one there, another life predestined to go down the drain. This was not very demanding work and Clotho and Atropos had plenty of time left over for interminable card games and the serving of the tea and pound cake on which the Fates lived. Only Lachesis needed to use judgment, determining how long a man should live, and, some say, in what manner he was to die. She was a tall, grim-faced old lady, related to Necessity by Chaos out of Night, an early Great Mother whom she visited on important holidays, spending the rest of the time working away at the lengths of flax, examining their individual fibers with indefatigable zeal, giving to each man his moira, his portion of fate.

The Fates were part of the heritage of the Age of Myth, and some might think they coexisted queerly with a cosmos that contained Christian angels and medieval demons. These and many other apparent paradoxes and inconsistencies were all explained finally in the Unified Field Theory of Spirit, whose existence was a matter of faith though no one had actually seen it.

It was no small task to visit the three Weird Sisters, as they were called, though not to their faces, for they lived in a little region of their own beyond space and time, a place that was unconnected to anything else except through the iron thread of Inexplicable Causality. Still, Azzie felt he had to go, because Lachesis, through her connection with Necessity, was reputed to be wise in the ways of the creatures of Dark and Light and skilled at reading their motivations.

First he went shopping for a little gift, for Lachesis liked getting presents, and kept them in a great storeroom that was attached to the modest Greek temple in which she and the other Fates worked. The storeroom had been enlarged over and over again, since the presents sent to influence the Fates never stopped coming. Azzie found a tea strainer in sterling silver, crafted in ancient China, and with this under his arm, suitably gift wrapped, he made his way to the little red star on the rim of the region of space known as the Coalsack, and, taking a deep breath, plunged in.

He was whirled and tumbled in the turbulence of this region, but at last came out at the place he had intended, a rocky meadow, and at the end of it the small brick house where the Three Fates lived, and, behind it, looming very much larger, the huge Greek temple they had built to house the presents that generation after generation of mankind sent in hopes of changing their destinies and winning a few more years or days of life.

"Come right in, dearie," Lachesis said, pushing open the door. "Atropos, Clotho, look who's come for a visit!"

"Why, it's that nice young demon, Azzie," Atropos said. Snip, snip went her shears. Cut fragments of twisted flax floated in the air.

"Take care!" Lachesis said to Atropos. "You cut off those

last lives a full inch below my mark. Every centimeter is ten years of life to a mortal!"

"What does it matter?" Atropos said. "They'd just waste those years like they've wasted all the others."

"That's not the point," Lachesis said. "Moira, the web of fate, gives them a certain amount of time to do with as they please. It's not for any god, mortal, or primordial spirit to change that."

"So I'll give someone else an extra inch or two," Clotho said defiantly. "It'll all even out."

Lachesis shrugged and turned to Azzie. "What can I do? Just last week I caught her tying knots in the strands of flax before cutting them. When I asked her about it, she said she just wanted to see what humans thought about having their life-cords tied in knots. And Clotho didn't say a thing against it! She doesn't care, either. I've asked Central Supply to replace Atropos, even if she *is* an old friend, but they tell me it's a Civil Service ruling, only Atropos can do the job, it wouldn't be traditional or within labor regulations to do otherwise! As if tradition and labor regulations were everything!"

"Indeed, you have many problems here," Azzie said. "I feel ashamed of coming to bother you with my own petty concern."

"Don't you give it a thought," Lachesis said. "The tea strainer is lovely and I know just the place for it. Now, what do you have on your mind?"

Azzie told her about the Millennial contest, and the ambiguous wording in the Protocols that had been drafted by the Archangel Michael.

"You're right to distrust Michael," Lachesis said. "His zeal for Good has become so great of late that he cares not what he does to win his point. It will get him a reprimand one of these days, I'm sure. But in the meantime he's able to get in his quibble about the uncertain nature of free will and the difficulty of making a judgment based upon it. That covers him for the situations he's going to put Faust into, or, rather, the false Faust. But I wonder how is Ananke to judge the intentions of he who makes the choices, beset, as he will be, by pressures on all sides? It seems that she will have to judge by outcomes rather than intentions. Taking this into account, Michael needed a contestant whose choices he could predict."

"So why not use the real Faust?"

"There are difficulties about the real Faust," Lachesis said. "The various stories we have about him present no unanimity in their assessment of his character. He is variously portrayed as a mountebank and boaster, on the one hand, and as a supreme magician and high-level thinker on the other. Michael knew he would have no difficulty getting Mephistopheles to accept Faust as a contestant; the problem came in trying to predict what Faust would do. Whereas Mack the Club was an altogether simpler proposition — a fallen divinity student, living out some hard times, doing some evil deeds, but possessed of an ineluctable urge toward bourgeois propriety; or such at least was the assessment of the Heavenly Investigators who checked him out surreptitiously for Michael."

"Are you telling me," Azzie said, "that Michael put Mack up to it? Put the idea in his head of clubbing Faust and going to his house, knowing that Mephistopheles would be there and would mistake him for the real thing?"

"You mustn't quote me on this," Lachesis said, "but that is the news that reaches me. Many of the Heavenly Host consider it a good joke on that presumptuous Mephistopheles. It was the angel Babriel who did the actual dirty work for Michael, appearing to Mack in a tavern and suggesting that Mack do it, and claiming that it would redound to his credit as a Good Deed. Mack, to his credit, expostulated, saying that it was difficult to justify murder, even for the best cause in the world. At which Babriel rolled his eyes in pious horror and said, 'We're not suggesting *murder!* Not at all! Not even maiming! We just want you to knock Faust over the head, take his purse, and then take some stuff from his house.' Mack then asked, 'But wouldn't that be stealing?' 'In a way,' Babriel replied. 'But if you put ten percent of your receipts in the poorhouse box, the sin will be rescinded.' "

Lachesis admired the tea strainer again, then put it down and said, "That, at least, is the information I have on the matter."

"This is most interesting news," Azzie said. "I don't know how to thank you for giving me this information."

"I gave it to you for the common good of all," Lachesis said. "We Fates assist neither Dark nor Light. But it is our bounden duty to expose skulduggery when we see it, no matter who commits it and for what purpose. The time may come, Azzie, when I may have to tell tales on you. Don't hold it against me!"

"Indeed I shall not," Azzie said. "He who gets caught deserves discomfiture, that is a rule for all. I must away, good mother!"

"What will you do with this information?" Lachesis asked.

"I don't know yet," Azzie said. "First I'll cherish it for a while, and gloat over it in my heart, then I'll see how I can put it to use."

And with that, he was away.

Chapter 15

Marguerite asked, "Where is this place?" She rearranged her gown and tried to do something with her hair, which had been considerably windswept from their recent trip.

They had just come plummeting down out of the blue, arriving near a large marble building with pillars situated on a hilltop. Nearby was an open-air market where small, dusky men sold rugs, cloaks, tapestries, and other goods. Behind the market were tents colored brown and dun and black, making the place look like a Bedouin encampment.

"Where are we?" Marguerite asked.

"This is Athens," Faust told her. "That marble building over there is the Parthenon."

"And these guys here?" Marguerite asked, indicating the rug sellers.

"Merchants, I suppose," Faust said.

Marguerite sighed. "Is this the glory that was Greece? It's nothing like they taught us in Goose School."

"Ah, well, you're thinking of ancient times," Faust said. "This is the modern age. It's changed a bit. And yet, the Parthenon is still here, its tall Doric pillars standing against the blue sky like a sentinel of all that is good and worthy and beautiful in the world of men."

"It's very nice," Marguerite said. "But why did we come here? I thought we were going right to the Styx now."

"The River Styx happens to run through Greece," Faust said.

"What? Here in Athens?"

"No. Somewhere in Greece. I thought I'd better come here first and ask directions."

Marguerite said, "One thing bothers me. We were taught the Styx didn't really exist. So how can you ask directions to it?"

Faust smiled in a superior way and asked her, "Does the Archangel Michael exist?"

"Well, of course."

"And what about the Holy Grail? Does that exist?"

"So they say," Marguerite said.

"Well then, believe me, the Styx exists, too. If one imaginary thing exists, then all imaginary things must exist."

Marguerite sniffed. "Well, if you say so."

"Of course I say so," Faust said. "Who's the autodidactic thaumaturge around here?"

"Oh, you are, of course," Marguerite said. "Don't mind me."

Faust knew from his old atlases that the River Styx comes to the surface somewhere in Greece, before it continues its downward and roundabout ways through the ages of time and space to the shores of Tartaros. The atlases said it came out of a cavern, issued along a darkling plain for a while, then plunged into a steep declivity which tended downward into a cavern measureless to man. This was the ancient classical road to the underworld that Theseus took when he went down to try to steal Helen away from Achilles. Faust mentioned this to Marguerite.

"Who is this Helen?" Marguerite asked.

"A famous lady," Faust said, "renowned for her beauty, over whom a famous war was waged and a great city destroyed."

"Oh, one of those," Marguerite said. "What do we need with her?"

"We probably won't get to meet her. But if we did, she might give us some important clues as to how to get to Constantinople in 1210 and displace Mack the Pretender and take our rightful place in whatever is going on."

"So who are you going to ask?" Marguerite said. "The people around here don't look like they know what city they're in, far less how to find a mythical place like the Styx."

"Don't let their look put you off," Faust said. "They just look like that to discourage strangers. I bet any of them could tell us."

He led Marguerite toward a group of people who were clustered around a man with a coffee pot. "What did I tell you?" Faust said to Marguerite. "Coffee! These people aren't so dumb. That stuff isn't even known yet in the rest of Europe."

Pressing forward, Faust said, in the mincing Corinthian accent he had picked up in Greek class, "Good citizens! Can you direct me to the famous River Styx, whose whereabouts is said to be somewhere in Hellas?"

The men in the coffee-drinking crowd looked at each other, and one said, in a broad Dorian dialect, "Alf, isn't there a Styx over near where your uncle's got his farm, in Thesprotia?"

"You're thinking of the Acheron," Alf said. "That runs into the Styx near Heraclea Pontica, but it takes its time about getting there. Meanders, as they say. But there's a more direct way. You go to Colonus, and pick up the Cocytus River. Just follow it downstream. It flows into the Styx after descending to the unplumbed caverns of Acherusia."

"That's the best way," another man agreed. "You can't miss it. You'll know you're in the Styx when the only vegetation on the banks is asphodel and black poplar. Then the river turns underground and things get a little uncanny, and there's no mistaking where you're at *then*."

Faust thanked the rustics and moved away with Marguerite. Utilizing his spell, Faust soared north, following the coastline of Attica. Marguerite rode on his back, for there was no spell strong enough to empower his arms to hold her while the wind was buffeting so. Marguerite's hair was all in a tangle again, and she feared that her complexion was getting reddened by constant exposure to the elements. But she was content, because she was the only girl she knew who had ridden on the air with a wizard, and that was a considerable distinction for a girl with so little education.

Faust flew past the city of Corinth, with its high citadel, and dipped over the ruins of Thebes, still much as Alexander had left them over a thousand years ago. The land below became less steep as they continued toward Thrace. After a while two broad rivers appeared, and Faust was able to ascertain that one of them was the Acheron. He put down to the ground immediately.

"Why are we stopping?" Marguerite asked. "Is this the Styx?"

"No, this is the Acheron, which runs into the Styx."

"So why can't we fly the rest of the way?"

Faust shook his head. He had depleted most of the puissance of his Traveling Spell by so much use, and it would need time to recharge. A few hundred yards away, on the riverbank, there was a dilapidated old farm, and there was an open punt tied to its dock. The area seemed deserted, so Faust untied the little boat, and, putting Marguerite in the bow and himself taking the stern, proceeded downstream toward the Styx.

Chapter
16

Their punt drifted like a dream on the slow-moving river. This, he knew, had to be Phlegethon. The stream narrowed, the region became more bleak, and soon there was no vegetation except for black poplars and mournful fields of asphodel.

"We're getting there," Faust said. He'd been doing most of the punting since they began. He had been able to get a little relief out of a poling spell that imparted a certain measure of energy to each stroke, like an artificial muscle.

The Phlegethon declined until it was no more than a narrow ditch. The time was twilight. Faust knew they'd finally reached the Styx when the banks suddenly opened out, revealing a dark expanse of water. At this he punted past a very large sign that was written in several languages. It read, THE RIVER STYX. NO PRIVATE BOATS BEYOND THIS POINT.

"We'll have to stop here," he told Marguerite. "Charon has the sole rights of passage on this river. And anyhow, no magician, no matter how clever, can sail the Styx unaided. For that, he needs to make a deal. Come, let us find Charon."

"But is there really a Charon?" Marguerite asked. "Isn't this counter to Church doctrine?"

"Not at all," Faust said. "These entities have very little to do with religion. These are energies that are left over from a former age, and still take a certain shape and form."

Then he saw the boat coming toward him across the dark river. As it approached, he could see it was a sort of a houseboat, and it was propelled by five dolphins who had their noses against the stern and were pushing. This boat was making good time through the water since men amidships were helping with oars and paddles. It was a high, unsteady old boat and you could see yellow lantern light shining out through the portholes, and hear sounds of music and merriment.

"And who might you be?" Charon cried out, directing the boat toward Faust's punt. He was a surly old man, lean and spindly, with unshaven white-stubbled jaw and sunken eye sockets out of which tiny black eyes glittered. A nimbus of grayish white hair floated above his bony forehead and knobby skull. He had a wide, withered mouth with many twists and turns in it, but all tending downwards. He broke off his talk with Faust to give some orders.

"Pass that beam over there! Pull that oar! Take that sail in! Turn that thing around!"

Faust knew through his excellent classical education that several of the people working on the boat were dead Greek heroes. There were Theseus, Perseus, Hercules, Jason, and several others whom Faust didn't know, but presumed were also heroes.

"What do you want?" Charon called out.

"We need passage across the Styx," Faust says. "We need to get to a certain place and time, 1210 in Constantinople."

"We don't call at 1210 in Constantinople anymore," Charon said. "Too much trouble and upset there. Too many souls wanting to be ferried away. I don't need to bring this boat into any trouble spots like that."

"I really need to go there," Faust says. "What will you take to bring us?"

Charon laughed. "You don't have anything that I want! And don't let that story that you can take the ride for one obol kid you. Doing anything on the Styx is damned expensive since I have the sole navigation contract. It's my territory exclusively so don't try going any farther in that punt. And don't try creeping around on the banks, either. I've got them planted with repel-me-not. You'd need a hell of a spell, magician, to deal with a constricting vine like the repel-me-not."

"I had no intention of sneaking around you," Faust said with dignity. "But I'm sure we can make a deal."

"What makes you so sure?" Charon asked.

"Because I have something you want."

"Hah! I can't imagine what that would be!"

"Listen," Faust said. "You noticed the person I came here with?"

Charon glanced at Marguerite. "The woman? Yes, I see her. So what?"

"Pretty cute, isn't she?"

"I see plenty of cute ones go by here," Charon said.

"Ah," Faust said. "But not *live* cute ones."

Charon stared at him. Faust said, "You *do* detect the difference between live ones and dead ones, don't you?"

"Just because you're alive," Charon said, "don't go putting on airs. I'm just as good as you and just as real, even if I haven't ever existed in the mundane sense."

"That's not the point," Faust said. "I'm offering you a live lady."

"Hey, wait a minute!" Marguerite said.

Faust said to Charon, "Just one moment. Trust me." He took Marguerite aside and said to her in an urgent whisper, "My dear, you mustn't believe I'm intending any impropriety when I offered you to Charon. That's not my way at all. But I thought that he might like to have dinner with you and perhaps go morris dancing after that. It would be a change of routine for him and harmless enough for you."

"What made you think I wanted a change of routine?" Charon asked. He had been listening in.

"Men, both alive and dead, desire a change of routine," Faust said. "It is the essence of being."

"Well, I *could* probably do with a little something different at that. I could use — What is that newfangled word for it?"

"A vacation," Faust said.

"Yeah, a vacation. We didn't have those in the ancient world."

"You have to get used to newfangled notions," Faust said. "It's the essence of keeping up an appearance in this universe. Why don't you set this boat for Constantinople, 1210, and have a nice dinner and dance with Marguerite on the way?"

"And what would you be doing?" Charon said.

"I'll just pop into your cabin and catch up on some back sleep," Faust said. "It's been a busy day."

CONSTANTINOPLE

Chapter 1

Mephistopheles seemed to have transported them to a wooded cove. Looking around, Mack saw that large trees grew thereabouts, and they were not trees he knew from Europe. Not even the grass underfoot was familiar, but seemed coarser and more robust than the stuff that greened the byways of home. More he could not tell, for large, drooping willows blocked the view, though he believed, from a certain saltiness in the air, that they were near the sea.

Despite the rush of fresh air that they encountered on their flight from the Witches' Sabbat, Mack was still a little drunk. They serve a heady brew at these witches' affairs! He was feeling very good indeed, though a premonitory throb in his head warned him he was going to feel otherwise later. Right now he wanted to talk about his rewards, to learn more about what Mephistopheles was going to give him.

He said to Mephistopheles, "I need to sit down and work on my wish list. You *did* say you'd grant my wishes, did you not?"

"Yes, of course," Mephistopheles said. "But that's the least of it."

"The least of it? For you, maybe, but not for me! Could I get a little something in advance? What I'd like right away is an ermine-lined cloak, of the sort kings wear, and a silver cup out of which to drink my wine. That pewter stuff is not fit for someone in the high position I have fallen into."

"Pull yourself together," Mephistopheles said sternly.

"Forget about the rewards. They will come in due course. For now, your work in this contest is to begin."

"Oh, dear," said Mack. "I'm really not feeling on top of my form. How about a day off first, and then we'll get serious?"

"We are serious now," Mephistopheles said. "You are renowned among men for your great intellect and powers of self-control. I took the occasion to read your dossier while you were carousing among the witches."

"My dossier?"

"In the Record Halls of Darkness there are dossiers on everyone living."

"I didn't know that."

"You were a swot at school, mastering the various disciplines of the lower form with a perseverance that some of your teachers found almost divine."

Mack gaped at him, for he had been an indifferent scholar during his brief years of education. Then he realized that Mephistopheles was talking about the real Faust, not him.

"Show some of that spirit now," Mephistopheles said, "for your time of testing is upon you."

"Yes, yes," Mack said. "I'll be all right." Despite his words, self-doubt seeped through his mind like an ink-leaking squid thrown into a crystalline pond. My God, what was he doing here? It had seemed the veriest madcap of a prank, to deceive this dark and splendid spirit into thinking he was the learned Dr. Faust. But now he was stuck with the consequences of his action. No longer could he be Mack, the bright but not brilliant student at the monastery school, the unruly and fun-loving lad who had spent but a year among the learned priests, learning the rudiments of scrivening, reading, and reckoning, studying little, getting by on charm and his glib tongue, until, due to a madcap adventure involving several young ladies from the nearby convent and a hogshead of potent German brew, he had found himself turned out to make his way in an inclement world. That was who he was, but who he could no longer be. The chance had been given him to become one of the great ones, to take his place among the famous archetypes, the intellectual movers and shakers of the world. It was also a chance to prove that he was as good a man as Faust, and what he lacked in learning could be put right by asking questions and applying quick-wittedness.

He felt a modest infusion of self-confidence. This was no time to think about his rewards. Mack forced his aching head to attend to present matters.

"Where are we?" he asked.

"On the shore outside Constantinople," said Mephistopheles, "close to the Frankish encampment. This is where I will leave you. Are you ready for your instructions?"

"That I am," Mack said, trying to put a good face on it but wishing that he had a cup of wine to buck him up. "What do you want me to do?"

"You have three choices," Mephistopheles said. "We require you to pick one."

"And what are these choices?"

"One, to kill Henry Dandolo. Two, to kidnap Alexius the Pretender. Three, to rescue the sacred icon of St. Basil."

Mack thought it was unfair, having to face so many choices before breakfast. But he knew he'd get no sympathy from the now stern-faced Mephistopheles, and so he said, "Which of those would you like me to perform?"

"My likes and dislikes have nothing to do with this matter," Mephistopheles said. "You must use your own judgment."

"But on what basis am I to decide?"

"You must come up with your own criteria, for this is an exercise in human judgment and free will."

"Dandolo? Alexius? But I don't know those people!"

"Obviously, you must acquaint yourself with them."

"And to kill a man—that was one of my choices, was it not?"

"It was indeed."

"Well, surely the forces of Good would take exception to that."

"I think I can speak for my friend Archangel Michael," Mephistopheles said, "when I tell you that you give Good too little credit if you think it never recognizes any grounds for killing. Good knows that there are worse things than that. Not that they condone killing in general; nor do we, for that matter, for intelligence and selection are the essence of both Good and Evil. But none of us gets too worked up over it, being immortals as we are, and used to the long view. We know that killing is a matter of very great importance to men, and so we include its possibility in our contest. And I will also tell you this: In killing, the motive is everything, and the ends are to be considered as well as the means."

"But how can I know the ends? How can I tell what the killing of this Dandolo will do in terms of future outcomes?"

"You face a problem common to all men. There is never enough evidence to know whether to kill or not. Yet sometimes it must be done, both from the point of view of Light as well as that of Dark."

"I'll be judged harshly if I make a mistake."

"No one will judge you but Ananke, Necessity, the judge of us all. Choose you must. That is the role of a Faust."

"Well, if you say so. Who am I supposed to kill again?"

"Henry Dandolo, the doge of Venice. And only if you decide that that's the best action under the circumstances."

"And the other guy? Alex something?"

"Alexius, Pretender to the throne of Constantinople."

"And the third choice again?"

"To rescue the sacred relic of St. Basil, protector of Constantinople. Really, Faust, you must pull yourself together. You are well known for your tenacious memory."

"It works better when I don't have a hangover," Mack said. "Now would you just mind telling me what a Frankish army is doing at Constantinople?"

Mephistopheles raised an interrogative eyebrow. "I thought an educated man like yourself would know all about this mighty event which took place only a few hundred years ago. I am surprised by your ignorance — though I also know this perhaps is but your bit of a joke. It is the Fourth Crusade, of course. But you must discover the situation for yourself, and take your best action."

"Well, I'll try," Mack said.

"You must do more than that," Mephistopheles said. "We have contracted with you to perform certain actions. If you fail to perform them in the time allotted, you will ruin our contest, and win for yourself something rather unpleasant."

"And what would that be?" Mack asked.

"Pain unspeakable in an everlasting pit in the bottomless places of horror where you will be killed unspeakably and then brought back to life to be killed again, and again, and again, until we can think up something worse for you. You have twenty-four hours in which to perform your deed. Adieu."

And with that Mephistopheles took to the air and soon vanished into the sky's sunny vastnesses.

Chapter
2

Mack stayed for a while in the cove, turning things over in his mind, until at last, deciding he had better get on with it, he began walking. He soon found himself on a vast plain that stretched, yellow and green, as far as the eye could see. A half mile ahead of him were the steep walls of Constantinople. These walls were higher and more massive than any he had seen in Europe. Sentries in brass cuirasses, with horsetail plumes on their bright helmets, marched along the battlements. Below, and a half mile back from the walls, there were hundreds of tents spread around the plain, and a multitude of campfires, and great crowds of armed men. There were also many wagons camped a little apart, in a place of their own, with women and children around them. As he came closer, Mack could see that forges had been set up, and smiths were even now hammering out arrowpoints and lance heads. There were other wagons from which provisions were being unloaded, and there were pavilions with brightly colored banners flying from lances set before them. These seemed to be the abodes of the leaders of this great expedition. Mack saw that this place was a veritable traveling city, a place that could pack up and move at any time. He realized that this city must have been moving almost daily since the host had left Frankland.

There was nothing to do but get on with it, and so he began walking toward the camp. As he approached, a group of horsemen rode by at a smart trot, and their leader raised a mailed hand to Mack, who waved in return. They must have mistaken him for one of the Frankish group, since his clothes were the good grays and browns and blacks of dear old Europe, not the gorgeous silks and satins of the fabulous East. He walked on, and soon he passed the first outliers, men-at-arms with lance and shield laid aside, reclining at their ease in the mild sunshine.

"What news bring you of the council?" one of them called out.

"What news I bring is not for your ears," Mack said, deciding to take a high hand lest he be undone at the very beginning.

"But is Boniface of Montferrat still at the meeting? That alone would be a sign of progress."

"I can tell you this much," Mack said. "Conditions haven't changed much in the last few hours."

"Then there's still hope of recovering honor out of this thieves' nest," another of the men-at-arms muttered.

Mack walked on. At last he came to a place that looked familiar. It was a wagon with a broad canopy to one side of it, and under that canopy there were chairs and tables, and there were hogsheads piled high, and men were sitting at the tables and drinking and eating. It was a tavern on wheels.

Grateful that he had found a place at last where he could feel at home, Mack entered and found himself a seat.

The tavern keeper appeared, and, taking in the finery in which Mack had been clothed at the Witches' Kitchen, louted low and said, "What might I bring you, my lord?"

"Your best wine," Mack said, realizing at once that his credit might be very good in this place.

The tavern keeper drew a piggin of wine and returned with it. "I have not seen you before, sir. Might it be that you have only recently joined our great company?"

"It might indeed be," Mack said. "Is that a roast of venison I smell on the back rack?"

"It is. My lord hath a discerning nose. I'll bring you a

gobbet of it forthwith. Prithee, sir, what can you tell us of any tidings you bring from your famous master?"

"What master is that?" Mack said, for the fellow's indirection left him grasping for the meaning, if any.

"I simply assumed, sir, that so great a lord as yourself did no doubt serve a greater; for it is written that all things serve another in this world, whether villein to master, ox to farmer, lord to God, and so on through the heavenly ranks where the rule is the same."

"Your loquacity is exceeded only by your perspicacity," Mack said, the wine having bucked him up considerably.

"My lord, might I enquire your name?"

"I am Johann Faust."

"And you have journeyed far to reach us?"

"Aye, passing far," Mack said.

"And tell me, sir, whom do you serve?"

The loungers in the tavern craned forward to catch the answer. But Mack merely smiled and said, "That is not for me to say at this time."

"Couldn't you give us a hint, though?" For a small crowd, indeed, a half multitude, had gathered around while the tavern keeper and Mack were holding their colloquy.

The landlord squinted one eye and said, "I'll bet you're an agent of the Council of Venice, which seeks to instruct and restrain the vainglorious Henry Dandolo, doge of Venice."

Mack shrugged.

"No," cried another, "he's no man of the Venetians, for note you not that look of proud piety on his face and how his hands seek his sleeves as if he were wearing a monk's habit? I'll bet he's a churchman in disguise, come from Innocent the Third, our Pope who organized this holy Crusade and now finds himself thwarted by the machinations of the diabolical Henry Dandolo."

They all stared at Mack, who said, "I wouldn't say yes and I wouldn't say no."

A third man, a soldier, declared, "It is apparent from his firm bearing and laconic replies that he is a soldier. No doubt he represents Philip of Swabia, a fighting man of few words, albeit many deeds that cry to Heaven for avenging. And I'll bet he brings an offer concerning who is to be ruler of Constantinople once the present incumbent, the inconvenient and stubborn Alexius the Third, has been reduced to a blind beggar scuffling for scraps in the dustbins of his once haughty city."

Mack gave no hint as to his political leanings. There was much conversation about whom Mack was representing, for there seemed no doubt that he was there on behalf of *someone*. The tavern keeper would accept no pay for his food and drink, asking instead that Mack remember him when the council met to regulate the use of strong drink among the Crusaders. And when Mack made to leave, a short, plump, well-dressed young man in clerk's gray introduced himself as Wasyl of Ghent and asked permission to assist Mack in getting quarters, since he had neglected to do so hitherto.

And so they walked together to the bright yellow double tent with the pennons flying in front of it, for this was headquarters of the Quartermaster Corps. There were loungers at the flap, but Wasyl cleared them out of the way with his announcement, "Make way for Johann Faust, a visitor from Frankland, and one who has not as yet announced his party and affiliation."

The quartermaster was impressed, and, asking no questions, assigned Mack to a high-peaked tent a little off to itself, since he had not associated himself with any of the factions. Wasyl, who seemed to have appointed himself servant and general factotum to Mack's certain but unspecified importance, went ahead to make sure that all was ready. When Mack arrived at his new quarters, he saw that a nice table had been laid for him, and there was a cold fowl and a bottle of wine and a half loaf of good wheaten bread. Not scorning a second lunch, for the tavern keeper had been niggardly with his gobbet of venison,

Mack tucked in, meanwhile listening to Wasyl prate of the affairs of the day.

"Everyone agrees," Wasyl said, "that Henry Dandolo, the doge of Venice, has turned what began as a religious matter into a thing of commerce. That is an advantage or a disadvantage depending on how you look at the rival priorities of religion and commerce." And he looked keenly at Mack to see which way his sympathies lay. But Mack merely waved a drumstick and took another bite of bread.

"Pope Innocent the Third," Wasyl went on, "is a pure man in his singleminded desire to free Jerusalem from the Saracen. Yet might not even his motives be suspect due to his overweening desire to bring the Greek Christians under the rule of Rome?"

"Interesting point," Mack said, finishing the bread and starting on some candied sweetmeats he found nearby.

"Then there is the question of Alexius the Fourth, as he is sometimes called, though as yet he has no kingdom, the son of the deposed Isaac the Second Angelus. They say he has promised to bring Constantinople under the sway of Rome if he becomes king. So he is seemingly allied to the side of piety. Yet it is true that his principal backing comes from Philip of Swabia, no friend to the Holy See, a violent man with ambitions as large as his domain is small."

"I see what you mean," Mack said, though he was making little sense out of the dissertation.

"And finally we must consider the position of Villhardoin, leader of the military expedition, a man both feared and respected, respectful of religion but not himself pious. A good man, one might say. Yet Villhardoin is noted for the extreme shallowness of his political opinions and his indifference to commerce. All he cares about is the clash of edged weapons. Is he the man we need to lead us?"

Mack wiped his mouth and looked around for a place in which to take a nap. The indispensable servant had provided a fine cot with comforter and newfangled pillow. Mack got up and walked toward it.

"My lord, I am your man," Wasyl said. "Will you not take me into your confidence, tell me who you favor and from whom you bring a message? I will fight and connive in your interests, lord. Do but tell me what they are."

Mack wished he could say, because he figured he needed people on his side in this contentious place. But he didn't know at this point what was the stronger party, nor on which side right lay, nor what he should do that would further the progress of mankind and preserve the city of Constantinople.

"Good servant," he said, "all will be vouchsafed to you in good time. Believe me, you will be the first to know where my sympathies lie. For now, go about the camp and see what rumors are extant, and then come back to me in an hour or two."

"I go!" Wasyl said, and left. Mack stretched out and was asleep almost immediately.

Chapter
3

Mack awoke with the feeling that there was someone in the tent with him. It had grown dark. He must have slept for hours. Someone had provided a lighted candle in an earthenware bowl. Wasyl, no doubt. Its flickering flame threw wild shadows on the walls of the tent. They looked almost like a man; a fantastic man with black and gray garments, piercing eyes, floating hair; the kind of man you wouldn't want to meet at night. It was strange how close to the real thing was the apparition. Mack reached out and touched. The shadows gave under his fingers and felt for all the world like flesh and bone. Appalled, he shrank back.

"You poke me," the apparition said, "but you don't greet me. What kind of manners is that?"

"I didn't think you were real," Mack said.

"Nor am I, entirely. But then, neither are you. For you are not who you say you are."

"And you?"

"I say not who I am, but you know who that is."

The apparition stepped into the light, revealing himself as one whose features Mack had reason to remember, since he had spied on his movements for several days before his accomplice, the Lett, had hit him over the head in the alley in Cracow.

"You are Dr. Faust!" Mack breathed.

"And you are a damned impostor!" Faust said in a grating voice.

For just a fraction of a second Mack quailed before the fury of that accusation. Then he pulled himself together. Those who do wrong have a code, too, just like those who do good, and like them they needs must strive to keep up their self-esteem, even their aplomb, in difficult times as well as good ones.

Now was an extremely difficult time: It was very embarrassing to be caught in an impersonation, and worse to be face-to-face with the man he was pretending to be. It was the sort of situation that would cause a lesser man to pale and squeak, "Sorry, sir, I didn't know what I was doing, I'll give it up immediately, just please don't have me hung." But Mack had not embarked on this role to give it up lightly. And so he strengthened his spirit, remembering that one who would play Faust on the stage of the world needs a little of the Faustian spirit if he's to get anywhere.

"We seem to be at cross-purposes here," Mack said. "I doubt not that you are Faust. Yet I am Faust, too, on the authority of no less a person than Mephistopheles."

"Mephistopheles was mistaken!"

"When the great ones make mistakes, those mistakes become law."

Faust drew himself to his full height, which was rather shorter than Mack's, and said, "Must I listen to this casuistic palaver from one who speaks in my name? By the powers, I'll have vengeance if you don't vacate immediately and leave this game to the player for whom it was intended, namely, me."

"You think highly of yourself, that much is evident," Mack said. "But as to who was chosen, it seems to be me. You can argue till kingdom come and you won't change that."

"Argue? I'll do a lot more than argue! I'll blast you with spells of greatest puissance, and your punishment will be most hideously condign."

"Will be what?" Mack asked.

"Condign. It means fitting. I intend to give you a punishment worthy of your transgression."

"You know a lot of words honest folk never use," Mack said hotly. "Now listen to this, Faust, I defy you utterly. And furthermore, I have the Powers of Darkness behind me all the way. The fact is, I make a better Faust than you!"

Faust felt rage turn his eyeballs into reddened jelly, and he fought hard for control. He wasn't here to get into a shouting match. He wanted his rightful place in the Millennial contest. And it seemed that threatening Mack — against whom he could do nothing anyway — was a waste of time.

"I'm sorry I lost my temper," Faust said. "Let's talk reasonably."

"Another time, perhaps," Mack said, for just then the tent flap was drawn back and Wasyl entered. He looked suspiciously at Faust.

"Who is this?" he asked.

"An old acquaintance," Mack said. "His name doesn't matter. He was just leaving."

Wasyl turned to Faust, who noticed that the plump, clerkly young man had a naked dagger in his hand and a nasty expression on his face.

"Yes," Faust said, "I was just going. Till next time . . ." He made himself say it. "Faust."

"Yes, till next time," Mack said.

Wasyl asked, "Who's the woman outside the tent?"

"Oh, that's Marguerite," Faust said. "She's with me."

"See that you take her with you," Wasyl said. "We don't want any stray strumpets crumpling the wicket."

Faust held his tongue, for he dared not reveal himself without first conferring with Mephistopheles. The great demon would not take it kindly if anyone aborted his contest.

Faust stepped outside and started walking. Marguerite, who had been waiting beside the tent flap, caught up with him and said, "So what happened?"

"Nothing, yet," Faust said.

"What do you mean, nothing? Didn't you tell him who you are?"

"Of course."

"Then why don't you simply take over?"

Faust stopped and looked at her. "It's not so simple. I need to talk to Mephistopheles first, and I haven't found him yet."

He turned to walk again, and found three soldiers in steel caps bearing pikes standing and looking at him.

"Hey, you!" said one of the soldiers.

"Me?" Faust said.

"There's nobody else here except her, and I'm not talking to her."

"Yes?" said Faust. "What do you want?"

"What are you doing here?" the soldier asked.

"None of your business," Faust said. "What makes it your concern?"

"We've been told to keep an eye open for fellows like you, skulking around the tents without anything to do. You'd better come with us."

Faust saw that he had spoken without thinking. Hasty grandiloquence was a fault of the Faustian character that Mack didn't seem to share. He would have to watch that. For now, he would talk nicely.

"Gentlemen, I can explain everything."

"Tell it to the captain of the guard," the soldier said. "Now come along quietly or we'll let you feel the end of a pike."

And with that they led Faust and Marguerite away.

Chapter
4

So what's new?" Mack asked, as soon as Faust and Marguerite had departed.

"Great news, lord," Wasyl said. "The doge Henry Dandolo himself wishes to see you immediately."

"Ah, indeed?" Mack said. "Do you know what he wants?"

"He didn't confide in me," Wasyl said. "But I have my suspicions."

"Share them with me, good servant, while I wash my face and comb my hair." He proceeded to do those things, and to wish that Mephistopheles and the witches had remembered to supply him with a change of linen. "What is Henry Dandolo like?"

"He is a fearsome old man," Wasyl said. "As doge of Venice, he is commander of one of the most powerful and well-disciplined fighting forces in all Christendom. We Crusaders are dependent on the Venetians for our transport and general stores, and they do not fail to remind us of it. Dandolo himself is blind and somewhat frail of body, being now in his nineties. He's at an age when most noblemen would be content to lie at ease in their country estates and have servants bring them sweetened gruel. Not Henry Dandolo! He has ridden all the way from Europe, and was seen in the battle lines at Szabo, where he demanded the Crusaders reduce that proud Hungarian city if they wished to secure Venice's cooperation in this Crusade. And so they did, but with much grumbling, because what began as a holy enterprise has been perverted into just another Venetian commercial venture. Or so some people say. I myself have no opinion on the matter until I hear your own."

"Wise of you," Mack said, running his fingers through his hair.

"Your opportunities in this meeting," Wasyl said, "are manifold."

"No doubt."

"An alliance of your interests with those of Venice could bring you wealth undreamed-of. And of course there is the other alternative."

"What's this?" asked Mack. For Wasyl had taken out his dagger, tested its point on the ball of his thumb, and put the weapon down gently on the table.

"That, my lord, is an instrument of good Toledo steel that you might find useful if your interests are *not* aligned with those of Venice."

Mack also tested the dagger's point on the ball of his thumb, for that was the customary thing you did with weapons in those times. He slipped the weapon into his sleeve, commenting, "This may come in useful if I need to make a point." Wasyl smiled obligingly.

Wasyl had commandeered two soldiers with torches. They went ahead and lit the way for Mack. Wasyl offered to go along, but Mack, realizing it was time he got down to business, declined the offer. It was prudent to work alone at this point, because he couldn't tell when Wasyl might realize that his interests didn't coincide with Mack's at all.

And so he started out. As he walked, he noticed that there was considerable commotion in the camp. Groups of soldiers were running here and there, and mailed horsemen rode past at a gallop. Many campfires were lit, and there was an atmosphere as of some great enterprise.

The doge's tent was a grand pavilion made of a white silken cloth through which lamplight gleamed. The doge himself was seated on a little chair before a table. There was a tray before

him, and on that tray was a quantity of precious gems, unset.
Henry Dandolo was fingering them. He was a huge man, still
imposing despite his great age. Now he seemed almost lost in
his stiff, brocaded clothing. There was a small velvet cap on
his head with the hawk's feather of Venice set in it at a jaunty
angle. His narrow face was unshaven, gray stubble catching
silver glints from the firelight. He had a thin, sunken mouth
tightly held, and his eye sockets showed the cloudy blue-gray
of cataractic sightlessness. He didn't look up as the servant
announced the presence of Lord Faust, newly arrived from the
west.

"Come in, take a seat, my dear Faust," Henry Dandolo
said, his voice booming and vibrant, speaking a correct but
accented German. "The servants have set out the wine, have
they not? Take a glass, my good sir, and make yourself at home
in my humble quarters. Do you like these baubles?" He gestured at the tray of jewels.

"I have seen their like from time to time," Mack said,
bending over the tray. "But never finer. These have a brilliant
luster and appear to be exceptional specimens."

"The ruby is especially fine, is it not?" Dandolo asked,
lifting a gem the size of a pigeon's egg in his thick white fingers
and turning it this way and that. "It was sent me by the Nabob
of Taprobane. And this emerald"—his fingers went to it unerringly—"hath a remarkable fire for its size, think you not?"

"Indeed I do," said Mack. "But I marvel, sir, that sightless
as you are, you can yet perceive these qualities and make such
distinctions. Or have you developed an eyesight in your fingertips?"

Dandolo laughed, a harsh bass cackle ending in a dry
cough. "Eyes in my fingertips! What a fancy! Yet betimes I
believe it to be so, for my hands so love to touch fine gems that
they have developed their own appreciation of them. Fine cloth,
too, is a favorite of mine, as it is of any true Venetian, and I

can tell you more about the tightness of warp and woof than a Flanders weaver. Yet these are but an old man's fancies. I have something more valuable than that."

"Indeed, sir?" Mack said.

"Take a look at this." The old man reached behind him and his fingers found and opened the lid of a large wooden chest. Reaching in, he took out the gorgeously painted wooden picture that had nestled in the crushed velvet.

"Do you know what this is?" Dandolo demanded.

"Indeed I do not," Mack said.

"It is the icon of the holy St. Basil. Its possession is said infallibly to ensure the continuing safety and prosperity of the city of Constantinople. Do you know why I show you this?"

"I can't imagine, my lord."

"Because I want you to take a message to your master. Are you listening carefully?"

"I am," Mack said, his mind filled with conjectures.

"Tell the Holy Father in Rome that I spit on him and his mean-minded excommunication. As long as this icon is in my possession, I have no need for his blessings."

"You want me to tell him that?" Mack asked.

"Word for word."

"So I shall, if it is ever my fortune to meet the Holy Father."

"Do not toy with me," Dandolo said. "Although you disguise it, I know you are his representative."

"I most respectfully beg to differ," Mack said. "I don't come from the Pope. I represent different interests."

"You're really not from the Pope?"

The old man's blind gaze was so fierce that even if Mack had been the Pope's emissary he would have denied it.

"Absolutely not! Quite to the contrary!"

The old man paused and took that in. "Quite to the contrary, eh?"

"Yes, exactly!"

"Who *are* you representing?" Dandolo demanded.

"I'm sure you can figure it out," Mack said, deciding to try some Faustian indirection.

Dandolo thought. "I've got it! You must be from Green Beard the Godless! He's the only one who doesn't have a representative here!"

Mack had no idea who Green Beard was, but he decided to play along.

"I won't say yes and I won't say no," he said. "But if I *were* representing this Green Beard, what might you have to say to him?"

"Tell Green Beard that we welcome him to our venture, and we are aware of the unique role that only he can play."

"He'll be interested to hear that. But what specifically?"

"He must begin his attack on the Barbary Coast no later than one week from now. Can you get that message to him in time?"

"There are many things I can do," Mack said. "But first I must know why."

"The reasons should be evident. Unless Green Beard, who commands the pirates of the Peloponnesus, neutralizes them, the corsairs of the Barbary Coast are apt to put a crimp in our plans."

"Yes, indeed," Mack said. "Which plans were those, by the way?"

"Our plans to take over Constantinople, of course. We Venetians have stretched our seapower to the utmost in getting this group of Franks hither to Asia. If a pirate attack should come on our Dalmatian dependencies while we are otherwise engaged, I fear we should be hard-pressed."

Mack nodded and smiled, but within he was boiling with excitement. So Dandolo was planning to capture Constantinople! By no stretch of the imagination could that be considered protecting it. It seemed clear that Dandolo had to go, and never would the time be better than right now, while he was alone with the blind old man in his tent, at a time when the camp of the Franks was in a state of excitement. Mack slipped the knife out of his sleeve.

"You understand," Dandolo said, fondling his ruby, "my plans for this fine city are far-reaching indeed, and no man but yourself and your pirate chief will know what I intend."

"It is a great honor," Mack said, trying to decide whether to insert the knife from front or back.

"Constantinople is a city that has seen better days," Dandolo said. "Once great and feared throughout the world, it is now an effete shadow of itself due to the ineffectual rule of its stupid kings. I'll bring that to a stop. No, I shall not reign myself. Command of Venice is enough for me! But I will put my own man on the Byzantine throne, and he will have orders to restore the city to its former majesty and greatness. With Venice and Constantinople allied, all the world will look with wonder at the age of great commerce and learning that will ensue."

Mack hesitated. He had been ready to strike. But Dandolo's words conjured up a vision of a great city restored to its full powers, a city in the forefront of learning and commerce, a place that could be a turning point in the history of the world.

"And what religion would these Greeks follow?" Mack asked.

"Despite my differences with the Pope," Dandolo said, "I am a good Christian. Young Alexius has made me promises of the most solemn sort, that once in power he will return his subjects to the rightful See of Rome. Then the Pope will lift my excommunication, nay, may even see fit to canonize me, for so great a feat of conversion has not been heard of in modern times."

"My lord!" Mack cried. "Your vision is holy and enchanted indeed! Count on me, my lord, to aid you in whatever way I can!"

The old man reached out and caught Mack in a close

embrace. Mack could feel the stiff bristles of the old man's face, and the warm salt of his tears as he raised his voice to praise Heaven. Mack was about to say a few words in favor of Heaven, too, because it could do no harm, when suddenly men-at-arms burst into the tent.

"My lord!" they cried. "The attack has begun! Villhardoin leads the soldiers even now to assault the walls!"

"Take me to the action!" Dandolo cried. "I'll fight in this just cause myself! My armor, quick! Faust, give my offer to Green Beard, and we'll talk more later!"

And with that the old man swept out of the tent on the arms of his servitors, taking the holy icon with him, but leaving behind the bag of jewels.

Mack stood in the tented room, with shadows dancing up and down its silken walls, and decided this was going to work out very nicely. He was going to save Constantinople and make a profit at it, just like Henry Dandolo was doing. But just in case anything went wrong . . . He found a little canvas sack and took a nice selection of the jewels, then hurried out into the night.

Chapter 5

The soldiers escorted Faust and Marguerite to a low wooden building constructed of heavy unpainted boards. It was the dungeon, and Faust knew at once that it was one of the portable models suitable for traveling armies. This dungeon was an exceptionally well-appointed one imported from Spain, where the Moors of Andalusia knew how to do these things. Upon entering, the soldiers showed Faust and Marguerite the torture chamber, a miracle of miniaturization and cunning joinery.

"We can't pull apart a whole man, like they can do back in Europe," one of the soldiers told him, "but we can sure rack hell out of his arms or legs, and it gets the same effect as the whole-body model. These finger pincers do the trick as good as the larger models, and are no bigger than what you'd use to crack nuts. Here's our iron maiden, smaller than the one they have in Nuremberg, but with more spikes. The Moors know how to put in more spikes per square inch than anyone else. Our pincers are not full size, but they tear the flesh in a very satisfactory manner."

"You're not putting us to torture!" Faust cried.

"Certainly not," the leader of the soldiers said. "We're common soldiers. Straightforward killing is good enough for us. Whether they torture you or not is up to the Director of the Dungeons."

As soon as the soldiers left, locking the cell door behind them, Faust crouched down and began drawing a pentagram on the dusty floor, using a twig he had found in a corner.

Marguerite sat on the backless stool that was the cell's only furniture and watched him.

Faust intoned a spell, but nothing happened. The trouble was, he hadn't brought along much in the way of magical ingredients, so great had been his hurry to find the impostor. Still, he had to try. He scrubbed out the lines and drew them again in the dust on the floor of the dungeon. Marguerite stood up and began pacing up and down like a caged pantheress.

"Don't step on the pentagram," Faust told her.

"I'm not, I'm not," Marguerite said in an exasperated voice. "Are you going to do anything with it?"

"I'm working on it," Faust muttered. He found a pinch of henbane in the bottom of his pouch, added a sprig of mistletoe he had left over from a midwinter ceremony. Shaking out his sleeves, he found some antimony. And there were two pellets of lead in his shoes. What else did he need? Common dirt would have to substitute for graveyard mold. And for mummy powder, he would substitute nose snot.

"That's disgusting," Marguerite said.

"Shut up, it may save your life."

All was in readiness. Faust waved his hands and chanted. A glimmer of rosy light appeared in the middle of the pentagram, a fiery dot at first, then it expanded.

"Oh, you did it!" Marguerite cried. "You're wonderful!"

"Quiet," Faust hissed. Then, turning to the growing light, he said, "O spirit from the darkest deep, I conjure you in the name of Asmodeus, of Beelzebub, of Belial—"

A voice came from the glowing light. It was a young woman's voice, and it said matter-of-factly, "Please stop conjuring. I am not a conjurable spirit."

"You're not?" Faust asked. "Then who or what are you?"

"I am a representative of the Infernal Communication Service. We cannot accept your conjuration in its present form. Please check your spell and if you think you have it wrong, please conjure again. Thank you. Have a nice day." The voice stopped and the rosy light dwindled and disappeared.

"Wait!" Faust cried. "I know I don't have all the right ingredients. But I've got most of them! Surely an exception can be made. . . ."

There was no answer. The rosy light was gone, and there was no sound in the dungeon but for the tap-tap-tapping of Marguerite's foot.

Then noises started up from outside. Running feet. The clank and ring of mailed vests. The squeak of big wooden wheels turning on ungreased axles. The sound of soldiers shouting orders. And there was another sound, too. The sound of a monotonous voice reciting what sounded to Faust like an incantation. He bade Marguerite shut up, and pressed his ear against the wall. Yes, that sound was coming from the next dungeon. But it was no incantation he was listening to. Instead, it was a prayer.

"Hear me, my Lord," the muffled voice was saying. "I have done no evil, yet I am sunk into an accursed double darkness, the darkness of mine own blindness, and the darkness of this prison cell. I, Isaac, who was once king of Constantinople and known as Alexius the Third, given to many deeds of piety and religious zeal, who gave to the churches of Constantinople the following items . . ." There followed a list of bequests to individual churches and churchmen, and the list was so long that Faust was able to turn to Marguerite and say, "Do you know who is in the next dungeon?"

"I really don't care," Marguerite said. "I just want to get out of this one."

"Be silent, girl! In that dungeon languishes Isaac, the old king of Constantinople, who was deposed by his cruel brother, who crowned himself emperor and had Isaac blinded."

"We're traveling in exalted company, no doubt of that," Marguerite said sarcastically.

"Be silent! Someone is opening his dungeon door!"

Faust listened and heard the key turn, the door swing open, then close again. He heard shuffling feet (the plank wall was very thin) and then a moment's silence. Then old Isaac's voice could be heard plaintively asking, "Who is it comes to me? Is it the executioner? Speak, for I cannot see you."

"Nor can I see you," a deep voice replied. "But I have brought you succor that needs no sight for its relief."

"Brought me what?"

"Succor. Aid. Help. Relief. Don't you recognize my voice, Isaac? I am Henry Dandolo!"

"It's the doge!" Faust whispered to Marguerite. "Henry Dandolo, the all-powerful doge of Venice!" Raising his voice, Faust called out, "Doge Dandolo! In here! We crave your intercession!"

There was a mutter of voices, a stomping of feet. And then the door to Faust's dungeon was thrown open. Two soldiers entered. And just behind them was the tall, erect old figure of Henry Dandolo, resplendent in his brocaded robes of scarlet and green, holding in his hand the holy icon of St. Basil.

"Who are you who thus calls me by name?" Dandolo demanded.

"I am Johann Faust," Faust cried. "I have come to this place to right a great wrong done to me. There is a fellow here who says he's me, and who has duped a gullible infernal power with his story. He claims to be a great magician, but he's not. I'm the great magician!"

"I see," Dandolo said.

"I beseech you, Henry Dandolo, release me from this place and I will prove a worthy ally to you!"

"If you're such a great magician," Dandolo said, "why don't you release yourself?"

"Even a sorcerer needs a few tools," Faust said. "I don't have any of my conjuring equipment here. Yet if I had just a single missing piece to complete the spell — that icon you hold in your hand, for example . . ."

Henry Dandolo looked at him with anger. "You would conjure with the holy icon of St. Basil?"

"Why, yes, of course, that's what holy icons are for!"

"The sole purpose of the icon of St. Basil," Dandolo thundered, "is to preserve the city of Constantinople from harm."

"Well, it's not doing a very good job of it, is it?"

"Don't you worry about that. It's nothing to do with you."

"Maybe not," Faust said. "At least release us, since we have done you no harm and are not your enemies."

"I need to look into your claim to being a magician," Dandolo said. "I will be back."

And with that he swung around, and, guided by the soldiers, left the dungeon. The door clanged shut and the key turned again.

"It's impossible to reason with these pigheaded Venetians!" Faust said.

"Oh, my goodness, what will we do now?" Marguerite wailed.

Marguerite was depressed. Faust was feeling none too chipper himself, though in his case it was more outraged pride that irritated him than fear of death. He paced up and down, trying to think of an expedient. It had been shortsighted of him to go chasing after Mephistopheles without making sure he had his magic in order. He remembered when he had traveled throughout Europe with a bag of tricks. He had always been prepared. Had respectability dulled his wits? And if it had, how was he to know it?

He toyed again with his pentagram, more just in order to occupy his hands than with any real hope of success. He was amazed to see a light growing again within the inscribed lines. It was a little light at first, just like the previous time, but it grew larger, and this time the light was of a red-and-orange hue, a color which presaged a visit from someone hellish.

As the light took on human shape, Faust called out, "O spirit! I have conjured thee from the darkest pits —"

"No, you haven't," the creature in the light said, taking on the form now of a smallish, fox-faced demon with short goatlike horns, wearing a skintight sealskin suit that outlined his well-turned figure.

"I haven't conjured you?"

"Certainly not. I came of my own accord. I am Azzie. I am a demon."

"I am very pleased to meet you," said Faust. "I am Johann Faust and this is my friend, Marguerite."

"I know who you are," Azzie said. "I have been observing your actions, and those of Mephistopheles, and of the other man who calls himself Faust."

"Then you know that he is an impostor! I am Faust!"

"Indeed you are," Azzie said.

"Well then?"

"Well, I have been considering the situation. And I have a proposition to make to you."

"At last!" Faust cried. "Recognition! Revenge! Eternal delights!"

"Not so fast," Azzie said. "You haven't heard the terms of my proposition."

"Well then, out with it!"

"No, not here," Azzie said. "A Frankish prison is not where I conduct my negotiations."

"Where, then?"

"I have in mind a certain mountaintop," Azzie said. "It is a high mountain in the Caucasus, not far from where Noah first found land after the Flood. There we can talk and I can lay forth my proposition with all due majesty."

"Lead on, then," Faust said.

"Hey, what about me?" Marguerite asked.

"What about her?" Faust asked.

"She can't come. My bargain will only be with you, Faust, not with a camp-follower jade."

"You've got a lot of nerve!" Marguerite said. "I'm with him! I've even helped him in his enchantments. He asked me along. Johann, you can't leave me here!"

Faust turned to Azzie. "It's not right, you know."

"I give you my word of honor," Azzie said, "she'll be all right."

"You're sure?"

"I'm never wrong about things like that."

"Then let's go," Faust said. "Marguerite, we'll be back together after a while. I hate to do this, but business is business." But actually, Faust was not sorry to leave her, because Marguerite hadn't proven quite as admiring and servile as he'd hoped.

"No, no! Take me along!" The unhappy girl rushed to Faust and tried to throw her arms around him. But Azzie made a gesture. Smoke and fire arose, and Marguerite had to back off. When it had cleared, Faust and Azzie were gone, she was alone in the dungeon, and there was the heavy tread of soldiers approaching the door.

Chapter 6

Azzie, with Faust in tow, flew high and fast, above the towers of Constantinople, then to the southwest above the great plain of Anatolia. They passed over an occasional mud village, homes of the Turks who had migrated to this place from the back of beyond, and were even now raiding as far north as the fortifications of the great city. After a while they were over a region of low, barren hills, and then they came to the first peaks of the Caucasus Mountains. Azzie gained more elevation to pass over them, and Faust found himself shivering violently in the thin, chill air. The mountaintops lay below them, their tops piercing the fluffy white clouds, illuminated by the bright sun.

"See that big one ahead?" Azzie asked Faust, raising his voice against the windstream. "That's where we're going."

They landed on its summit, on a flat tableland that was drenched in brilliant noonday sunshine. Faust wanted to ask Azzie how he had brought this about, since it had been nighttime when they left the Crusaders' camp. But he didn't want to appear ignorant, so he said instead, "Where are we?"

"This is Mount Crescendo, highest peak in the Caucasus," Azzie said. "It is not far from Mount Ararat, where Noah first found dry land after the Flood."

Faust walked to the edge. Through the crystal air he could see for miles and miles, all the way down to peaceful settlements on the flatlands below. Beyond that he could just make out a pink stone palace, decorated with white walls and turrets and looking very like a birthday cake.

"What is that?" he asked.

"That is Castle Carefree," Azzie said. "It will be yours if you do my bidding."

"What are the special qualities of Castle Carefree?" Faust asked.

"You notice that pink stone that Carefree is constructed from? That is happiness stone, and it comes from the Golden Age of mankind, when all was well with everybody and everything. This stone is so permeated with the essences of good luck and happiness that one tends to walk around most of the time in a state of mild euphoria. It is a place where you can be happy and blithe, Faust. And this palace has the usual assortment of maidens of the most exquisite form, with heartstoppingly beautiful faces, and figures that would make an angel weep, though he'd better not let his superiors catch him in such an unangelic attitude."

"Castle Carefree looks very tiny from here," Faust said.

"The properties of light and air on this mountain are such," Azzie said, "that by squinting your eyes slightly you can magnify your view and see whatever you wish."

Faust squinted, too hard at first, because he found that he was looking at a blank wall from an apparent distance of perhaps two inches. Relaxing his squint slightly, he was able to move his gaze away from the wall and so get a panoramic view of the palace. Castle Carefree was indeed an enchanting place. Faust saw the many splashing fountains, neatly graveled walkways which meandered through a large and well-kept garden, he saw the multitude of tame deer that roamed its shaded confines, and the many bright-winged parrots who lived in its trees and converted the place into a shifting pageant of color. He saw the servants, dressed in white garments, strolling back and forth with brass trays filled with sweetmeats, fruits, trays of nuts, and dishes of spicy condiments. They offered these treats to the guests, who were clad in rich robes of many colors. Faust could see that several of the guests were tall and nobly bearded, and had such finely shaped heads as he had not seen since he had studied ancient sculpture in Rome.

"Who are these men?" he asked.

"These are philosophers," Azzie said. "And their purpose would be to converse with you about the how and why of things, and add their learning to your lightning-quick intelligence. Now shift your gaze a little to the left — that's it — and notice that dome-shaped building standing apart from the other structures."

"Yes, what is it?" Faust asked.

"That is Castle Carefree's treasure store," Azzie said. "Therein are treasures aplenty: gems of the first water, pearls beyond compare, jade of an ultimate exquisiteness, and other fine things."

Faust squinted his eyes again and tilted his head somewhat.

"What is it that I see far ahead on the horizon?" he asked. "It seems to be a moving cloud of dust."

Azzie looked. "That is of no account."

"But what is it?"

"If you must know, that is a band of wild Turkish warriors," Azzie said.

"Do they belong to Castle Carefree?"

"I'm afraid not. They provide quite a menace hereabouts. But they leave Castle Carefree alone."

"But what would I do if they came to attack me?" Faust asked. "Then my riches and cheerful life-style would not help much, would they?"

"Change is ever upon us," Azzie said. "There are savage warriors outside every palace, clamoring to get in. And sometimes they succeed. But never fear, I would not leave you in peril. I can provide palaces for you in various regions of the world. There are many fair cities where you might live. And you would not be confined to your own time, either. If you wanted to walk in Athens with Plato, for example, or ancient Rome to converse with Virgil or Caesar, I could arrange that."

"That sounds pretty good," Faust said. "But what about my rightful place in this great contest of Dark and Light?"

"I think I can do something about that," Azzie said. "You understand it was not my fault that this mistake was made. It was that stupid Mephistopheles, and I intend to teach him a lesson. But first I'll need to make some enquiries, for the contest is already underway and the Powers of Light and Dark would not be pleased to have it interrupted. But with a little luck and a word or two in the right places I think I can get you switched into the game in Mack's place."

"And you would do this for me?"

"Yes, I would," Azzie said. "But there is a condition."

"What is it?"

"You must bind yourself to me by the strongest oath you know to obey me in every instance, and, especially in matters of the contest, to be bound by me and do what I say."

Faust drew himself up proudly. *"Me,* obey *you?* I am Faust, and who are you? Merely some almost anonymous unclean spirit!"

"I wouldn't say unclean," Azzie said, offended. "That's a vile canard on us demons. Anyhow, there's nothing dishonorable about obeying a demon. Men do it all the time."

"Not Faust," Faust said. "Why do you consider it necessary?"

"It is because I have a plan, by means of which you can regain your rightful place in things, and I mine. But you must do what I say. You won't find me too hard a taskmaster. Come now, will you do it?"

Faust considered and was sore perplexed. He was tempted. Being ruler of Castle Carefree was a step up from being a professor of alchemy in Cracow. But he couldn't bring himself to agree to obey Azzie. A deep-set inner reluctance held him back. It was not so much that Faust the man had to have his own way. It was more that, as the embodiment of the archetypal spirit of Faust, he could not make himself subservient to a spirit who, by the nature of things, was supposed to be serving him, not the other way around.

"I can't do it," he said.

"Ah, but consider," Azzie said. "How about if I also throw in that quintessence of beauty that all men seek. I refer of course to none other than the incomparable Helen of Troy."

"Not interested. I already have a girlfriend."

"But you don't have Helen of Troy!"

"I'm not interested," Faust said.

Azzie smiled. "Just take a look."

So saying, the demon made a gesture. And there on the mountaintop, before Faust's eyes, a woman began to take shape. And then she stood before him. She looked at him with eyes of a deep color, though Faust could not say which, since they seemed to shift color as the clouds passed over the sun. One moment gray, another moment blue, and yet another green. She wore a classic Greek outfit, a white tunic well pleated, with a strap passing over one shoulder, the other bare. So excellent in all her proportions was she that it would have been ridiculous and futile to try to pick out some feature above the others, saying, her nose is very good, or, her eyebrows arch nicely, or, she has a well-shaped bosom, or, her legs are of a comely disposition. All these statements were true, but Helen beggared description and undercut comparison. She was of that perfection, which men glimpse sometimes, murkily, in their dreams. She was in her own way an absolute, an ideal more than a human being, and yet she was human. And whatever flaws might be found in her served only to enhance her perfection by their very humanity.

Faust looked at her and was sorely tempted. She was a great prize to be won because—completely apart from her inherent desirability—there was the pleasure to be gained by taking her away from all other men, and having all men in the world except the gay ones envious of you. To have Helen make a man richer than the treasures of a king of kings.

But there was a price to be paid, too. For a man who possessed Helen would also be possessed by her, and could call neither his soul nor his destiny his own. His fame would suffer by comparison to hers. In his own case, no longer would he be thought of as Faust the archetype. He would probably be referred to as Helen's boyfriend. And his own excellences could not fail to dim in comparison with hers. Paris had probably been a good enough man, back there in ancient Troy when he won her from Menelaus. Yet who thought about Paris now?

There were all those reasons, and there was another one: Faust knew that desiring Helen was one thing but, for him actually to take her would be archetypically unsound. He was Faust, a solo act who stood on his own. He was not to be any man's puppet, no, nor woman's, either.

He spoke rapidly, before the sight of her fatal loveliness could undermine him. "No, no," he said, "I'll not have her and I'll not be your man."

Azzie shrugged and smiled. He didn't seem to be entirely surprised at this decision. He must have known what stern stuff Faust was made of, and realizing this, Faust felt a glow of pride in his heart. It's something when even a demon admires your steadfastness!

"All right," Azzie said. "I'll get rid of her. But it was worth a try." He made a series of hand movements, of a dexterity that Faust had to admire: magicians know each other's skills and excellence by the sinuosity of their hand and finger movements. Azzie's was second to none.

The light shimmered for a moment around Helen, who had

been waiting rather passively through all this. But then the shimmering went away. Azzie made passes again. This time there wasn't even a shimmer.

"Well, isn't that weird?" Azzie said. "Usually that Disappearing Spell works just fine. I'll have to look it up again later, when I have time. Tell you what. Helen's a nice girl and she needs a little vacation from Hades, where she currently resides. How about if she sticks around with you a while, and I'll take her back later?"

Faust looked at her and his heart throbbed in his breast, for, although his intellectual reasons for refusing her were impeccable, his heart still went out to her. But he controlled himself and said, "Well, all right, I'll look after her for a while if you'd like. Of course, there *is* Marguerite."

"Don't you worry about her," Azzie said. "She'll come to no harm. And anyway, I could tell that she wasn't right for you."

"You really think that?" Faust asked.

"Trust me. A demon knows by the glow in his chest when a love match is doomed to destruction. I'll catch up with you later, we'll have another talk. You're sure I can't tempt you with something?"

"No, but thanks for trying."

"Right, then. I must be off."

"Wait!" Faust said. "Could you supply me with a few ingredients that I need for my Traveling Spell? Otherwise Helen and I might be stuck on this mountaintop for quite some time."

"Good thing you mentioned it," Azzie said. And, opening the pouch that all demons carry with them, but which, because of witchcraft, does not make a bulge in their clothing, Azzie removed a variety of herbs, simples, nostrums, purified metals, recondite poisons and the like, and gave these to Faust.

"Thank you," Faust said. "With these at my disposal I'll

work my own destiny. Your offer was kind, Azzie, but I can take care of this matter of the impostor by myself."

"Farewell, then!" Azzie cried.

"Farewell," Faust said.

They both struck a pose, right arms upraised in the air, palms outward, thumbs folded in — the magician's gesture — then Azzie vanished in a flash and Faust, a moment later, accompanied by Helen, vanished in one also.

Chapter
7

Marguerite couldn't believe it. She had always heard that magicians were a fickle lot, but this, in the old German expression, really took the apple kuchen. She had gone from a tavern in Cracow to a cell in Constantinople, and she didn't even know what she'd been arrested for. And here she was, abandoned by Faust and probably in a lot of trouble. She paced up and down the cell, then cowered back as she heard the sound of heavy footsteps marching down the passageway. The footsteps stopped, the door to the next cell clanged open.

Marguerite waited, listening. There was a brief pause. Then the steps started up again. They stopped in front of her cell. She heard the sound of a key rattling in the crude lock. Then the lock turned. She cowered as the door to her cell swung open.

And saw, entering the doorway, a tall, yellow-haired young fellow dressed in fine clothing. He paused in the doorway, looking at her with a gaze of some attentiveness. For a while the two of them formed a tableau there in the gray light that filtered into the cell from the guttering horn lanterns hung in the corridor. The newcomer was little more than a boy with a sheen of perspiration dappling his upper lip, staring, while she, her long, chestnut hair tangled in an attractive way, long skirt slightly raised to show her attractive ankles, cowered in a posture most pathetic yet most enticing, too.

Then Mack, for such it was, said, "Who are you?"

"I am Marguerite," the girl said. "And you?"

"Dr. Johann Faust, at your service."

Marguerite blinked twice, and it was on her mind to say that he couldn't be Faust because the real Faust had just abandoned her to go off joyriding with a demon. But a moment's reflection convinced her that this line of talk might not be a good idea, since this fellow presumably had rescue in mind, and might not care to be contradicted so vehemently at the very beginning of their relationship. Let him be Faust, or Schmaust, or Gnaust, or whatever he pleased, so long as he got her out of here.

"What are you doing here?" Mack asked.

"That's a long story," Marguerite said. "I was with this other fellow, and, well, he sort of went off and left me here. And you?"

Mack had come to the prison cell in pursuit of Henry Dandolo, hoping to get from him the icon of St. Basil, because this, it seemed to him, was very much what he needed to bring this situation to a successful conclusion. When he reached the first cell he saw that Dandolo, along with blind old Isaac, had left. He was about to leave himself, when some presentiment made him look into the next cell. It was strange: it was not his usual way, to look into cells. But this time it had seemed quite urgent that he do so. And so he had done it. But how to tell all this to Marguerite?

"Mine's a long story, too," he told her. "Do you want to get out of here?"

"Does a pig like to wallow?" Marguerite said, using an old expression which was common in the part of Germany where she had been a goosegirl.

"Come, then," Mack said. "Stick with me. I have to find somebody."

They left the dungeon and went out into the camp. It was a scene of confusion and riot. A thousand torches flared, illu-

minating people scurrying back and forth. Trumpets were blast-
ing, and most people were moving in the direction of the city
walls. It seemed that an attack was in progress.

Mack and Marguerite made their way through the crowd,
walking in the direction most of the people were going. Everybody was hurrying toward the walls of Constantinople, and it
seemed there was fighting going on there. Bloodied men were
being helped back from the fray, many of them stuck with
Byzantine arrows, which could be distinguished from others by
the red and green hexagonal patterns painted on their shafts,
and by their feathers, which were of Muscovy duck rather than
English goose.

Other soldiers pushed past them to get into the fight. There
were signs of struggle on the high battlements. But below, with
a sudden clang, the great gates that guarded Constantinople
swung open, unbolted by Frankish sympathizers within the city.
The mounted Crusaders, seeing this, quickly formed up and
galloped toward the open gates in an armored wedge. There
were Greek soldiers barring the entrance, and there were
Northmen, too, who had been enlisted to fight in the city's
armies. They tried vainly to stem the tide. But the maddened
Crusaders slammed into them, battle-axes and maces swept
through the air in short, sharp arcs, and there were cruel sounds
as, with terrible effect, they landed on bodies. A group of Greek
women atop the wall had brought up a huge cauldron of boiling
oil. They tipped it over now, and it came down in a sizzling
golden cascade. Frankish soldiers caught in the flood screamed
as the hot oil poured over their armor and came through the
neck and arm openings, to broil them inside like so many lob-
sters. Then a flight of arrows swept the women away, and the
Frankish host was charging again, shouting their battle cries
and advancing into the city with irresistible force. A small group
of Turkish mercenaries were now the only ones left guarding
the inner keep. Their arrows flew hard and fast, darkening the
sky, making conversation difficult with the ominous hiss of their

passage. Rank after rank of Crusaders were thrown down, rolling away from horses that bristled like porcupines as the Turkish arrow storm struck home. Then the tide of maddened Franks reached the ranks of the Turks, who, small of stature and lightly armored, could not stand up to the big, hairy, unshaven European men in their heavy mail. There was a great lopping of limbs and beating in of heads, and the blood-maddened Franks burst through the Turkish lines into the city streets.

Mack raced through just behind the fighting, pulling Marguerite along by the hand. Finally he spied Henry Dandolo. The old man was on foot and clutching an enormous sword. He was waving it around so that everybody near him had to duck out of the way. "Lead me to them!" Dandolo was shouting. "Let me at those Greeks!"

Mack ran up, ducking under the sword, and, clutching Dandolo's arm, said, "Henry, it's me, Faust! Let me guide you!"

"Ah, the messenger from Green Beard!" Dandolo said. "Yes, fine, just point me in the direction of the enemy and give me a push."

"I'll do that," Mack said, and turned Henry around so that he faced the city walls. As he did so, he deftly removed Dandolo's silken sling, from which he had seen, peeking, the icon of St. Basil.

"Best of luck, sir!" he called out, and Henry Dandolo waved his sword and went charging into the battle, a precursor of Don Quixote if there ever was one.

Mack turned to Marguerite. "All right, let's get out of here!"

Mack, with Marguerite in tow, now turned away from the city walls and made his way back into the camp. He was in search of a place of safety. One thing he knew for sure was, he had fulfilled his first test. He had made a choice, had saved the icon of St. Basil.

Already it was late. Darkness suddenly fell. The night had

turned quite chilly. A cold wind was blowing. Rain was falling. Shivering, shaking, Mack and Marguerite slogged across the muddy battlefield.

"Where are we going?" Marguerite asked.

"There's somebody I have to meet," Mack said, wondering where in hell Mephistopheles was.

"Did he say where?"

"He said he'd find me."

"Then why are we running like this?"

"We're getting away from the battle. You could get killed out there!"

And then they ran into a group of soldiers. These were not the same soldiers who had arrested Faust earlier. These looked quite similar, though, being large and unshaven and hairy and foul-spoken and loaded down with weapons. These fellows had been doing some fighting and they looked all the worse for it. They were beaten and bruised and their armor was dented. They were crouched over a pile of logs and a couple of chairs they had plucked from a passing caravan, trying to get a fire going. Over and over they struck flint and steel, but the rain, which had begun just past sunset, was coming down harder and they were meeting with no success.

"Hey there, you! Stop a moment!" a voice cried as Mack and Marguerite came up. "Haven't got a bit of dry firewood on you, have you?"

"No, no," Mack said. "Sorry, but we don't have any. Excuse us, fellows, we have to go."

The soldiers crowded around them. Marguerite felt something lumpy press against her side. She was about to slap somebody's face when she realized that Mack was trying to get her to take a small sack he had taken from Henry Dandolo. She concealed it on her person as the soldiers grabbed Mack.

They searched him roughly, and then turned to her. Marguerite, fearing rude hands on her person, dumbly handed over the sack.

"Aha!" one of them cried in a triumphant voice, taking out the icon of St. Basil. "What have we here?"

"Careful with that," Mack said, "that's a special holy icon."

"What does it do?" the soldier asked.

"It works miracles," Mack said.

"Works miracles, does it? Let's see if it'll start this fire. *That* would be a miracle!" He struck flint and steel. Sparks flew. One of them caught in the varnish on the icon's painted face. The icon sprang immediately into flames.

The soldiers bent down over it, trying to get the burning icon under the other logs. Mack took the opportunity to get away, followed by Marguerite.

They reached the edge of a little woods that bordered the battlefield. Loud lamentations could be heard from the direction of the city, now that the hiss of arrows had ended. The Crusaders were running wild. Already a pall of smoke hung in the clear moonlit air. It looked like it was going to be Troy all over again.

Mack looked away. A flash of lightning revealed a tall, sinister figure standing not ten feet from him, wrapped in a crimson cloak, picturesquely posed at the margin of the woods.

"Mephistopheles!" Mack cried. "Am I glad to see you!" He hurried up to him. "Did you see what I did? I took the icon option."

"Yes, I saw," Mephistopheles said. "Frankly, I'm not impressed."

"You're not? But it seemed the best choice. When I heard of Henry Dandolo speak about his plans for the future of Constantinople, I knew that I shouldn't kill him. As for Alexius, I never did get close enough to him to kidnap him even if I'd wanted to."

"Fool!" Mephistopheles said. "Henry Dandolo was deceiving you. His hatred of Constantinople is implacable."

"How in hell was I supposed to know that?" Mack asked.

"Read his lips," Mephistopheles said. "If you had killed

him, a better emperor might have been found, who could have saved the city from the terrible sacking and burning that the Crusaders are giving it even now."

"I did the best I could," Mack said sullenly.

"I don't really mean to scold you," Mephistopheles said. "As I said, it's not you yourself being judged, it's mankind as exemplified by you. You made just the sort of silly choice a human *would* make. To try to save an illusion rather than perform a practicality!"

"Well, I'll do better at it next time," Mack said. "I won't try to save any more illusions, I can tell you that. What's next?"

"Your second adventure awaits you," Mephistopheles said. "Are you ready?"

"I could use a bath and a night's sleep."

"You will be able to get those things at your next stop. You are going to the court of Kublai Khan."

"What am I going there for?"

"I will explain when we get there. Prepare yourself."

"Wait!" Mack cried, for Marguerite was tugging at his sleeve. "Can I take her along?"

Mephistopheles looked at Marguerite, seemed about to refuse, then shrugged. "Oh, I suppose so. Hold hands, close your eyes, and the thing will be done."

Mack and Marguerite did as they were told. Marguerite also held her breath, because she hated the dizzying sensation of being conjured to another place and time.

Mephistopheles made hand gestures, there was the familiar flash of fire and curl of smoke. And they were gone.

MARCO POLO

Chapter
1

When Mack opened his eyes, he found he was on a busy street corner in what looked like a very large city. Mephistopheles and Marguerite were standing on either side of him. Mephistopheles was looking as dapper as always. He had a fresh red rosebud in the buttonhole of his dark lounge suit. His black shoes glittered with a new shine. And Marguerite was pretty as a picture. She'd found the time to repair her makeup since leaving Constantinople, and to change into a flowered gown with low-cut bodice.

Mack looked around, and saw at once that this city had many large and noble buildings of a peculiar design that had to be Chinese. This impression was further reinforced by the inhabitants, who, wearing silks and furs, and with their hands in their long sleeves, hurried back and forth holding high-pitched conversations. The air was crisp and cold and smelled of charcoal and five-spice powder. The sky overhead was a cold northern blue. Men in fur hats with flat orange faces passed by. These, Mack was pretty sure, were Mongols. There seemed to be a lot of them around, all armed to the teeth. They walked past Mack and the others as if they were not there.

"What's up?" Mack asked. "Don't they like us?"

"They can't see us," Mephistopheles said. "I have put us under a temporary Invisibility Spell. It's cheaper than hiring a conference room."

"If you say so," Mack said. "Now, what am I supposed to do here?"

"There in front of you," Mephistopheles said, "down at the end of the street, is the great palace of Kublai Khan. Within that palace live the great Khan, his nobles, relatives, concubines, and hangers-on. Also in that palace is Marco Polo."

"The famous Venetian explorer?" Mack asked.

"None other. His uncle and father would normally be there with him, but they've gone on a trading trip to Trebizond."

"Where's Trebizond?" Mack asked.

"Never mind. You don't need to know that. What you need to know is what you're supposed to do here."

"Yes, right," Mack said. "Better fill me in."

"The situation is like this. Marco is planning to leave Peking and return to Venice. Kublai Khan has reluctantly agreed to let him go because Marco is the only one who can provide safe escort for the Princess Irene, whom he has betrothed to one of his lords in Persia. There are plots 'gainst Marco's life, however. Some of the Mongol lords resent the favors Kublai has bestowed on him. There are people who want to kill him. One of your choices is to prevent Marco Polo from being killed before he leaves Peking."

"Now, wait a minute," Mack said. "He *did* leave Peking, didn't he?"

"Yes, but that was in the past. This is happening now. So it all must be done over again. And it could go a different way. Because even though it's happening over again, this is also the first time."

"But if it *did* go a different way," Mack said, "wouldn't that play hell with events in our own time?"

"You needn't worry about that," Mephistopheles said. "Think of it as a game within a game. You are brought here and given a moment in time. You will have three choices of what to do with that moment. From your choices, we will see how you will affect the future, whether for good or for ill."

"No, it makes no sense at all," Mack said. "Why should

I have to help Marco? He has already won out against any plot there might have been against him."

"You don't seem to understand," Mephistopheles said. "When we send you here, it's as if the story is happening for the first time. No outcomes are fixed. For that matter, who knows how many times the Marco Polo story has been replayed? The history of Earth is like the old morality plays one sees over and over again, but the outcomes are not fixed. It's like the commedia dell'arte. The basic cast assembles every evening, the situation is begun, but sometimes, quite unexpectedly, the outcome is different."

"And these new endings don't affect the main course of history?"

"How could you know what the main course of history is if you're immersed in its stream? And yet, although it is all deadly serious, it is all a game. At least, to *us* it is a game. But to you it had better stay serious or you'll suffer for it."

"What are my other choices?" Mack asked.

"There is the matter of the Princess Irene. She is from a far country and Kublai Khan has betrothed her to a lord of Persia. Yet if she were to marry someone else, that would change the course of history, too. You can decide to change that by getting her to marry someone else."

"What happened with the one she did marry?" Mack asked.

"History doesn't tell us," Mephistopheles replied.

"All right," Mack said. He saw he wasn't going to get anything much clearer out of this high-flown demon. "And what is the third choice?"

"Kublai Khan possesses a magic scepter that brings good luck to the Mongol forces, and hence bad luck on his enemies, which include the countries of the West that Kublai opposes. You could steal that scepter."

"I tried that last time with the magic icon."

"This time is completely different. Forget about the last time. Now, if you're quite ready, I'll take away the cloak of invisibility and you can begin."

"Wait a minute!" Mack said. "How do I explain my presence here?"

Mephistopheles pondered for a moment. "Tell them you're the ambassador from Ophir."

"And what is Ophir?"

"Ophir," Mephistopheles said, "is the city mentioned in the Old Testament from which King Solomon got his gold, silver, ivory, apes, and peacocks."

"And where is this Ophir located?"

"No one knows for sure. Various sites have been mentioned, among them East Africa, the Far East, Abyssinia, and Arabia. We can be sure Marco Polo has not been there, otherwise he would have mentioned it in the long and boastful list of travels he will leave behind. So you can safely claim your ambassadorship since there is no one to refute you."

"Well, all right," Mack said. "So I'm the Ophirian ambassador. Or is that Ophirese?"

"As you please," Mephistopheles said, showing signs of impatience. "Now, if you're quite ready?"

"Wait! One more thing," Mack said. "What about my clothing?"

"Look at yourself," Mephistopheles said.

Mack looked. Evidently, when redressing himself and Marguerite, Mephistopheles had found time to give Mack black-and-white tights, a wool-lined jacket, and a little cap with a feather in it. So that part was all right. But Mack felt there was something else, some other problem. Mephistopheles was beginning to make his disappearing gestures. Then Mack had it.

"Wait! How can I talk to these people?"

"What do you mean?" Mephistopheles said.

"Unless they know German and a little French, I'm going to be stuck."

"Oh." Mephistopheles frowned. "But, Dr. Faust, you are a renowned scholar and linguist."

"You know how it is," Mack said. "People exaggerate these things. Anyway, I've been a long time out of languages. They all need brushing up."

"Very well," Mephistopheles said. "I'll give you a Language Spell that will enable you to understand everything anybody says. Be careful with it. It's not for general circulation."

"A magic Language Spell will help," Mack said.

Mephistopheles gestured. "It is done. You have to give it back when you are through with it."

"What about me?" Marguerite asked.

"You're just along as his friend," Mephistopheles said. "The Language Spell doesn't pertain to you. Ready, then?"

Mack gulped and nodded. Mephistopheles disappeared, this time without a flash of fire and smoke, just a rather rapid fading out. At the same moment, a short, squat man with a long beard bumped into Mack.

"Ogrungi," the man said.

"No, no, it was my fault," Mack said. And then marveled at the fact that he had understood the fellow perfectly. The man moved on and Mack turned to Marguerite.

"I wish Mephistopheles hadn't been so peremptory," Mack said. "He really doesn't set these things up very well. Let's see now. What is the first thing I'm supposed to do?"

At that moment a tall, fierce-looking warrior in fur hat and lacquered armor, with sword and shield and a lance on his back, said, "Hey, you!"

"This is familiar," Mack murmured to Marguerite. Turning to the warrior, he said, "Yes?"

"I haven't seen you around before. Who are you?"

"I," Mack said, "am the ambassador from Ophir. Take me

to your khan. And by the way, this is my friend, Marguerite."

"Follow me," the warrior said.

Staying a few steps behind the warrior, out of whose way people scurried with much kow-towing, they walked through the teeming marketplace that lay on their way to Kublai's palace. There were smells aplenty here and they were Chinese smells for the most part, not European smells, though there were also curry smells from India, and hibiscus smells from the South Seas. Once they began walking among the stalls, the air became redolent with the odor of five-spice powder and Ac'cent. Blocks of pressed seaweed, which people ate like knockwurst, exuded their characteristic odor both miasmic and iodinic. Mack could detect the clean smells of bamboo and sandalwood above the more insistent odors of garlic, charcoal, rice-wine vinegar, and lichee nuts. There were baskets of barbecued pork and platters of General Khu's chicken. Duck Peking style could be seen everywhere, most of it doused in the ubiquitous Peking sauce. People with brownish yellow faces and straight black hair, of all sizes and shapes, gazed at them and passed comments. Because of the Language Spell that Mephistopheles had given him, Mack was able to understand all of the comments.

"Martha, will you take a look at that."

"What is it, Ben?"

"Sure looks like foreigners to me."

"What a funny skin color!"

"What ugly eyes!"

"And the way he's dressed! Nobody wears them velvet jackets around here."

"And look at her in them high heels! We don't even wear high heels around here, they're so tacky, so you can figure what they're like."

"Hell no, we don't!"

Noisy but cheerful, the crowd offered no violence. Mack, Marguerite, and the warrior left the market with its many smells and came to an altogether more neutral region in terms of odoriferousness, a great boulevard beyond which lay a noble palace.

They crossed the street and entered a long stone courtyard leading to a high gate. The gate was open and a captain of the guard stood before it in lacquered armor with sword and shield, and challenged them. "Who goes there?"

"Anonymous soldier," the Mongol warrior replied, "bringing with him the ambassador from Ophir and his girlfriend to present to the Khan."

"What good timing!" the guard said. "Kublai Khan and his whole court happen to be assembled now, they've finished talking business and it's not yet time for dinner, and so are hoping for something amusing to come up. Pass, anonymous soldier with honored guests."

The halls of the Khan's palace were rich beyond description. So none will be attempted. Down the corridors they marched, past scrolls covered with Chinese poetry extolling the virtues of water-watching. The final doors before the audience chamber were tall, oval-shaped, richly ornamented, and made of bronze. They swung open of their own accord.

"Who shall I say is calling?" a small, dark man asked.

"The ambassador from Ophir," Mack said. "And his girlfriend."

The great audience room was lit by flambeaux, which, being a newly imported French kind of torch, burned with a cold, pitiless intellectual light. By that light Mack saw, ahead of him, on a stage, a group of richly garmented people. In the center, elevated on a small plinth above the others, was a middle-sized, middle-aged, middle-tempered sort of a man of medium coloring and average good looks, a small beard, and on his head a turban from whose summit blazed a diamond so great that Mack knew even without a program that this fellow had to be Kublai Khan.

On either side of the Khan were various people who turned out to be dignitaries, aunts and uncles, perhaps a few brothers

and sisters, and some of their relatives. There were many court-
iers in the room. There was a pale blond woman sitting on a
small throne beside and slightly below Kublai who might have
been the Princess Irene. At every hand there were archers,
bows half drawn, arrows ready, watching the movements of
the guests, trusting none of them. At a little table all by himself
sat a wizened old man wearing a robe with stars on it. This no
doubt was the court wizard. Not far from him was a young
European-looking man sprucely dressed in pantaloons and
doublet and wearing on his head a small felt hat with a hawk's
feather. This was Marco Polo.

"So, you're from Ophir?" Kublai Khan said. Remembering
what Mephistopheles had told him, Mack noticed that Kublai
Khan had a scepter. It didn't look especially magical, but Mephistopheles was presumably correct in his information.

The Khan said, "You're the first Ophirean we've had visit.
Or do you say Ophirese?"

"Whichever Your Majesty prefers," Mack said.

"Look, Marco!" Kublai said. "A fellow European!"

The young man in the hawk-feather cap looked up and
scowled. "He's nobody I know. What's your name, fellow, and
where do you come from?"

"I am Dr. Johann Faust," Mack said. "I was born in
Wittenberg in Germany, but of late I'm the acting ambassador
from Ophir."

"We have not seen your like in Europe," Marco said.

"No. We Ophirese are pretty much content to stay home.
We're not a great trading nation anymore like your Venice,
Marco."

"Ah. You know me, then?"

"Certainly. Your fame has spread even as far as Ophir."

Marco tried to maintain his frown, but he was flattered.
"Tell me, what are your principal products?" he asked.

"We export a lot of stuff," Mack said, "but our main products are gold, silver, ivory, apes, and peacocks."

"Apes! That's interesting," Marco said. "The great Khan has been looking for a good source of apes."

"We've got the best," Mack said. "We've got big apes and little apes, tiny apelets, huge gorillas, orange-furred orangutans, and so on. I guess we can fill about anything you might need in the ape department."

"Great, I'll get back to you on that," Marco said. "The great Khan might want some peacocks, too, if your prices are competitive."

"Talk to me," Mack said, "I'll make you a price."

At that moment the court wizard spoke up. "Ophir, eh? The city that is near Sheba?"

"That's it," Mack said. "You got the right one."

"I shall check on this further," the wizard said.

"I'm sure you'll find our city is in order," Mack said. He chuckled, but no one else laughed at his little joke.

Kublai Khan said, "Welcome to my court, Dr. Faust, ambassador from Ophir. We shall wish to speak to you at some later time, because, let it be known, we love to hear stories of distant lands. Our dear son Marco regales us with many tales. But it is always good to get a new slant on these things."

"At Your Majesty's service," Mack said, and, noting that Marco's face had changed from a scowl into a rictus of annoyance, decided that he had made no friends here this day.

"And what of the woman?" Kublai Khan asked.

Mack hissed at Marguerite, "He's talking to you!"

"What's he saying?" Marguerite said. "I can't understand a word!"

"I'll speak for you," Mack said. To Kublai Khan he said, "This is Marguerite, a friend of mine, but she doesn't have a word of Mongol."

"No word at all? But we would fain hear her story!"

"I'll just have to translate it for you," Mack said, "which is a shame because she tells it so well herself."

"That won't be necessary," Kublai said. "Luckily, we have recently instituted a rapid-learning center for subjects and friends who don't understand Mongolian. You speak it perfectly, my dear Faust."

"Thank you," Mack said, bowing. "I've always had a bit of a knack for languages."

"But the woman is going to have to learn. Explain to her that she is to go to class now and come out when she can speak to us."

Mack said to Marguerite, "Look, I'm sorry about this, but they're taking you off to language class."

"Oh, no," Marguerite said. "Not school again!"

"Yes. I'm sorry. There's nothing I can do about it."

"Darn it!" Marguerite said. "This is no fun at all!" But she let herself be led away by two serving maids.

Chapter
2

Mack was aware of a strangeness in the outer corridors as he followed Wong, a servant who had been assigned to lead him to his quarters. He noted how Wong's lantern flame would suddenly sway when there was no breeze to stir it. As they moved through the silent hallways and corridors they came to one that was roped off with a crimson cord.

"And what is down there?" Mack asked.

"That is the spirit wing," Wong said. "It is dedicated to the spirits of dead poets. Entrance to it is forbidden to the living. Only the Khan himself and the servants of the Arts may go through with the sacrifices."

"What sacrifices?"

"Brightly colored stones, seashells, moss, and other things that are pleasing to the spirits of dead storytellers."

Wong told him that there were few monarchs as hospitable as Kublai Khan, and none as desirous of hearing the converse of strangers. Kublai was different from other Mongols in the pleasure he took at travelers' tales. He encouraged people from all over the world to come call on him, tell him where they were from and what the customs were like there. He liked to hear about their families, too, and the more extended, the better. And Kublai had a whole wing of his palace put aside for hospitality to strangers. This wing was arguably the world's first luxury hotel where people were welcome without a reservation and without money. Just a story.

There were beggars in the Khan's palace as well as ambassadors. But they were not ordinary beggars. In the Khan's estimation, a beggar was one with an insufficiency of stories. All the beggars in the Khan's palace were persons who, for one reason or another, were or could be considered story-dead. The Khan supported these unfortunates as a public charity.

Not only were there luxurious rooms for travelers, there was also the special wing for the wandering spirits of poets and storytellers. For it was the Khan's belief that the spirits of poets live forever, in a special celestial kingdom that had been constructed for them alone by the Powers That Be. And these spirits sometimes went a-wandering back to the Earth, for poets draw inspiration from revisiting the scenes of their former triumphs and defeats. And in their peregrinations around their old-time countrysides and city streets, sometimes these spirits were susceptible to outside influences. At such times, the Khan believed, a man could perform a certain ritual, lay out certain offerings, and these would attract such spirits, and they would come to the Khan's palace, for they knew they were welcome. Once there, they would find all the things that a spirit might crave: bits of soft fur, shiny shards of mirror, pieces of amber, antique silver coins, curiously colored pebbles. These were some of the things that were said to give pleasure to the spirits of dead poets, and the Khan had collected many of them. These were laid out in the chambers where the spirits were invited to visit. Incense was burned around the clock in these chambers, and candles were kept lit. And sometimes, a spirit would come to such a place, enjoy the feast of memory that had been laid out for him, and, when he left, deposit a dream in the Khan's head as a gift.

Due to this, the Khan had many remarkable dreams, for he had been visited by spirits telling of savage white whales, of conspiracies in the Roman forum, of great armies moving across a frozen white landscape. He had dreamed of journeying through a dark wood, gone from the path direct. He had dreamed of choosing between a lady and a tiger. Thus the Khan piled up a treasure of stories and dreams by day and by night, until he no longer knew which was which, and he worked on his own secret dream, which was to be an audience for dead poets after he had left this life.

Mack's apartment was of a luxury rarely encountered in the West. And the Khan had thought up many niceties. The servants who fetched him food and drink and hot water for his bath were trained to act as if he weren't there, so that their gaze would not intrude on his inner solitude. Mack found all this very nice, but he could not enjoy it properly for worrying about getting on with his choices. After all, he wasn't a sightseer. He was there to work.

To do something with and about Marco Polo seemed a good place to begin. Saving Marco Polo's life ought to be quite a Good Thing. In any event, he could see no harm in it. Nobody gets angry at you for saving their life. Whereas finding a new husband for Princess Irene seemed a little risky, and besides, he hadn't even met the princess yet. As for taking Kublai's scepter, it hadn't escaped Mack's attention that there were Mongol bowmen always near the Khan, arrow on bowstring, and whenever anyone even made a gesture in the Khan's direction, the bowmen stiffened and half drew their shafts. It was apparent that nobody got close to Kublai Khan. He'd risk being transfixed by arrows if he tried.

And then there was Marco Polo to consider.

"Tell me," Mack said to Wong, "does Marco Polo live anywhere around here?"

"He keeps an apartment in this complex," Wong said. "But he also has several fine mansions in the city and numerous farms, pleasure domes, and the like elsewhere."

"I didn't ask for his real estate holdings," Mack said. "I merely want to know where to find him."

"Right now he's in the Main Banquet Room, supervising the decorating for a great banquet tonight in the Khan's honor."

"Be so good as to take me there."

Chapter 3

The Main Banquet Room was filled with workmen putting up paper streamers, banners, brightly colored tapestries, and other gewgaws of a festive nature. The ceiling was lofty and was held up by eight pillars. Each of those pillars rested on a square block that gave some room at its corners for decorations. The main decoration for the festivities was severed human heads. Marco had heads piled on these corner stones, great piles of severed heads, some of them still bleeding, some rather dried out, some in a state of mummification, others in a state of moldiness, decay, or even putrescence. In the middle of the room was a vat of blood, with two cowled figures stirring it so it wouldn't coagulate. Marco was standing near to it, hands on his hips, supervising the placement of the heads.

Mack paused a moment to take it in, then walked up to Marco. "Nice-looking arrangement of heads," he commented.

"Thank you," Marco said. "But they're still not right."

He shouted to the men on ladders piling the heads, "Tighten up that pyramid! I don't want those heads scattered around. I'm after a concentrated effect. I want them piled high! A pyramid of heads about seven feet high, that's what I'm after on each of the corner stones. I know they won't balance by themselves. You'll have to devise some way to get them to look like they're balancing. Find some bracing material, or use twine or haywire, but make sure it doesn't show. And take those dried-out old heads out of the pile. They look like they've been lying around for decades. This isn't a tribute to the past. We're celebrating the Khan's present and future conquests and all we want here are freshly severed heads, preferably with the blood still dripping. If the blood isn't fresh, add some from the vat."

Mack and Marco watched for a while. The workmen made adjustments. Mack commented, "The display looks much better now."

"Do you think so?"

"Oh, yes. You Venetians have an eye for these matters."

"Thank you. So you're from Ophir?"

"Yes," Mack admitted. "But let's not talk about me. I just wanted to tell you how nice it is to meet you. I admire you, Marco. It's an honor to meet the foremost fabulist of your generation, perhaps of any generation."

"That's good of you," Marco said. "But you're a fabulist, too, aren't you? I mean, Ophir, what's that if not fabulistic?"

"Oh, only in a very minor way. After all, who cares about Ophir? After you've mentioned the ivory, peacocks, and apes, there really isn't much to say about the place."

Marco smiled a thin, dangerous smile. "I hope not. There's only room for one fabulist at a time in a royal court."

"Hey, you're the resident fabulist," Mack said. "As a matter of fact, you're the reason I came here. I want to get your autograph."

"You have my book?"

"It's my dearest possession. Was, I should say, for thieving Arabs stole my copy from me one night in High Tartary."

"That sounds like quite a tale."

"Not at all," Mack said, remembering who was supposed to be the storyteller around here. "Actually, it was the most banal burglary imaginable. But it was bad luck for me because I don't have a copy for you to sign. But if you could put your signature on a piece of paper, I'd paste it in when I get a copy again."

"I just might happen to have a copy," Marco said carelessly. "I suppose I could let you have it at cost."

"Your only copy? I couldn't!"

"As a matter of fact, I have several."

"I'd consider it a privilege if you'd sign a copy for me. And I'd consider it a privilege if you'd let me guard your person and keep you safe from the plots and cabals that swirl around your glorious person."

"How did you know about the plots against me?" Marco asked. "You just got here."

"It is common knowledge," said Mack, "that a man as talented and famous as you must have enemies. It would be my desire to protect you from them."

"If you really want to help," Marco said, "there *is* something you could do for me."

"Just tell me," Mack said.

Marco said, "As ambassador of Ophir, I take it you speak quite a few languages."

"It's a prerequisite of being an ambassador," Mack said.

"I already know that you speak German, French, Mongol, and Persian."

"They're necessary, of course."

"And what about Turkestani? Farsi? Turkoman? What about Oglut and Mandarin?"

"I can get by in them," Mack said.

"What about Pushtu?"

"I'm not sure," Mack said. "What does it sound like?"

Marco held his mouth in a special way and said, " 'This is how a sentence in Pushtu sounds.' "

"Yes," Mack said, "I can understand that."

"Perfect," Marco said. "The Princess Irene speaks only Pushtu, having never mastered the Mongol tongue. She has no one to talk to."

"Except for yourself, surely?"

"The only sentence I have learned thus far is, 'This is how a sentence in Pushtu sounds.' I've had no time to study it, you see."

"That's too bad."

"What I want you to do," Marco said, "is go to the princess and converse with her. It'll be such a pleasure for her to speak again in her native tongue. And I think she'd be interested in the customs of Ophir."

"I wouldn't waste her time with that," Mack said. "Ophir is much like any other place. But if you think my prattle may get her into a better mood, you can depend on me. I'll go to her at once."

Mack left, congratulating himself on how quickly he was penetrating into the inner circles of the Mongol court.

Chapter
4

It was lucky that Mack had precise directions, because the palace of Kublai Khan had been laid out with the complexity of a maze. Mack went down long polished corridors that seemed to fade into infinity, up hushed ramps glowing in reflected sunlight, down gleaming staircases. Sounds were muted in this place. Here and there a birdcage swung from the ceiling. Cats and dogs and ocelots roamed the passageways. From time to time Mack could hear the sounds of high-pitched pipes played against the boom of bass drums. Twice he ran into corridor vendors, who purveyed potstickers, beef on a stick, and Mongolian enchiladas, free of charge, provided by the Khan for the guests who sometimes got ravenously hungry as they searched for the corridor leading to the commissary.

There were no windows in this part of the interior palace, but the traveler passed occasional dioramas giving scenes of nature—birch trees with chipmunks, lazy rivers with otters, jungles with monkeys. With these, he need no longer feel deprived of some connection with the natural world, even if it was only symbolic and fanciful. And here and there a break had been made in the even regularity of the corridors, and there would be an open space, sometimes a tiny one, no more than a patch of land with a little shrine on it, and sometimes it would be larger, a half quaa of land, and sometimes even a whole quaa.

So it was that Mack, after following courtyard after courtyard at the end of corridor after corridor, came to a large paved plaza, and in this plaza were many armed men and they were doing exercises. The men were fully armored, and they carried swords and shields and lances. There were drill instructors with red headbands who led them in exercises of arms and in calisthenic drills that Mack thought looked very tiresome. He made his way through the ranks of sweating men, because his route to the princess' suite continued on the other side of the plaza.

It was a colorful sight he passed through, because these men wore uniforms from the different armies of many different countries and nations, and they all spoke different languages. There must have been two dozen different tongues spoken in that crowded courtyard, and Mack could understand them all because of the gift of tongues that Mephistopheles' spell had given him. Mack pretty much ignored them, because the things soldiers say during calisthenics are not interesting in any language. But he suddenly paid attention when he heard Marco Polo's name mentioned.

The mention had come from two warriors who were fencing together. They were bearded, clad in leather with plates of bronze, and their hair was oiled and curled in the Phoenician manner. One of them had said, "Now, what were you telling me about this Marco Polo?"

The other said, "We shouldn't be speaking about him here in this public place."

"Don't worry," the first one said. "Nobody around here except us speaks the Haifa dialect of Middle Aramaic."

It *was* a pretty obscure language, but Mack, due to the all-inclusiveness of Mephistopheles' Language Spell, understood it perfectly well right down to the glottal stops. He paused to adjust a boot and heard the second man say, "I was telling you that the time has come for our plot to reach its maturation. You and I have been selected for guard duty at the Banquet Hall tonight. That's when we'll do for him."

"It's to be death, then, eh?"

"That's what the Potentiator of Phoenicia wanted done

according to the carrier pigeon message I received from him earlier. We're to get him now, before he can leave Peking and make other trade treaties that will exclude our city of Tyre."

"Long live Tyre!" the first man said.

"Quiet, you fool. Just be ready to act tonight."

And with that the two soldiers returned to their fencing exercise with renewed vigor. Mack finished adjusting his boot. He straightened up and got out of there. Everything was working out for him. He had detected this plot against Marco, and would tell the Venetian about it as soon as he finished his conversation with Princess Irene.

Chapter 5

Princess Irene was in her chambers, was decent, and she was pleased to admit the ambassador from Ophir.

"You mus' unnerstan'," she said, in broken Mongolian, leading Mack over the many carpets to an interior room, "I likee visit but I no speaka da Mongol lingo so good."

"That is precisely why I have come to call on you, Princess," Mack said, in flawless Pushtu. "Since I have some slight proficiency in your native tongue, I thought you might like to converse a bit apace ere it gets to be banquet time, if you know what I mean?"

The princess drew in her breath sharply, because hearing her own native language spoken by this yellow-haired young man with a flawless accent and with all the particles in place and no breathing signs omitted and with full value given to the fricatives was more wondrous to her than seeing violets bloom in the January snow, her previous high point for new and unusual experiences.

"The dear old mother tongue!" she cried. "You speak it like a native!"

"To whatever small extent as might please Your Highness," Mack said, using the subjunctive as though he'd been born to it.

"How delightful that I no longer need to speak in broken Mongolian," the princess said, "for it annoys me to have to display myself as an ignorant person when actually I have a degree in Ophirese literature as well as in that of Kush and Sheba."

"I haven't read a lot of that stuff, myself," Mack said. "But I know it's important."

"What is more important is that you can talk to me," the princess said. "And, what is even more important, I can talk to you. Come here, sit down, have a fig canapé and a glass of palm wine, tell me about yourself. What are you doing here in Peking?"

Mack allowed himself to be seated on a low divan with plenty of brightly colored pillows. The princess Irene sat down beside him. She was a tall pale blonde, with not very interesting shoulders, and with eyes of an ambiguous sea green color. Her manner was one of imperfectly controlled hysteria. Bracelets jangled as she gestured. Mack ate a date from a nearby bowl, hoping to calm himself.

"They brought me here from the Land of the High Flags, and eventually decided I must marry this shah in Persia," Irene said. "Do you think that's fair? Daddy promised I could marry whomever I pleased. Then he changed everything because the great Khan needed a princess of my line. First I was to marry a Vigur, but he was poisoned."

"Among nobles," Mack said, "a marriageable woman's role in society is often to cement some treaty. What's the matter with the shah of Persia? Sounds like a good match to me."

"I have seen his portrait," Irene said. "He is fat. Old. Ugly. He has a cruel mouth. He looks impotent. He seems unintelligent. He speaks only Persian."

"Well, you can't hold that last against him," Mack said.

"I don't want to hold anything against him," Irene said, shuddering. "If his portrait turns me off, imagine what the man himself would do! I would never bear him any children. His line would die out."

Mack nodded, wondering if that would make any difference to future generations. Yes, it would probably make a difference. Everything did. But what difference would making a difference make? They hadn't told him how to figure out that one.

"Try one of these candied figs," Irene said. "I'll bet they're not as sweet as you are."

"Princess!" cried Mack, for, hardened man of the world though he was, or at least fancied himself to be, the open invitation in the princess' voice shook him down to the upturned toes of his soft leather boots.

"I have to be direct," Irene said. "I might not get another chance." She moved close to him and put her arms around his neck. "What did you say your name was, cutie?"

"Johann Faust, at your service. But Princess—"

"Johnny, you have won me over with your sweet tongue. Don't struggle so, I'm trying to get this unlaced." She was referring to the tight bodice that cinched in her tiny waist. Mack tried to escape from her, but he sank into the soft pillows of the divan, and the princess seemed to be all over him, simultaneously unlacing her bodice, stroking his hair, taking off her shoes, unfastening his doublet, and eating a candied fig. Mack had no fear of aggressive women, but he was turned off and frightened by the circumstances, which were dangerous. He wondered if Princess Irene had ever done this sort of thing before, and if those she had done it with had been caught, and if so, what had been done to them. And for a fleeting moment it seemed to him that Marco could have warned him about this.

But before he could pursue this thought, there was a sudden sound as of doors opening. And Mack struggled to his feet and saw that a young woman had appeared in the princess' chambers, though how she had gotten there he could not say.

The young woman was dark, and beautiful, and clearly not human.

"Who are you?" Mack quavered.

"I am Ylith, a worker in the forces of Good, and a certified observer for the contest. And you, Dr. Faust, are up to no good at all."

Chapter 6

Ylith had been doing good deeds in one of Earth's alternative and highly provisional alternate time-lines when Michael had paged her on the angel hot line. Ylith had come at once. She liked being an angel of the Good, even though she was still in training. The main difficulty with life in the Good was that there seemed nothing to do. She had gotten Hermes Trismegistus to put her into this other time-line so she could practice Good Works. It was nice, but of course it wasn't the real Earth so she was happy when Michael had paged her.

"Ah, there, Ylith," Michael said. "I've been wanting to see how you were getting on."

"Fine," Ylith said. "The only thing is, I'd like to be doing something."

"That's the spirit!" Michael said. "As it turns out, we have a job for you. You know our great contest between Light and Dark?"

"Of course," Ylith said. "Nobody in the spirit world talks of anything else."

"Well, both sides in the contest are allowed observers. That's to make sure no one takes advantage of the situation or coaches the contestant in what he is to do. I'd like you to go to Earth and check on what Mephistopheles and Mack are doing."

"You got it," Ylith said.

"Here, take this." He handed her an amulet.

"Why, Michael!" Ylith said.

"It's not meant as a present," Michael said. "That is an amulet which confers invisibility on its holder. It will allow you to observe things unobserved."

"Okay. See you later!" She vanished.

She caught up with Mack just at the end of his time in Constantinople. Utilizing the charm of invisibility she saw Mack and Irene together on the couch, and came to her own conclusions.

Princess Irene, as stunned as anyone by the sudden appearance of the black-haired witch with the feathery haircut and the virginal yet somehow provocative angel costume, said, "Oh, my goodness! What is going to happen?"

"Nothing to you," Ylith said. "But I need to hold converse with this fellow." She indicated Mack, who edged away but didn't quite do what he wished to do, which was to run like crazy from this probably demented spirit.

"However," Ylith said, "I will take him away, for what I have to say to him is not for innocent ears." She turned to Mack and said, "Come with me, young fellow," in tones that brooked no interference.

She led Mack into the hall and down the corridor to the next chamber, which was identical to Irene's but untenanted, awaiting the arrival of another monoglot princess from another tiny country. There Ylith took a chair, and, sitting with her back very straight, stared at Mack, who stood before her like an abashed schoolboy.

She said, "Dr. Faust, I am very disappointed in you."

"Me?" Mack said. "What did I do?"

"Don't play the innocent with me. I was in the next room and I heard everything."

"Did you, indeed?" Mack said, trying vainly to remember what he and the princess had been talking about before Ylith made her entrance.

"I heard you trying to seduce that poor innocent young princess, taking advantage of the Language Spell that Mephistopheles gave you, the better to work your wiles."

"Hey, wait a minute," Mack said. "You've got it all wrong. I wasn't *doing* anything!"

"Then how do you explain the hanky-panky that was going on when I came into the room?"

"She was trying to seduce *me,* not the other way around!"

Ylith's beautiful wide lips curled in scorn. Ylith had once been a witch. But that had been back in the bad old days when she had served the forces of Darkness with all the passion of naive lusts. Her eyes had been opened to the spiritual aspects of love when she had met Babriel, the gelid-eyed, blond young angel with whom she had fallen in love back in the days of the last Millennial contest. That was the time when Azzie produced his updated Prince Charming story. Ylith had been Azzie's girlfriend up to then. But she forgot all about the fox-faced, red-haired young demon when she met the golden-haired Babriel. Love transformed her values. She turned fervently to Good, did this splendidly haunched and handsomely thewed young witch, since Good was *his* way, and she found it good, even kicky. Out of love for the handsome but extremely proper young angel, she had changed her ways and made new spiritual vows, embracing Good with a fervor that commended itself highly to those who like such things. From being a carefree, party-going sort of witch, she had changed into a bluestocking and prude of a sort not even seen much in Heaven in these days; but of course there is no greater zealot for the Good than the once-fallen. Ylith pursued Goodness and Proper Behavior (two qualities that she habitually conflated) as she had once pursued Badness and Impropriety, and with such energy that she was sometimes an embarrassment to the older representatives of Good, who had learned a little about how things really work during their long years of working for Light. "She'll learn," they said. But she hadn't, so far.

"You have misused your position," Ylith said to Mack. "You were not sent through space and time to seduce maidens with your devil-given gift of language. You are supposed to be working in a serious contest dealing with important matters, not flibbertigibbeting around like an adolescent gazook. I am going to lodge a strong complaint with the Board of Governors about your behavior. And in the meantime, I shall see to it that you don't repeat your unwarrantable actions."

"Lady, listen, you've got me wrong," Mack said, and was about to explain in detail what had actually happened. But Ylith wasn't interested in listening to the lies of a not-bad-looking young yellow-haired seducer with a spell for languages.

Ylith said, "I'm going to put you where you can do no further mischief until I get a definite ruling on this case. It's the Mirror Prison for you, my lad."

Mack raised his hands to remonstrate. But he wasn't quick enough. Nothing comes on faster than the spell of an irate witch. Between two blinks of an eye and a lightning-fast gesture of long, blood-red fingernails, Ylith was gone. Or so it seemed at first. But when Mack looked more closely, he saw that it was himself who was gone. Or, if not gone, at least somewhere else.

He was in a small room with mirrors. There were mirrors on all the walls, floor, and ceiling. There seemed to be more mirrors than the number of walls would accommodate. They formed reflecting quicksilver tunnels and precipices, a baroque topography of mirrors. He saw himself reflected and re-reflected in a hundred mirrors at a hundred angles. He turned, and saw himself turn in a myriad of surfaces. He took a tentative step forward and saw his doubles do the same, though some seemed to go backwards. Another step, and he bumped into a mirror. He recoiled, and his many likenesses did the same, except for a few who hadn't bumped into anything. Mack found it strange and somewhat sinister that some of his mirror images weren't doing what he was or what the others were doing. One of those aberrant images was sitting in an armchair reading a

book; he looked up and winked at Mack. Another appeared to
be sitting on a riverbank, fishing. He didn't look up. There was
even one who was sitting backwards on a chair, legs stretched
out, grinning into Mack's face. At least Mack assumed it was
his face. Suddenly he was no longer sure what the front of his
face was wearing.

He began walking again, arms outstretched, trying to lo-
cate the glass surfaces, hoping to find a way out of the mirror
maze. Some of his reflections were doing the same. But at least
one of him was sitting at a table eating roast beef and Yorkshire
pudding. And another of his images was asleep in a big feather
bed, and another was sitting on a little hilltop, flying a kite.
When he stared at these images most of them looked up and
nodded at him, and smiled, though some paid him no attention.
And then they went back to whatever they had been doing.

Mack stared, disbelieving. A voice in his head said, "I'm
going crazy!" And another voice said, "I wonder if they've left
anything to read around here." Mack realized there was nothing
he could do about any of it, and so he closed his eyes and tried
to think pleasant thoughts.

Chapter
7

Mephistopheles flashed into existence in the Princess Irene's chambers, accompanied by a roiling of sulphurous yellow smoke that gave some hint of his mood. He had been plucked from his favorite chair in front of a nice log fire reading *Memories of an Evil Childhood*, one of the most inspirational books he had come across in a long time. He had just reached the place where the story's young demon hero-prince discovers the pleasures to be gotten from betraying those near and dear to him in morally ambiguous circumstances.

And then the telephone had sounded, tearing him out of his daydream, and he heard a message from one of the unseen witnesses to the contest, reporting that an interference of a serious nature had just occurred; *viz.*, the protagonist had been unlawfully removed from the drama and exiled to a mirrored room of tumultuous reflecting surfaces.

Mephistopheles had had to put down his book and come hurrying to Constantinople, even though he was technically off duty at that moment. He didn't really resent it, though, because those who are serious about evil are ready to hurry off whenever the call to iniquity comes, leaving behind more passive pleasures when the chance to do something really bad comes up.

"Ylith," Mephistopheles said, "what are you trying to do? Why have you locked up Faust?"

"I am correcting a great wrong," Ylith said, with bravado, but with some of the certainty already leaking out of her, punctured by the demon's sharp look.

"What did you do with Faust?"

"I locked him up on a morals charge, that's what," Ylith said.

"Woman, how dare you! You have no right to interfere in this contest! You are here purely as an observer."

"As an observer," Ylith said with sudden asperity, "I have an observation to make. You have obviously been tampering with Faust and suggesting unsavory things to him, and permitting him to stray from the narrow path on which he has been set; otherwise explain how he finds the time to seduce innocent princesses when he should be making one of the choices offered in the situation?"

"Me? You dare accuse me? I had nothing to do with it!" Mephistopheles replied hotly. "If he seduced the wench, he did so on his own responsibility!"

Then they both remembered that Princess Irene was there. They turned and looked at her, then at each other. They reached an unspoken agreement. Ylith raised an eyebrow; Mephistopheles nodded. Ylith produced a small Sleep Spell, light as fairy's down, which she cast over the princess. It carried sleep, with a retrograde memory blank-out for the last half hour.

With Irene safely out of the way, and Mack still in his mirrored prison, Ylith turned to Mephistopheles, fury in her dark blue eyes.

"It's all your fault! And don't think to get around me with blandishments and so-called learned arguments. Remember, I was once of your camp."

"Woman, control yourself," Mephistopheles said. "The Language Spell I gave to Faust was simply to enable him to operate in this oriental babble of tongues. Anyhow, whatever the rights and wrongs of it, you can't just take the protagonist out of the drama. That's a worse crime than anything Faust might have done."

"You are a liar," Ylith said.

Mephistopheles nodded. "Yes, of course, but what has that got to do with it?"

"I want Faust replaced with a more moral creature!"

"Woman, you presume! There is no place for dogmatic moral judgments in Heaven or in Hell. Release Faust at once!"

"No! I am not yours to command!"

Mephistopheles glared at her, then, reaching into the pouch he carried under his cloak, he took out a small red portable telephone. He punched a number into it — 999 — the number of the Beast upside down — which is the number of the Angel — and stood, tapping his toe.

"Who did you call?" Ylith asked.

"One who will talk a little sense into you, I hope."

In a moment there was a puff of light-colored smoke, and a chord of harp music. The Archangel Michael appeared, looking annoyed, dripping wet, and dressed only in a very large fluffy white towel.

"What is the emergency?" he said, as annoyed as an archangel ever gets. "I was just having my bath."

"You're always in the bath," Mephistopheles commented.

"So what? You know what they say about cleanliness."

"It is a vile canard! Evil is easily as fastidious as Good. Cleanliness itself is neutral. But we have no time for disputation."

"Correct. Why have you called me here?"

"This witch," Mephistopheles said, pointing a long, sharp fingernail at Ylith, who stood defiantly, arms folded across the light-creased bulge of her small but sharply pointed bosom, jaw set, eyes set with a hard glitter, "this *silly* woman, this mere angel-in-training, this former hellot turned zealot, has seen fit to remove our Faust from the stage of events, and has gone so far as to incarcerate him, thus bringing our Millennial contest to a grinding halt. That is why I've called you here."

Michael turned to Ylith. His broad brow was puckered

into an expression of annoyance rarely seen on the brow of an archangel. His face had taken on the contours of bemused quizzicality. "Removed Faust? Can this be true?"

Ylith, in a voice not quite as certain as before, but still defiant, said, "What was I to do? His Faust was seducing the princess Irene."

Michael said, "And who is the princess Irene? No, don't tell me. It doesn't matter who the princess Irene is. Why by all that is holy did you see fit to interrupt our Millennial contest because of some silly little seduction?"

"*Alleged* seduction," Mephistopheles put in.

"Even worse," Michael said. "How could you so presume on our gracious pleasure in appointing you an observer, which we did only to quiet down Babriel, who is besotted with you, for something as trite and unimportant as a seduction, and only an alleged one at that?"

"We are taught that seductions are Bad," Ylith said in a small voice.

"No doubt they are," Michael said. "But you should know by now it is not our policy to step in whenever anyone does something Bad, just as the other side doesn't step in whenever anyone does something Good. Didn't you read about Moral Relativity and the Joining of Opposites in the *Angel's Practical Guide to Everyday Earth Matters*?"

"I must have missed that one," Ylith said. "Look, don't shout at me, please. I'm just trying to be good and to have everyone else be good."

"Acting ingenuous won't get you out of this one," Michael said. "Angels are supposed to temper Goodness with Intelligence. Otherwise Good would become an insensate, all-devouring force, bad by nature of its totalitarianism if nothing else. And we don't want *that*, do we?"

"I don't see why not," Ylith said.

"You shall find out. Release the man at once and restore

him to his place in this drama. And then report to the Fervor Defusion Center for chastisement and retraining."

"Oh, don't be so hard on the poor girl," Mephistopheles said, seeing a chance to score a point for the magnanimity of Bad. "Let her go on observing. Just no more interfering."

"You hear him?" Michael said.

"I hear and I obey. But to think I'd ever hear an archangel tell me to obey the commands of a demon from Hell!"

"You've got some growing up to do," Michael said. He hitched his towel more closely about him. "And now may I return to my bath?"

"Enjoy," Mephistopheles said. "Sorry to have disturbed you."

Michael said to Ylith, "As for you, be good, but not too good, and don't make waves. That's an order."

He vanished. Ylith quickly collapsed the Mirror Prison. Mack stepped out, blinking. Mephistopheles smiled and disappeared.

"I seem to be back," Mack said. "Did you talk to the princess?"

"Just watch yourself," Ylith said to Mack, and then she disappeared.

Chapter 8

After Mack was released from the Mirror Prison, he said good-bye to the bewildered Princess Irene and hurried back to warn Marco of the plot. But getting back to Marco's apartment proved more difficult than leaving it. Mack stumbled into unfamiliar corridors that spiraled up and down steep ramps he couldn't remember passing before. There were many people in the corridors, so many that he thought he had somehow gotten outside the palace, into a covered bazaar that apparently spread for acres around the palace. But then he heard the sound of the royal pipes and drums again and knew he was on the right track. Puffing and out of wind, he finally reached Marco's apartment and burst in without knocking.

"Marco! I have word of the utmost urgency for you!" But he was talking to empty walls, because Marco was no longer there.

Mack realized that some hours must have passed while he was in the mirror maze. It was probably evening now, though you could never tell from inside, since the corridors always had the same even lighting, day and night. He rushed out again, and, with a stroke of luck, found the Banquet Hall without incident. He pushed past the guards and entered.

The celebrations were in full progress. Kublai and the other dignitaries were arranged on the dais as he had seen them that morning. Marco was there, and so was the princess Irene, and so was the court wizard in his star-spangled gown. A small orchestra was tuning up, and on a little stage a Mongol comedian in baggy goatskin pants and painted nose was saying, "Take my yak . . . please, take my yak." But no one was listening. All eyes were turned to Mack.

Mack felt more than a little embarrassed by the attentive silence with which his arrival was greeted. He coughed and cleared his throat, and said, "Marco, I'm glad I've reached you in time. There's this plot against you. I overheard it in the courtyard where the soldiers were exercising. There were these two guys from Tyre, see, and they were saying—"

Marco held up a hand, stopping him in midword. "Are you referring to these two over here?"

Mack saw the two bearded soldiers he had overheard in the courtyard. "Those are the guys," he said.

"Very interesting," Marco said. "*They* came here an hour ago to warn me of a plot that they say was instigated by *you*."

"That's not the way it was," Mack said.

"They said you paid them to assassinate me."

"They're just trying to get out of it themselves! Marco, I've told you the truth!"

"Your behavior has been suspicious," Marco said. He turned to the Khan. "May I proceed to demonstrate the duplicity of this fellow?"

"Do proceed," Kublai Khan said. "Western techniques of litigation and interrogation have long fascinated me."

"I call upon the princess Irene," Marco said.

Princess Irene arose from the little throne that had been set out for her on the main dais. She had had time to change into a sky blue mantle decorated with embroidered buttercups. She looked the model of innocence as she said, in broken Mongol, "This long-legged jackanapes came to my chambers, which no man is allowed to do. He made indelicate suggestions toward me, speaking to me in my native tongue, but in the familiar dialect that is used only among family members, or by uncultured persons with a homicidal streak. I was in fear of my life, for when strangers talk to you in that dialect, it means, if they're not related, they're planning to kill you. I fainted, and when I awoke he was gone, frightened away, perhaps, by some noise in the corridor — for he seems a cowardly lot — and I changed into my sky blue mantle and ran down here."

"Lies, all lies," Mack said. "You, Marco, sent me to talk to the princess yourself!"

"*I* sent you to the princess?" Marco said, rolling his eyes and glancing at the Khan with a showman's gift for innuendo. He turned to the assembled nobles. "You know me, gentlemen. I have been here seventeen years. Would I do something that is prohibited by Mongol law, to say nothing of common decency?"

The only sound that could be heard in Kublai's Banquet Hall was the creaking of necks as heads among the audience shook, no, no. And even the severed heads piled up in pyramids seven feet high on the corner stones of the pillars seemed to shake, no, no.

"This is a setup!" Mack declared hotly. "It is clear to me now that Marco Polo, for his own reasons, is out to get me. He probably can brook no rival at the Khan's court. And he probably feels inferior since he's only a Venetian merchant, whereas I am the ambassador from Ophir."

"As to that," Marco said, "let the court wizard speak."

The wizard stood up and rearranged his star-splattered robe. He adjusted the wire-rimmed spectacles on his nose, cleared his throat twice, harrumphed a few times, and said, "I have made enquiries of all the learned men in Peking who are especially skilled in geography. They agree that there is no such place as Ophir. They further assert that if it ever did exist, it perished long ago in a natural cataclysm. And they conclude that if it *did* exist today, it would never employ a German as its ambassador."

Mack waved his hands in frustration. Indignation raged in his brain, annoyance set his fingers to clicking and his toes to tapping, but he couldn't think of a thing to say.

Kublai Khan said, "I don't like to do this, because my court is renowned for its gentleness and high standards, but this man has been found guilty before a jury of his peers of being an impostor and a fake representative of a nonexistent country, as well as being a seducer of royal women. Therefore it is the judgment of this court that he be taken from here and brought to the common prison, where he is to suffer such tortures as are indicated for impostors, and then be strangled and disemboweled and drawn and quartered and burnt."

"It is a good sentence," Marco said. "But it is a commoner's doom. This man might have some noble standing. May I suggest that you have the fellow killed here and now? It will amuse the court, and then we can get on with the rest of the entertainment."

"An excellent suggestion," Kublai said. He raised his magic scepter and made a gesture. From the back of the room a fat bearded man came forward. He was dressed in a chamois loincloth and matching waistcoat, and he wore an enormous turban.

"Royal executioner at your service, Great Khan," he said.

"Do you have your bowstring handy?" Kublai asked.

"I always keep it on me," the executioner said, untying it from around his waist. "You can never tell when it might come in handy."

"Guards," Kublai said, "seize that man! Executioner, do your duty!"

Mack turned and tried to run from the place, hoping to hide himself in the interminable corridors of the Khan's palace until some better notion came to him. But Marco, smiling maliciously, stuck out a leg and Mack stumbled over it and fell sprawling. Bowmen seized him and held him tightly. The executioner approached, twirling the bowstring in his hand like the professional he was. Mack called out, "Your Majesty, you're making a mistake!"

"If so, let it be so," Kublai said. "To err with confidence is the prerogative of power."

The executioner bent over and whipped his bowstring around Mack's throat. Mack tried to shout, but no sounds came. He had a moment to reflect that one's life really doesn't flash in front of one's eyes at the moment of death as they say it does. All he could think of as the bowstring tightened around his throat was an afternoon lying on the banks of the Weser during a school holiday, and remarking to a student friend from the monastery, "You know, a man can never guess how he will die." And that was true, because he could never have imagined at that time (he was no more than fourteen then) that he would end up a couple of hundred years in the past, being executed at the court of Kublai Khan at the instigation of Marco Polo while engaged in a contest on behalf of the forces of Light and Dark.

And then there was a flash of light and a puff of smoke, and Mephistopheles appeared.

Mephistopheles was annoyed, and at such times he made extremely spectacular entrances, as he did this time, employing an entire panoply of fireworks and causing various prodigies of vision to appear in the air and then fade away mysteriously. He had found that spending a few moments setting up the atmosphere saved time in the long run, because those to whom he appeared were in such awe that they never thought to oppose him.

"Release that man!" Mephistopheles thundered.

The executioner fell back as though struck by lightning. The bowmen collapsed in terror. Kublai Khan cowered back. Marco ducked under the table. Princess Irene fainted. Mack stepped forward, a free man.

"Are you ready to go?" Mephistopheles asked.

"Ready, my lord!" Mack replied, getting up and dusting himself off. "Just one last thing."

He walked up to Kublai Khan. As Kublai looked around for help, Mack lifted the magic scepter from his hands and tucked it into his pouch. "Now see how long your reign lasts!"

he cried spitefully. And then Mephistopheles made a gesture and both he and Mack had vanished.

There was silence in the Khan's court. After their departure there was a short adjustment period during which time no one did much of anything. Then Kublai said, "Marco, what was that all about?"

Marco said, "I think we have witnessed a genuine supernatural occurrence. It puts me in mind of something that happened to me when I was in Tashkent. It was spring, and the flowers of the valley — "

Just then the great bronze doors of the Khan's Banquet Hall opened again. Marguerite entered. She was wearing a new Chinese dress of watered silk with high collar and form-fitting lines. She had also been freshly made up, washed, perfumed, had her hair set and her nails done. They knew how to make language lessons interesting in Kublai's court.

"Hi," she said. "I'm just back from class. Listen to this, everybody." And in crude but understandable Mongol she said, "The swain from Spain is standing in the rain." She smiled and waited for words of approval.

"Shall we execute her?" Marco asked Kublai, getting out from under the table and dusting himself off.

"Might as well," Kublai said, the thought of cruelty helping him regain his dignity. "It's better than nothing."

Marco called out, "Guards! Executioner!"

Once again the grim charade proceeded. Marguerite was seized. The executioner, resolutely, despite the fact that his legs were shaking, approached. And then Mephistopheles appeared again.

"Sorry, I forgot all about you," he said. He gestured. Marguerite disappeared. Then Mephistopheles disappeared. The Khan and his guests stared in stunned silence at the places where they had been. And then the waiters came in with the main course.

FLORENCE

Chapter 1

Well, Faust, we are sending you on your way again for the next contest. In this one, you are going to the city of Florence, in the year 1497. How I envy you, my dear fellow! You will see at firsthand the city that can claim to be the artistic inventor of the new world. Many scholars argue that the Renaissance began in Florence. How does that sound?"

Mack and Mephistopheles were in a little office perched in Limbo. Limbo was wide and expansive in that part, and the office was the only thing in sight. It was the sort of place Mephistopheles often used for late-night paperwork. Quite simple; a wooden frame structure about ten feet to a side (you can build as large as you'd like in Limbo, at no extra cost, but Mephistopheles had wanted to keep a homey look). A few oil paintings of pastoral subjects on the walls. A small sofa covered in green satin on which he sat, and a straight-backed wooden chair on the edge of which Mack perched. Mephistopheles had given Mack a glass of barley wine to buck him up after his close call. But he had been anxious to get on with the contest.

"All right, then," Mephistopheles said at last. And so, with barely a chance to catch his breath, Mack knew he was to be off again. To a place with an odd name.

"What's a Renaissance?" Mack asked.

"I forgot," Mephistopheles chuckled, "the term 'Renaissance' didn't enter usage until long after the Renaissance was over. It refers to a period in history, my dear Faust."

"What am I supposed to do about this Renaissance?" Mack asked.

"Why, nothing, directly. The Renaissance isn't anything you can *do* anything about. No, I was merely making conversation, pointing out to you how important this time is in history, and how your choices here could make a big difference."

"What *am* I supposed to do? Are there choices?"

"Yes, of course there are choices," Mephistopheles said. "We're going to put you into Florence at the time of the Bonfire of Vanities."

"What was that?"

"A great burning of objects of vanity, such as looking glasses, amusing pictures, light novels, precious manuscripts, comfits, and the like. All these and many other things were heaped into a pile in the great courtyard of the Piazza della Signoria, and put to fire."

"Sounds a little extreme," Mack said. "You want me to stop this bonfire?"

"No, not at all," Mephistopheles said.

"Then what am I supposed to do?"

"A deed," Mephistopheles said. "That is why we put our Faust into these contests. So that he may perform a deed that will redound either to Good or to Bad, and so be judged by Ananke."

"Who?"

"Ananke is the Greek name for the ancient primordial force of Necessity, that which must be. All things must finally be judged by Ananke."

"Where is this Ananke?"

"She is ever-present," Mephistopheles said. "But immaterial and elusive, since Necessity is that final force that binds things together, but has no substance itself. When the time comes, however, Ananke will take on bodily form and tell us her judgment."

It was getting a little deep for Mack. "What, specifically, am I to do?"

"That I cannot tell you," Mephistopheles said. "This particular episode has been structured differently from the others. In this one, it's up to you to find something to do."

"But how am I to judge what's to be done?"

Mephistopheles shrugged. "There are many ways. You might see a person in peril, and choose to save his life. Then the judgment would depend on whose life you saved, and what he did with his life in the years left him."

"But how am I supposed to know?" Mack asked.

"You just have to take your best guess," Mephistopheles said. "Niccolò Machiavelli is in Florence at this time. You might advise him not to write his masterpiece, *The Prince*, that caused such a stir in celestial circles." Mephistopheles hesitated and examined his fingernails, then said, "Or you might look around for a Botticelli for me, if you can't think of anything else to do."

"That would be good?"

Mephistopheles hesitated. There'd be hell to pay if anyone found out about it. But he knew just the spot on the west hall wall of his palace in Hell where he'd hang the painting. The other archdemons would be sick with envy when they saw it.

"Oh yes," he said, "getting a Botticelli wouldn't be bad at all."

"The trouble is," Mack said, "I wouldn't know a Botticelli from a Dürer. Painting is all Greek to me. In fact, I know more Greek than painting."

"Well, that's not right," Mephistopheles said. "I'm sure no one would object if I improve your knowledge of art. It might be necessary in order for you to carry out your assignment."

He made a gesture. And Mack's knees buckled for a moment as his memory was suddenly burdened with the knowledge of comparative art values from the Hellenic period to some

"Get you a painting by Botticelli? Is that what you want me to do?"

"It is not for me to tell you," Mephistopheles said. "I merely give some background so you'll have some feeling for conditions." He hesitated, then added, "Of course, if, during your time in this construct, you *should* happen to come across a Botticelli, I'd be happy to buy it from you at a very good price."

"If I don't come across the painting," Mack said, "what else ought I to do?"

"I can't tell you. My dear Faust, there are no simple choices in this game. It is not a matter of just finding out which is the 'best' move in terms of some preestablished criterion. There's no morality involved in this. This is pure nuts and bolts. It gives you, a mere man, a chance to make the sort of decision usually reserved to spiritual beings. We are going to see how well a human being does at this sort of thing."

"All right," Mack said dubiously. "But I'm still not sure that I get it."

"My dear fellow, it is exactly like a quiz show."

"Beg pardon?"

"I forgot, those haven't been invented yet. Think of it as a man standing before an audience and answering questions for money, and being paid for each one he gets right. Now, for ten thousand louis d'or . . . You are at the Bonfire of Vanities in Florence in 1492. In front of you is a huge bonfire. Being thrown on it are all sorts of vanities. Among them is a priceless Botticelli. It is in your power to rescue it. What do you do?"

"I get the idea," Mack said. "And if you like the answer, I get the money?"

"That's the general idea," Mephistopheles said. "To go on. Next we say to you, all right, same situation. Now you are at the palace of Lorenzo de' Medici. He is a great and terrible tyrant, but also a great and inspired patron of the arts. He is dying. Here. Take this." He handed Mack a small glass vial filled with a green liquid. "You now have in your hand a medicine that will give him another ten years of life. Do you give it to him or not?"

"Wow," Mack said. "I'd need to think about that. Can you tell me any more?"

"Sorry, these are the only clues I can give you. The essence of this matter is speed. We're testing the quickness of your understanding, and looking into depths you didn't even know you had. Get in there, Dr. Faust, and do a job for the human race! Are you ready?"

"I guess so," Mack said. "Oh. What about Marguerite?"

"I've sent her ahead to meet you in Florence. You'll find her at the silk market. She says she wants to do some shopping while there's time."

Chapter 2

Meanwhile, in another part of the universe, a soppy, dismal evening had come down over west Downtown Hell. Big black birds squawked disconsolately as they flew overhead to no-one-knew-where. The squalid streets were wet, the garbage cans were overflowing, and there were cries of torment from the boarded-up windows of the tenements on either side, where spirits newly released from the Pit lived in perpetual peonage. The only cheerful spot was Maladroit's Ichor Club, in the middle of the block. Inside the club, all was lively, fast, trendy — the good side of Hell.

In that Ichor Club, in a private booth off to one side, sat Azzie Elbub. He had a date that evening with Etta Glber, a young lady who had been elected Miss Sycophant of the year 1122 at her witches' coven, and had received as her prize a date with a top-drawer, upwardly mobile young demon of handsome aspect. She had been a little surprised when she got Azzie, because she hadn't been prepared for an orange-headed, fox-faced demon, but had adjusted quickly with the adaptability that had won her the sycophant contest. Azzie had set up the scheme several years back, as a surefire way of getting dates with Earth girls.

It was a moment to be tucked away in the memory file that holds sleazy acquisitions. The lights were low. A discreet spotlight lit up Miss Sycophant's creamy décolletage. The jukebox was playing "Earth Angel," because in Hell they get all the hits sooner or later, though never on time. Everything was perfect. But somehow Azzie couldn't get into the spirit of fun.

In Hell, fun is a religion, but Azzie was in a rebellious mood. He had serious work to do. He had to decide how to ensure his own best position in the contest between Light and Dark, and that necessitated doing something about Faust.

Faust was proving very difficult to tempt. Azzie had had no luck so far. He wondered if he was offering the right things. But after you come up with fame, riches, and Helen of Troy, what else is there?

Faust was a difficult customer, there could be no doubt about that. Spiritually, he was a wild man. There was no telling what he would do next. In actual fact, the forces of Dark were better off not having him in the contest. Faust might not be a good man, but he was a long way from being bad. Whereas Mack, his stand-in, was altogether simpler and so could be expected to produce a more predictable and hence satisfactory result.

Azzie thought it over a while longer. The more he thought about it, the more difficult he found Faust. Finally he came to a decision.

"Listen," he said to Miss Sycophant, "it's been fun and I've really enjoyed meeting you. But I have to be going now. Don't worry, the bill's paid for."

And so saying he set out at once, stepping into a handy conjuring booth that the club had put aside for those fastidious members who didn't like to conjure in public. He directed himself toward the past of the Earth, because he had gotten somewhat ahead of himself. The spell kicked in and years flipped backwards like leaves off a calendar in some future age when such things exist. Moving faster than the speed of recollection, Azzie saw the panorama of time coiling back on itself, swallowing its own tail. Old men grew young, volcanoes receded and returned to their caps, icebergs flowed north and south, and the race of man shrank and dwindled.

At last he passed entirely out of human territory and came

into the lands of legend that Homer and others had caused to come into being. There was Lethe ahead, and then the great cavern of Avernus was in sight, and he streaked into it, following its winding and turning as it descended into the depths of Hell and joined up with the Styx. It was like traveling through the intestines of a snake. The whole thing was lit in pale and ghastly colors by towering phosphorescent crags, and sometimes Azzie could see men standing on those rocks, heroic naked men draped in sheets like refugees from a Doré etching. But now he was at the place he had conjured himself to, where the territory of Hell began.

Azzie turned and flew over the Styx itself, until finally he came upon Charon's houseboat, nestled close to the muddy bank. In the back of the craft, Faust and Helen sat and watched the black rippling water and made small talk.

Azzie swooped down and made a neat landing on the houseboat. The boat barely rocked when he set down, so lightly did he step, though Charon did look up to see who had alighted on his boat. Azzie paid him no mind.

"How now!" Azzie cried. "Dr. Faust! Good day to you!"

"Hail to thee, foul spirit," Faust said. "What brings you to these parts?"

"I just thought I'd look you up." Azzie sat down on a folding chair that was propped against the rail. "How are things going?"

"Well enough," Faust said. "Charon is not so easy to get along with, but I think I have convinced him enough so that he will cooperate with me."

"Convince Charon? How did you manage to do that?"

"I pointed out to him that I was giving him an opportunity to be in on the very beginning of a brave new myth."

"What myth is that?" Azzie asked.

"Why, it is the story of the great meeting between Faust

and Charon; of how, with Charon's cooperation, Faust traveled to places unheard-of before, bringing with him the beautiful Helen."

"Hah!" said Helen, who had been sitting nearby paddling her toes in the water and listening to the conversation.

Azzie ignored her. He said to Faust, "I've got another proposition for you."

"I told you before. I will not obey you."

"That's not what I'm asking," Azzie said. "Look. The game for the rulership of the Millennium is running. This guy Mack is doing it, playing your role. It's not the way I would have done it, but that's what's happened. He's already gone through two episodes. Whether he did well or badly is beside the point. What's done is done, and there's nothing either you or I can do about it. So I say, let it alone. Stop trying to take over Mack's part. Drop out of the drama. And I'll make it worth your while, Doctor."

"How do you propose to do that?"

"I'm going to pick a period in history that's just tailor-made for your talents. You will be rich, and acclaimed by everyone."

"Is it just me doing this?" Faust asked. "Or will I have a suitable consort along with me?"

There was Faust, bargaining again! Azzie said, "All this will be with Helen at your side, for she goes along with the bargain. Johann, you'll be the envy of all mankind. And you'll be rich, Doctor, rich beyond even your dreams of wealth."

"With your talent for trickery," Faust said, "you'll give me all that but have me brainstruck or paralyzed so that I can't enjoy it. I know your way, demon!"

"You think I would do something like that?" Azzie said. "I may be evil, but I'm not bad. But I'll tell you what, to make it all even better, I'll throw in the full rejuvenation treatment. It'll make you look, feel, be, a new man, intellectually and physically. You'll have many many years of vigorous life ahead of you. And it will be good, Doctor, oh, my, it will be so good!"

So much did Azzie get carried away with his selling job that he kissed his hand in a florid gesture that was not his typical style. But Faust was unmoved.

"No," Faust said, "I'm sorry, I understand your feelings. But I just can't do it."

"But why not?" Azzie wailed.

"It would not be Faustian, you see. I know you have to think about your contest. But I have to think about the greatness of Faust, and, if there's any time left over, to think about the future of mankind in general. I'm sorry, foul fiend, but I cannot oblige you."

"Well, it was worth a try," Azzie said. "What will you do now?"

"I propose to take my rightful place in the contest. I don't know if I have time to get to Florence. But after that, the next act is to begin in London. I have already proposed to Charon that he take me there. It would be a pleasant change for him, to spend a day boating on the Thames."

Charon had been listening. Now he shuffled over, and, laughing his uncanny laugh, said, "Yes, Faust, it was agreed upon, but only on condition that you give me a Traveling Spell that will provide the motive power to take us there. The ship of the dead doesn't run through space and time on oars alone, you know."

Faust turned to Azzie. "About that Traveling Spell. My own is considerably depleted. Do you think you could spare me a spell recharge? Or better yet, give me a whole new Traveling Spell and Charon and I will be on our way."

"Certainly," Azzie said, and took a small spell out of his pouch, surreptitiously tore away the DEFECTIVE—DON'T USE label the Board of Spell Standards had given to it, and handed it to Faust. "Best of luck," he said, and then conjured himself away.

He was very pleased with himself. He didn't have to worry about Faust. The fellow was going to neutralize himself, with a little help from a sly, fox-faced, spell-giving, egg-sucking demon.

Chapter 3

"Earlier," Faust asked Helen, while Charon was preparing the boat for a new destination, "what did you mean by 'hah'?"

Helen, beautiful and unapproachable, stood at the rail, watching the time fish gulp up odd moments. The dark water turned and roiled, and reflections of the deeds of men and gods played dimly on its surfaces. Without turning she replied, "It is an expression of contempt, which is the emotion I feel for you and your sexist ways."

"Sexist? Me? But I'm Faust!"

"Good for you! But what about me? You may have a great intellect in some matters, but you still consider a woman an object to be fought over and won as a trophy in the ridiculous wars you men fight to prove such things."

"This line of argument doesn't sound like the Helen we've come to expect," Faust said. "You're talking like an intellectual rather than the pretty piece of puff pastry men have always taken you for. History doesn't record your views on the subject of men."

"That's because History is sexist," Helen said. "The winners get to tell their version of things. And why should it be otherwise? Might makes right and we become what you say we are. Talk about unfair typecasting!"

"What do you have to complain about?" Faust asked. "You're beautiful and famous!"

"But they've got me in an eternal ingenue role. My friends laugh at me. And why? Because fools like you keep on mooning about me and think they're hot stuff because they can enslave me."

Faust said, "Me, enslave thee? Say nay, fair Helen! For rather am I slave to *thee,* and stand obedient to your slightest whim."

"Yeah? Then how about taking me back to Hades where the demon stole me from?"

"Oh, well, that's out of the question," Faust said. "Come now, I'm trying to be gallant. You have to try, too."

"Like hell I have to try," Helen said. "You may own my body, but you don't own me."

"Hmm," Faust said, eyeing her with salacious eye. "A wise man might think your body good enough reward."

"You don't get the body, either," Helen said. "You'll have to kill me first."

Faust found himself thinking it might come to that. But he gritted his teeth. The funny thing was, he didn't even desire this woman very much. To own her, possess her, dominate her, yes, sure. But to make love to her? Faust found her formidable even when she was silent, and a virago when she was vocal. He marveled that the ancient world had never commented on Helen's conversational style.

"Look," Faust said, "let's be reasonable. There are only a few roles to play in this world of ours. I'm playing the role of possessor, though I can assure you it doesn't entirely suit me. I'm not at my best with imperious women. I like goosegirls, to tell the truth. But having you is the big time of aspiration, even if I don't go for it much personally. So I play my part. Now then, Fate, or Necessity, or Chance, or whoever it was, cast you in the role of the ultimate desired woman. You're supposed to be a paragon of seductiveness. It does no good for you to wish yourself something else. You've got your role and it's a good one. A lot of women would give anything to change places with you. And it's not bad, as roles go. Even if you don't like it, at least try to not let down the side."

Helen considered for a while. Then she said, "Well, Faust, you say well and you talk bluntly. Now let me be equally blunt. Are you up to me? The Helen archetype is known everywhere. But I never heard of the Faust archetype."

"It came along after your time," Faust said, "but it is no less potent than your own. In the ancient world, men might have wished to be an Odysseus or Achilles. Nowadays, young men aspire to the Faustian ideal."

"Can you sum up that ideal for me?" Helen asked.

"It is difficult to capture in words the veritable quality of one's own numinosity. Let's just say that Faust wants more. It's quite a bit more than that, but that gives you an idea."

"A sort of latter-day Prometheus?" Helen asked.

"Perhaps so, Helen," Faust said, chuckling. "But with a difference. Prometheus ended up on a rock with a vulture tearing out his liver. Whereas Faust ranges free over space and time. With a little help from his friends, of course. And that's the difference between the old world and the new."

"I see you can keep up your end of a conversation," Helen said. "If nothing else." She chuckled, and Faust's titillation receptor cells went into a frenzied fibrillation until application of his powerful will caused them to quiet down again.

"Let us go on, then, Faust," Helen said. "I confess, I'm interested in seeing the contours of this new myth you're creating. Can you give me a hint as to what happens next?"

"Next we're going to get out of here," Faust said. "Charon! Is the boat ready?"

"You got that Traveling Spell?" Charon asked.

"Here it is," Faust said, handing it over. Charon felt along the lapstraked side of the boat and found the Motive Slot. Carefully he inserted the spell. Faust said the words that brought it to life. A spirit stood amidships and cast off the lines as the first ripple of motion rocked the boat. The motion came again. There was a great cloud of smoke, green and gray in color, with ochre backlighting and little wispy nebulosities hanging from its extremities. Then the Traveling Spell kicked in. And suddenly, just like that, the boat took off.

An observer on the bank, however, watching the boat of the dead disappear, might have noted that green and gray clouds of smoke are not the usual byproducts of spell conjuration, but rather bespeak a defective Motive Spell. That's not the way boats usually move when they're powered by magic. The observer might have conjectured that something was very wrong. And had he so conjectured, he would not have been very wrong.

Chapter
4

Mack found himself walking on a road that ran straight between rows of poplars. He topped a little rise and saw, in the near distance, the spires of a noble city. The weather was warm and sunny. There were other people strolling along the road. They wore hose, tunics, soft boots, just like in Cracow, but with an Italian panache. Mack saw that Méphistopheles had dressed him in the same way. He proceeded through the gates into the bustling wonder that was Florence.

There was a lot of stir and turmoil in the narrow streets. Everybody seemed to be out, most of them in holiday clothing. Florence was in festive mood on this fine spring day. There were multicolored banners snapping in the breeze, flying bravely from many balconies and rooftops. They represented the various communes of the city. Food vendors were out in force, selling the newest taste sensation, tiny Renaissance pizzas. Armed riders in steel helmets coursed through the streets, pushing people out of the way in the manner of policemen of all times and ages. Mack passed close-packed stalls selling cloth, kitchenware, spices, swords, and knives. One stall had large porcelain plates for sale, another watermelon, a third, smelts.

As interesting as it all was, Mack decided he'd better find a place to stay. First he checked his purse and found that he had plenty of expense money. Mephistopheles had not been stingy in that regard. An inn just up the street appealed to him with its well-painted pastel walls and gold-leaf sign proclaiming it the Paradiso. The owner, a stout, red-faced man with a carbuncle on his nose, was suspicious at first, since Mack hadn't sent a messenger ahead to announce his arrival. But he became all affability when Mack handed him a gold florin.

"Our best room for you, my dear Dr. Faust! You come at an auspicious time. This is a public holiday, you know, the time when we Florentines burn our vanities."

"Yes, I know," Mack said. "Will it be held far from here?"

"Just a couple of streets away in the Piazza Signoria," the innkeeper said. "You'll have a great view of one of the most remarkable phenomena of our time. Savonarola has promised that this year's bonfire will be something truly remarkable."

"What sort of man is this Savonarola?" Mack asked.

"He is a most holy monk and friar. He lives simply, unlike the princes of the Church who lord it over us. He speaks out against simony, indulgences, and other bad practices in the Church. And he's in favor of the French alliance."

"What's that?"

"It's our pact with the French king, which keeps us protected from the Pope's desire to force the Medicis back on us."

"You don't like these Medicis?" Mack asked.

"Oh, they do well enough," the landlord said. "Lorenzo is called the Magnificent, for good reason. There has never been a greater patron of the arts. Under his rule, Florence has become the most beautiful city in the world."

"But you still don't like him?" Mack asked.

The landlord shrugged. "It's the people who pay for his magnificence. And besides, we don't like any family lording it over us. We Florentines are free people, and we intend to stay that way."

Mack inspected his room and found it was up to the standard he was rapidly getting used to. Time to find Marguerite. The owner told him that the silk market was held in a small piazza on the Fiesole road. To Mack it looked like an oriental bazaar with its stalls crowded close together, its casual bathroom fa-

cilities, and its pigtailed retinue of observers from Cathay. Here
were piled high the watered silks that were de rigueur in Flanders and the Netherlands; the twice-dyed material that was
making such a hit that year in Amsterdam, and the raw silk
estofados and open-necked sanbenito sport shirts for the Spanish trade. Spotted here and there among the stalls were little
espresso bars, and near them were spaghetti houses, already
selling the concoction that Marco Polo had brought back from
China, where they unaccountably called it noodles. Mack found
Marguerite at a progenitor of the boutique system that was to
make such a change in the habits of luxury buyers. She was
looking at herself in a tall mirror that was tilted this way and
that for her by the proprietor, a small man with a harelip but,
perhaps in compensation, very good teeth.

"Ah, signore," he said, "you have come just in time to see
your lady in all her glory!"

Mack smiled indulgently. It was not his money. He could
afford to be generous.

"Go for it, babe," he said huskily.

"Look," she said, "I've picked out these darling ball gowns.
You must look at Signore Enrico's men's store, Johann. He
carries the latest in doublets and camicia."

"Camicia?" said Mack.

Signore Enrico smiled with extreme twinklings of his warm
brown eyes. "It is the latest thing from Hungary," he said. "A
casual style. For evening wear we have the most divine tights,
which come with a codpiece that whispers masculinity rather
than shouting it to the skies."

"I just love the way he talks," Marguerite said.

Mack felt more than a little foolish trying to respond to
this conversation. But he consoled himself by remembering that
buying expensive clothes for a beautiful woman is one of the
delights of masculine success. And as soon as Marguerite was
finished, he could start looking for some stuff for himself, perhaps asking Mephistopheles for an advance on his reward, if

need be. Of course, Mephistopheles hadn't specifically mentioned what his reward would be. Mack knew he should have pinned it down earlier. But as soon as he had a chance, he'd check it out. In the meantime, taking a foretaste of his reward seemed only reasonable, because if he didn't like what he was going to get he was really wasting his time.

"You look beautiful, my dear," he said. "Please finish your business so I can get on with mine."

"And what business is that, my love?"

"I need to find a Botticelli. I can make a very good deal if I find one."

Enrico said, "A Botticelli? Perhaps I can help. I know all the painters. It would give me great pleasure to offer my assistance, and, of course, my expertise. Not," he added quickly, "that I think it will be needed. Because the signore is obviously a connoisseur."

"Good idea," Mack said. "Let's check it out now."

He turned to go. Just then a heavyset man in nondescript clothing burst in.

"I am looking for Faust! The German doctor! They said at the Paradiso that he had come this way!"

"I am he whom you seek," Mack said. "What seems to be the trouble, my good fellow?"

"It's my master! He's dying! When he heard there was a new German doctor in town, he sent me out to find him. Oh, sir, if you can cure him, you can name your own reward."

"I'm a little busy," Mack said, not wishing to put his imaginary healing skills to the test, especially in an excitable place like Florence. "Who did you say your master is?"

"My master is Lorenzo de' Medici, the Magnificent!"

"Things seem to be falling into shape rather rapidly," Mack remarked to Marguerite. "Come, my dear, pack up your things and wait for me at the hotel. I have an errand of mercy to run."

Chapter
5

$\mathbf{M}$ ack followed the servant to Medici's palace, which was in a small, exclusive suburb of palaces close by the Arno. It was a fine-looking place, with white marble pillars and a porch in the Attic style. The doors were of varnished mahogany and extensively carved in the manner originated by Damiato the Damned. There were servants at the door, wearing lounge suits and white-on-white shirts in the latest Neapolitan style. They looked askance at Mack, because his clothing here, uptown, as it were, didn't look half as good as it did in the clash of illusions that was the marketplace. But they passed him through in response to the old servant's plea.

Weeping and wringing his hands, the servant led Mack down quiet corridors with oil paintings on the walls, down to a big rosewood door at the far end. Tapping to make his presence known, the servant pushed open the door and Mack looked in on a room that would not have disgraced a king.

There were fine paintings on the walls, and small sculptures scattered here and there on end tables. There was a rich oriental carpet on the floor, and a crystal chandelier overhead which gave forth a rich yellow light. The windows were hidden behind heavy drapes, through which scarcely a hint of sunlight peeped. There was a smell of sulphur and sickness in the air, wine and whining, feasts on the table above, faeces on the floor below where the dogs lay gnawing bones.

A large, tall, gorgeously carved, and sumptuously canopied bed dominated the chamber. Tall wax candles had been brought in and put around the bed on more end tables. A fire in the fireplace flickered and glowed red.

"Who is there?" asked Lorenzo de' Medici.

Lorenzo, well tucked up in the bed, looked every one of his seventy years, plus a few more. Dropsy had robbed his body of vigor. He peered at Mack from a fat, gray face. It was a countenance in which shrewd little eyes struggled to make a deal with mortality and stay alive a little longer, but with class, of course, since he was Lorenzo de' Medici and class was his middle name. He wore a long white cotton nightgown embroidered with unicorns, and a black cap with bobbin lace was tied under his chin. His face, where it bore any flesh at all that was not puffed out with rottenness, sagged toward the bone clearly visible beneath. His lips, formerly ruddy in the days when a Medici Pope considered announcing the unique existence of a Medici God, were withered, having tasted the bitterness of the world for so many years. An artery in his neck pulsed, as though wondering why it hadn't collapsed like the others. The fingers of his left hand, palsy stricken, made little fluttering movements.

"I'm Dr. Faust," Mack said. "What seems to be the trouble?"

"I," said Medici, in a voice that, even as a shadow of its former timbre, was enough to excite the dust particles on the top of the chandelier, "am the richest man in the world."

It was one hell of an opening line, but Mack was not to be thus put down.

"And I," he said, "am the world's most expensive doctor. How fortuitous that we have met!"

"How do you propose to heal me?" Medici growled, with such dominance that the very maggots in his flesh stopped their gnawing for a moment out of respect.

Mack knew that the cure was simple enough. Just take out the vial that Mephistopheles had given him and pour its contents down Medici's throat. But he wasn't going to let Lorenzo know that. Who'd pay a fortune for something as simple as a slug of elixir? No, the contents of the vial might be the final step, but procedure, as Galen and others had pointed out, was the irreducible framework. And the procedure had to be impressive.

"First we'll need a gold basin," Mack said. "Only twenty-four karat will do."

It had crossed his mind that a gold basin would be a good thing to have on hand in case anything went wrong. Funny, the things you think about in a crisis.

"See that it is done," Medici said to the servants.

The servants scurried around. There was a brief delay while they searched for the key to the bin where the gold pots and pans were kept.

The servants brought the gold basin, and also the alchemical equipment Mack asked for. That was not difficult to come by, since Lorenzo was a collector of all sorts of things, and he had a whole room full of alchemical equipment of the latest models. His alembic alone, all gleaming glass and polished bronze, was a sight to behold. And his furnace could perform such miracles of calibration that it was a wonder Medici hadn't cured himself with all his fancy junk on the basis of his pillaged knowledge.

Mack set up his test tubes and burners and was about to begin when there came a resounding knocking at the chamber door. The door burst open and in strode the most famous friar in the world, Fra Girolamo Savonarola.

Tall and ghastly pale was this monk who was the talk of all Italy. He fixed his burning eyes on Medici and said, "They said you wanted to see me about something."

"Yes, Brother," Medici said. "I know we've had some differences, but I think we can both say we stand for a strong Italy, a balanced lire, and no more Church corruption. I'd like to make my confession and receive absolution."

"Delighted to arrange it," Savonarola said, taking a parchment out of his cloak, "if you will sign over all your goods and monies to a nonprofit organization I have founded, which will see that they are distributed to the poor."

He slid the parchment beneath Medici's rheumy eyes with an alacrity that belied his slender frame and fever-swept body; for the friar was suffering toothache and so far hadn't been able to pray it away.

Medici's rheumy old eyes swept the manuscript, then narrowed in suspicion. "You drive a tough bargain, Brother. I'm prepared to make a good bequest to the Church. But I've got relatives who have to be taken care of."

"God will provide," Savonarola said.

"No insult intended, but I don't think so," said Medici.

"I think we're about ready with the medicine," Mack said, seeing that he was losing out to the newcomer.

"Sign the parchment!" shouted Savonarola. "Confess yourself a sinner!"

"I'll talk to God in my own heart, Girolamo! But I'll not say it to you!"

"I am a monk," Savonarola said.

"You are vain, and proud," Medici said. "To hell with you. Faust! The medicine!"

Mack hurriedly took out the vial and struggled to uncork it. It had one of those thin little wires wrapped around it that are so hard to cut if you don't have pliers. And back then, before even the circle was standardized, hardly anyone had pliers. Medici and Savonarola were screaming at each other. The servants were cowering. Outside, church bells were ringing. Mack finally got the bottle cap off. He turned to Medici.

The Magnificent had fallen suddenly silent. He lay in bed motionless, jaw agape. Blind eyes, still rheumy, but over which a milky film was beginning to form, stared up at nothing.

Medici dead? "Don't do this to me," Mack muttered, and

forcing the vial into Medici's mouth, poured. The liquid came bubbling out of Medici's mouth, untasted. The great man was finally and definitively dead.

The servants were muttering angry curses when Mack backed away at last from the Medici's corpse, with Savonarola standing over it still scolding in a high-pitched voice. Mack made his way out the door and down the corridors to the exit.

He stood for a moment on the street, wondering if he had forgotten something. Damn it, he had forgotten the gold basin! He turned to go back in. But it was too late now. He was swept up into the crowd and carried along by the laughing, screaming, singing, praying multitude. It was the time of the burning of vanities, and all was madness.

Chapter
6

People were running, their footsteps echoing on the cobblestones. There was an air of holiday glee. Many drunks had gotten an early start and were sleeping it off in doorways. Children were everywhere, darting here and there in an ecstasy of pleasure. The shops were all closed, with boards nailed up over their doorways. A clatter of hooves was heard as mounted lancers rode by, brilliant in uniforms of scarlet and black, and Mack ducked back into a doorway to avoid getting trampled on. As he did so, he ran into a man's solid body.

"Watch where you're going!"

"Sorry!" said Mack. "It was the soldiers."

"What did soldiers have to do with you stepping on my foot?"

The man whose foot Mack had stepped on in the doorway was tall and finely shaped, with a head that could have modeled for a Grecian Apollo. He was fashionably dressed in a cloak of dark fur, and from his hat floated an ostrich feather, proof that he either had contacts abroad or knew someone in the Florence Zoo. He peered intently at Mack with large and brilliant eyes.

"Excuse me, stranger," the man said, "but haven't we met?"

"I doubt it," Mack said. "I'm not from around here."

"That's interesting. I'm looking for a man who doesn't come from around here. My name is Pico della Mirandola. Perhaps you've heard of me?"

Indeed Mack had, from Mephistopheles, as one of the great alchemists of the Renaissance. But Mack, foreseeing trouble, was not going to admit having heard of him.

"I don't think so," Mack said. "Anyhow, it's just a coincidence us meeting this way. It's very unlikely that I'd be the man you seek."

"So it might seem in the ordinary course of things," Pico said. "But when you put magic to work, coincidences suddenly become much more probable. I was supposed to meet someone here. Might it not be you?"

"What is the name of this person you're supposed to meet?"

"Johann Faust, the great magician from Wittenberg."

"Never heard of him," Mack said promptly, because it was immediately obvious to him that the real Faust, or, as Mack preferred to think of him, the Other Faust, must have used his magical powers to contact this fellow. Pico della Mirandola was or had been a magician of great and sinister reputation. He and Faust had probably been corresponding across the centuries. It was said that magicians could do that, since even death was no impediment to real magic.

"You're sure you're not Faust?" Pico said.

"Oh, yes, quite sure. I suppose I know my own name, ha, ha! Excuse me, I must be off, I don't want to miss this Bonfire of Vanities." He hurried off. Pico gazed after him, then began to follow.

Mack hurried on and saw a great open plaza. In the middle of it, there was a tall pile of wooden furniture, paintings, cosmetics, and ornaments of various sorts.

"What's going on?" Mack asked a man near him in the crowd.

"Savonarola and his monks are burning the vanities," the man told him.

Mack moved closer. He saw that there were many pretty things carelessly thrown on the great pile. There were babies' embroidered gowns, and crocheted tablecloths, there were well-wrought candlesticks, there were oil paintings by artists of no great reputation, and a lot of other stuff.

As Mack came closer, he saw, on the edge of the fire, a large painting in an ornate frame. Since Mephistopheles had gifted him with a knowledge of art, he saw at once that it was a Botticelli, one of the middle period of the master's paintings. It was worth a lot of money, and was rather pretty, too.

Surely, Mack thought, in all this great mass of paintings, it wouldn't matter if I took one?

He looked around, saw that no one was looking at him, and pulled the painting out before the flames had reached it. It looked as good as new. He put it to one side and looked around for others. There was a Giotto, but the surface had already begun bubbling in the heat. He sought hungrily after others. If saving one Botticelli was good, saving two ought to be excellent. And lucrative as well! And surely it was not wrong to serve Art! Especially when it was just lying around waiting to be burned! Those other choices Mephistopheles had given him had just sounded too weird. He was sure no one could object to a man who rescued great art.

Then there was a hand on his shoulder. A thin, splendidly dressed man with a short beard was staring at him severely.

"Sir, what are you doing?"

"Me?" Mack said. "I'm just watching the fun like everyone else."

"I saw you take a painting off the bonfire."

"A painting? Oh, you mean this." Mack gestured at the Botticelli and grinned. "The servant put it out by mistake. We had taken it down to have it cleaned. It's a Botticelli. You just don't burn Botticellis in bonfires, not even vanity bonfires."

"And who might you be, sir?" the man demanded.

"I'm just a local nobleman," Mack said.

"Strange I haven't seen you before."

"I've been out of town. Who are you?"

"I," the man said, "am Niccolò Machiavelli. I work for the commune of Florence."

"That's a coincidence," Mack said. "I've been told to tell you not to write that book you're planning, the one you call *The Prince*."

"I have written no such book," Machiavelli said. "But it is a catchy title. I just might try it out."

"Do what you please," Mack said. "But remember, you've been warned."

"And who is the warning from?" Machiavelli demanded.

"I can't disclose the name," Mack said. "But I can assure you he's a devil of a good fellow."

Machiavelli stared at him, then turned and walked away, shaking his head. Mack picked up the painting, preparing to get out while the getting was good. But just then Pico della Mirandola came back.

"I've been checking with certain infernal powers," he said. "What have you done with the real Faust?"

Pico advanced threateningly. Mack cowered back. Pico raised one of those newfangled firearms that fired a ball large enough to tear a man apart. Mack looked for a place to hide. Nothing was immediately forthcoming. Pico's finger tightened on the trigger.

At that moment, Faust appeared. "Don't do it, Pico!" he cried.

"Why not? The man is trying to pass himself as you!"

"But we are not allowed to kill him. He *is* impersonating me. But it is necessary for him to stay alive as long as he occupies my role."

"What role is that, Johann?"

"All will be revealed later. For now, old friend, desist."

"You are a wise man, Faust!"

"I may call upon you later, Pico. I have a plan!"

"Count on me!"

Faust vanished. Then Mephistopheles appeared. "Ready?" he said to Mack. "Let's go. What's everybody gawking at?"

Mack decided not to tell him about Faust. "You know how people are. They'll stare at anything." He got a tight grip on the painting and Mephistopheles conjured them both away.

Chapter
7

Mack and Mephistopheles arrived in Limbo, conjuring themselves into existence at the entrance to a small building on a hill close to where the judgments for the Millennial contest were to be held.

"What's this place?" Mack asked.

"This is the Waiting Room of Limbo. I've got a storage facility here where you can store your Botticelli. Unless you want to sell it to me immediately?"

"I think I'd like to hold on to it for a while," Mack said. "So how did I do?"

"I beg your pardon?"

"On the contest, in Florence."

Mephistopheles didn't answer until they were inside. He indicated a room that Mack might use to store his painting.

"You didn't get anywhere with trying to get Medici and Savonarola to patch up their quarrel. You get a zero for your ineffectuality."

"But I told Machiavelli not to write *The Prince*. That was a good thing, wasn't it?"

Mephistopheles shrugged. "We don't know. It's up to Necessity to judge these matters. Good and Bad must remain subservient to What Must Be. By the way, who was that man? He seemed to know you."

"What man?"

"The one who kept Pico della Mirandola from killing you."

"Some nut," Mack said, deciding not to mention Faust. "I have no idea who he was. The painting's nice, isn't it?"

Mephistopheles held the painting at arms' length and gazed at it for a while. "Yes, it's very nice. I'll be happy to take it off your hands."

"Not just yet," Mack said. "I'd like to see what the market is worth, that sort of thing."

"A good idea," Mephistopheles admitted. "Here's a spell to get you to London. Don't dawdle, though. We need you for the next appearance."

"Don't worry, I won't be late," Mack said.

Mephistopheles nodded and vanished. Mack looked around the room and found a large metal box with a key in its keyhole. He unlocked it and was about to put in the painting. As he lifted it, he heard a scratching sound under his feet. He stepped hastily out of the way. The floor cracked, a small pick poked through the hole, then was replaced by a shovel. The hole was rapidly enlarged. Soon a diminutive shape clambered out. It was Rognir.

"Hi," said Mack, remembering the dwarf from the Sabbat.

"Nice painting," said Rognir. "Where'd you get it?"

"This painting? I picked it up in a place called Renaissance. It's somewhere in Italy near Florence."

"Oh? What were you doing there?"

"I'm in a contest," Mack said. "It's to decide the destiny of mankind for the next thousand years."

"Is that what they sent you to the Renaissance for, to get a painting?"

"I don't really know what they sent me for. I did some other stuff. But I got the painting because Mephistopheles said he'd like one, and he'd pay me a pretty price for it. But I haven't sold it yet. I decided to see what the market's worth."

"He wanted you to get a painting, did he?"

"Sure he did. Since I was going to be there anyway. Sorry, gotta go. I'm due in London next. It's a big one."

"Good luck," Rognir said. "Maybe I'll see you there."

"I look forward to it," Mack said. He hesitated, looking at the hole in the floor. "You're going to clean that up before you leave, aren't you?"

Rognir told him not to worry, his painting was safe. He left musing about just what kind of stupid jerk this guy Mack was. He didn't even know he was being manipulated. The idea of making up his own mind had never occurred to him. He was still trying to please other people. As he'd probably been doing all his life. And yet, there was something about him that roused an odd bit of sympathy.

ACHILLES

Chapter
1

In the meantime, there were consequences that emanated from Azzie's taking of Helen of Troy from her place in Hades, where, together with her husband, Achilles, she reigned over the social aspects of the underworld. Azzie had conjured Helen away rather casually, not stopping to wonder why this sort of thing was usually not done and what the consequences might be. A moment's thought would have reminded him that the dead have some powers and it is not good to run afoul of them.

Achilles really didn't take it well when he returned one evening from hunting ghost deer in the mist-covered meadows that lay just past the Slough of Despond, and found that Helen was missing. That was unlike her. At first he thought she was off visiting neighbors. He enquired, but no one had seen her. Still, people just don't go missing from Hades. Someone has to take them out. Achilles went at once to his old friend and neighbor, Odysseus, for help.

Odysseus had fared pretty well in the battle of the archetypal ratings. He had his own problems, of course. Although he was a pretty tricky fellow, it was hard to think up any new stunts that would deserve the term *Odyssean wiliness*. The spirits behind archetypes can reach their prime and fade away, but they have to continue trying to surpass themselves anyway. You know what they say about teaching old gods new tricks. Odysseus' later schemes tended to be pretty obvious. And some-

times a little nasty. There was a mean streak in Odysseus. He
liked to win, and he'd do anything to achieve victory.

And he didn't like being dead. He hated not having a body.
He scorned the way everyone just lay around Hades all the
time, complaining about conditions and talking about the good
old days on Earth. He himself wouldn't stoop to complain. Show
a little spirit, he told them. Stay in condition. Even though the
dead aren't able to build muscle, Odysseus exercised faithfully.
"You have to retain the ability to do things," he told dead people
who asked about this, "even if what you do makes no difference."

Odysseus was sitting on the front porch of his house when
Achilles came to ask his help. Odysseus lived by himself in a
marble house near a tributary of the Styx. Asphodel grew in
the moss on his front lawn. The place was shaded with the
inevitable black poplars, which one gets very tired of after a
while, in Hades and elsewhere. It was a gloomy day, like all
the other days in Hades. It was just chilly enough so you weren't
comfortable sitting outside, but not cold enough to be invigo-
rating. Odysseus had a fire going in the living room, but it
threw very little heat. Not that it mattered: the dead can never
get warmed up properly anyway. Odysseus brought Achilles
into the kitchen and offered him a breakfast of dates and porridge. They weren't real food, of course. But the dead are
attached to the habits of the living and go right on eating, and
even plan elaborate banquets. Eternity goes on for a very long
time, and food is a way of passing it.

Sex is a way of passing time, too, even though dead people
can't be properly said to have sex, ectoplasm being devoid of
sensation as well as immaterial. But sex is something they used
to do, so they go on doing it after death, or at least going through
the motions.

Odysseus was currently unmarried. He and Penelope had
split up long ago. Odysseus had always had his suspicions about
what she'd really been up to with the suitors during the twenty

years he was away fighting Trojans. For a while he kept the family together for the sake of the boy, Telemachus. But then Telemachus found his own archetype, nothing big, but quite steady, and now he lived in another section of Hades and had as his friends the sons of other famous men.

So Odysseus was alone, and he had little to occupy him. He did his exercises faithfully every day. Sometimes he visited his friend Sisyphus. Sisyphus was still rolling the big boulder up the mountain. He didn't have to do it. He had been set free long ago. But, as he said, it gave him something to do, and, above all, it kept his archetype alive.

Sometimes Odysseus went to visit Prometheus, one of his oldest friends, who was still spread-eagled on a rock, with a vulture eating away his liver. Prometheus had been a difficult case for the gods. Setting him loose would have endangered everybody, since the world still wasn't ready for personal freedom. And the guy wouldn't promise to shut up about his ideas. Again, a modus vivendi, so to speak, might have been worked out — sooner or later, all of the dead compromise their values — but Prometheus was interested in keeping up his reputation. Recently he had turned moody and some days wouldn't even talk to Odysseus. People said that his only friend was his vulture.

So Odysseus was bored. He used to go out hunting ghost deer with Achilles or Orion, but that sport soon palled. The main disadvantage of a ghost deer was that you couldn't kill it. And even if you could, you couldn't eat it.

Odysseus was in a receptive mood when Achilles came over and told his problems. Odysseus suggested that they go at once and talk to Dis, king of Tartaros, in the black palace he shared with Persephone.

Dis had his own problems. He was engaged in jurisdictional disputes with the Roman chthonic deity Plutus, who had recently become the chief deity of the Roman underworld, and had pulled strings to be declared a separate deity in his own right and not subsumed under the Hades concept. Because of this ruling, Dis immediately lost control of a large section of the classical underworld, and no longer had jurisdiction over the Latins who had formerly been his subjects. In one way he was glad to see them go. Latin dead had never gotten along well with the Greeks. On the other hand, losing the Latins diminished his kingdom, and shrank his archetype.

And he was engaged in other jurisdictional battles, because there were always claims from other underworld constructs who proposed that Hellenic Hades should be subsumed under them. The gods of the Sanskrit-speaking people had put together a lot of material to show that all the Greek gods originally had come under their aegis, and should do so again. So far, Dis had been able to stave off any final vote on it. But it was still a touchy matter.

Problems, problems. And then suddenly there were Achilles and Odysseus, demanding justice.

"What do you expect me to do about it?" Dis said. "I don't have any power up there. To hell with Dis, that's what they say. They've got new constructs."

"There must be something you can do," Achilles said. "If you're so ineffectual, you should step down and let somebody else rule Hades. I've got a good mind to bring it before the Hellenic General Assembly at the next Bylaws of Hades meeting."

"Hell, no, don't do that," Dis said. "Let me think about this. Do you know who took her?"

"There was a demon involved," Achilles said. "Alecto told me that. He was one of those spirits from the cycle that came after ours."

"Which side is this demon on?" Odysseus asked.

"Alecto said he represented Darkness or Badness," Achilles said. "I can't remember which."

"Darkness," Odysseus mused. "I suppose that equates

with Badness? In that case we know which party to apply to for redress. I've never been able to understand the distinctions between Good and Bad. People only started making them some centuries after our time."

"Beats the hell out of me too," Dis said. "But people seem to like the Good and Bad stuff."

Odysseus said, "Meanwhile, there's a wrong here we must right. If you'll give us a provisional reality card so we can get out of here, and your authority to act for the classical infernal construct in this matter, Achilles and I will bring this matter to the attention of the proper authorities."

"All right, you've got it," Dis said. He felt pleased with himself. One of the most important things about having authority is being able to delegate responsibility. Now it was up to Odysseus to right this wrong.

Chapter 2

After Odysseus received permission from Dis to accompany Achilles to the world of the living, he decided to seek out Tiresias, the most notable magician of the ancient world. Tiresias would know what they had to do and how they could get where they were going.

First the heroes had to prepare a blood sacrifice, because Tiresias wouldn't do anything without blood. He was hopelessly addicted to the stuff. Blood was always in short supply in Tartaros, but Dis felt it his duty to supply a skinful from his private store. (It is not true that you can't drink well in Hades, but you have to know somebody.)

The two heroes set off for the grove of Persephone, with its black poplars and aged willows, at the point where two rivers of Hades, Phlegethon and Cocytus, flowed into the Acheron. There they dug a trench and poured in the blood, heroically desisting from drinking it themselves. Whenever dead people came by asking for some, they turned them down. They wouldn't even give a sip to Agamemnon, their old commander-in-chief, who drifted by, drawn by the scent. This blood was for Tiresias alone.

Dark and oily, the blood lay in the trench. Then it suddenly frothed, then diminished, drunk by an unseen presence. Immediately after that Tiresias appeared, a slight figure in a long gray wool mantle, his face painted with ochre and blue clay, his dank white hair hanging down over his eyes.

"A very good day to you, gentlemen. Thank you very much for the nice sacrifice. Some of Dis' private store, isn't it? Lovely stuff! Don't have any more, do you? Too bad! Well then, what can I do for you?"

"We seek Helen of Troy," Odysseus said. "She has been unlawfully abducted from her husband, Achilles, here."

"Somebody always seems to be stealing the fair Helen," Tiresias said. "Do you know who did it?"

"We are told it was a demon from the new age," Odysseus said. "But we do not know his name or where to find him. We need your advice and assistance."

"All right," Tiresias said. "The demon's name is Azzie and he is part of the new Dark-Light overview which has captured the minds of mankind."

"We will go seek him out!" Achilles said.

"You're going to find it a different world out there," Tiresias said. "You will have to go to the main place from which Evil is commanded, which is called Hell, and make your enquiries there. I can provide you with a Traveling Spell, as long as you have Dis' permission to use it. As a matter of fact, I happen to know who Helen is with at present."

"Tell us!" cried Achilles.

Tiresias cleared his throat and turned toward the trench, now drained of blood.

"We have no more to give you," Odysseus said. "But at the first chance we will provide another sacrifice."

"The word of Odysseus is good enough for me," Tiresias said. "But I warn you, finding Helen won't be easy. She's moving around a lot since she is now the consort of a famous magician named Faust."

"Faust?" Achilles said. "That doesn't sound like a Greek to me."

"He's not. Other races have come up in the world and are now the physical as well as intellectual masters. This Faust is engaged in a game with the gods themselves. I mean the new gods."

"Where *are* our old gods, by the way?" Odysseus asked.

"They've been pretty much subsumed under different names," Tiresias said. "They've taken on new identities. Most of them don't even remember Greece and Olympus. Except for Hermes, of course, who is still active as the Trismegistus."

"Well then, where do we find Faust and Helen?"

"They are traveling," Tiresias said. "But not only on the Earth. They are traveling in time as well."

"Can we get to where they are by boat?" Achilles asked.

"Not unless it's an enchanted boat. Traveling by spell is really the only way."

"You're sure we can't get there by land?"

"Not that way, either. It takes a bit of magic to get where Helen has gone to. Luckily, I have brought along my bag of spells." From beneath his mantle he took a horsehide bag. It bulged and creaked suspiciously, and gave off little sighs and whines.

"The spells are restless today," Tiresias said. "Use them with care and mind your fingers when you take them out of the sack. Do not be precipitate. Remember, the matter must proceed step by step. First you have to visit Hell and get permission from the Powers of Darkness to take Helen back. There's always a procedure in these matters."

"And will you accompany us there?" Achilles asked.

"No, I will not. But I'll be looking around for information. Don't forget, you owe me a sacrifice! Now, I must away."

Odysseus would have liked something a little more definite. But Tiresias had said his last word. So Odysseus agreed. Tiresias vanished. Odysseus reached into the horsehide bag and separated one spell from where it lay coiled around the others. He brought it out and hastily tied up the sack again. The spell writhed and squirmed, but Odysseus held it firmly and muttered the necessary words. The spell quivered, and then gave a mighty lunge. Odysseus held on, and Achilles held on to him. With classical simplicity, and no baroque nonsense about fire and brimstone, Odysseus and Achilles found themselves in the anteroom of the Kingdom of Dark.

Chapter 3

The door to Belial's office burst open. Belial gave a jump of startlement. The fat, toad-bodied demon with the blue-gray complexion and the bulging orange eyes had been gazing into a mirror of illusion, lost in contemplation of his own cleverness and beauty, since in hell self-love replaces self-respect, and he hadn't heard the knock. In strode two brawny figures in pleated white kilts and tunics.

"Who are you people?"

"I am Odysseus," Odysseus said, "and this is Achilles."

"Oh. Really?" Belial peered at them closely and saw that they had the classical Greek look—big men with straight noses and curly brown hair. Even dead and without a vestige of reality about them, they were impressive. Some awed clerk at a lower gateway to the realm of Darkness must have issued them a pass of temporary reality. Otherwise they could not have ventured into this place. The inhabitants of the classic underworld had been judged unreal. In the end, it was the only way to get rid of them, and even that didn't work all of the time.

"Achilles and Odysseus," Belial said. "I've heard about you, of course, but I never expected to actually see you."

"They don't let us out of Tartaros," Odysseus said. "We were too strong for them once. Now they won't permit us any manifestation except the archetypal one, which doesn't affect us anyway except in the form of publicity."

"Oh, really. Too bad! It's a pity that you're not real. Some of our younger devils would enjoy hearing a lecture or breakfast meeting discussion with you. I'm sure you could teach us a great deal that would be useful."

"We can discuss that some other time," Odysseus said. "A lecture tour is not completely out of the question. But now I'm here speaking on behalf of my friend, Achilles. A wrong has been done to him by one of your people."

"You're representing Achilles, eh? Can't he speak for himself?"

"Of course I can," Achilles said, piping up abruptly. "The trouble is, my speech is impetuous, like my nature. I tend to speak hastily and get myself into weird situations. They often end up in a fight, which I win, of course. But people don't usually like me. Everyone likes Odysseus, though."

"That's enough, Achilles," Odysseus said. "Remember, I was going to do all the talking."

"Sorry, Odysseus," Achilles said.

"That's all right. If I am well liked it's because I'm sort of a demigod, interested in customs and ways, unlike you, Achilles, who thinks of nothing but war and killing."

"I sure wish I could kill something now," Achilles said. "I'm nervous."

"Calm yourself," Odysseus said. He turned again to Belial. "We have it on good authority that a demon of your command named Azzie captured one of our people, Helen of Troy, grabbed her out of Hades and away from her husband without so much as a by-your-leave. He gave her to a magician named Faust, who is having her engage in un-Greek adventures."

"This surely can't be true," Belial said. "We servants of Darkness don't just grab dead people without their permission."

"Perhaps you should check on it," Odysseus said.

"Indeed I will." Belial pressed a button on his intercom. "Miss Siggs?"

"Yes, Your Excellency."

"Did you listen in on this conversation?"

"Well, sort of, but it was purely accidental."

"Never mind. Check into it and get back to me at once."

"I don't have to check, Your Excellency. What those Greeks say is quite true. People are already making up stories about Azzie's abduction of Helen. It ought to make a very popular myth."

"But damn it, he had no authorization to take her! There are rules, you know!"

"Yes, Your Excellency. But no one seems to know quite what they are."

"It's clear enough in this case," Belial said, for he was not about to give up an opportunity to get even with Azzie, who had been rude to him several times in self-criticism meetings.

He shut off the intercom and turned to Odysseus and Achilles. "There seems to be some basis to your claim. I had nothing to do with it myself, however, and there's nothing I can do about it. You'd better talk to Mephistopheles, or to Azzie himself."

"Where do we find them?" Achilles asked.

"Actually, right now they're both busy with the contest."

"What contest?"

"It is the great Millennial contest between Dark and Light to decide who will rule mankind for the next thousand years."

"What does Helen have to do with all that?" Odysseus asked.

"I believe Azzie seized her to give to Faust as a prize."

Achilles suddenly said, "We don't want any more talk. We want Helen back!"

"Yes, that's right," Odysseus said. "That's the bottom line."

"My dear fellow," Belial said, "I understand your position. But what can I do?"

"Let us go do something ourselves," Odysseus said. "We don't need your help to rescue Helen."

"You're fine upstanding fellows," Belial said. "But you have no power in this construct."

"Perhaps not. But we have some important friends."

"And who might they be?"

Odysseus laid a finger along the side of his nose in a gesture of caution. "Don't speak their names unless you want them in the office here with you."

Then Belial got it. Odysseus was talking about the Eumenides! Also know as Erinnyes, and as Furies! Some of those ancient constructs still had power, like Ananke herself. Belial decided this was not a good line for him to pursue.

"If you think you can handle it," Belial said, "you go right ahead. You've got *my* permission." He frowned. "I don't want to seem critical, but you two don't have much in the way of bodies."

"This is the best we could do," Odysseus said. "We're dead, you know."

"Tell you what," Belial said. "Here are two free passes to the Witches' Kitchen. Tell them to fix you up with bodies. Not all of us in Hell are as bad as some I could name."

Chapter 4

The hulking Arabian demon who stood guard at the door had seen some strange sights in his years of working at the Witches' Kitchen. But this was the first time this flabby, sloe-eyed, former citizen of Gehenna had seen two Greek heroes straight out of Homer come walking into his beauty salon. The demon knew at once who they were, because he had been a classical scholar before becoming doorman to an afterlife beautification service.

"We never had any Greek heroes in before," he muttered. "Do you spirits have a certificate of reality?"

Odysseus showed the certificate of temporary reality which Dis had given them. The senior witch put down her branding iron and came over and looked at the certificate, and at the passes Belial had given the heroes.

She said, "It's all right, Tony, let them in."

In the corporealizing treatment that followed, the big question was how much heroic musculature to give them. The witches decided not to go in too heavy for bulk, since speed and agility were necessary in most demigodlike pursuits.

Several hours later, Achilles and Odysseus finished the beauty treatment that made them men again. They had used another spell from Odysseus' horsehide bag to take them back to Earth. They were resting under a tree now, not entirely sure of their exact whereabouts. But that didn't worry them. They had brought several days' provisions with them from the Witches' Kitchen. At least, it should have lasted for several days. But overcome by the novelty of corporeal food again, they had devoured it all for lunch. After dreaming about food for all those centuries, they hadn't known when to stop.

"I'm full," Achilles said.

"Me too," Odysseus said. "This is one day in which the wise Odysseus didn't eat too wisely. The pickled herring was delicious, though, wasn't it?"

"I preferred the pâté," Achilles said. "I think chopped liver is probably the greatest discovery of the world since our time. Remember how it used to be back in classical times? We always had to eat our liver grilled, with onions on the side. There wasn't even soy sauce in those days. Odysseus, how did we stand it?"

"We didn't know any better," Odysseus told him. "It would be hard to go back to the Trojan War and army provisions now, though, wouldn't it? Not that there's any chance."

"I suppose not," Achilles said. "That was a good war, wasn't it, Odysseus?"

"The best," Odysseus said. "There'll never be another like it. Remember when I defeated Ajax?"

"I never got to see it," Achilles said. "I was already dead then, remember? You were fighting him for my armor."

"Yes, and I won," Odysseus said.

"It was a really great suit of armor," Achilles said wistfully. "With armor like that it was hard to lose. Wearing it I killed Cycnus and Troilus. But my greatest hit, of course, the one I'll always be known for in the record books, was killing Hector."

"I know all about it," Odysseus told him.

"I was just reminiscing. It was later that Paris got me with that sneaky arrow shot. . . . In the heel, yet! Oh, well." He sighed and rubbed his belly. "That pâté . . . Odysseus, about these bodies we have now . . ."

"Yes?"

"They're supposed to be good ones, aren't they?"

"Yes, as I understand it, the best."

"Well, I've got this pain right down here."

He pointed to his abdomen.

"That's nothing," Odysseus said. "It's a little muscle pull, or, more likely, overeating."

"Are you sure it doesn't mean there's something wrong with me?"

"They said these were sound bodies. You've had muscle pulls before."

"I don't remember ever getting anything like this before. And my feet hurt."

"That's because we've been running. Feet get sore when you run on them. Even when you walk on them."

Achilles said, "Is this how it felt, back when we had bodies?"

"I suppose it is," Odysseus said. "But we made much less of it then. We were in training. We were accustomed to the joys and sorrows of having bodies."

"I don't mean to complain," Achilles said. "I'm stuffed, but I'm hungry again, too. And there doesn't seem to be anything to drink around here."

"It's lucky there's not some chronicler around, listening to you," Odysseus said. "Imagine the great Achilles complaining about hunger and thirst!"

"I must have said and felt those things back when we were living."

"I don't remember you ever admitting you were hungry, Achilles. Mere food was beneath you. Your entire being was dedicated to glory."

"It still is," Achilles said, standing up, wincing. "I think I'm developing a low back pain. Never mind, come on, let's go."

"I'm quite ready," Odysseus said. "But the thing is, I don't know where we should go."

Achilles looked around. He saw they were in a sunny meadow. There was a forest ahead, dark and verdant. Small birds flew overhead, singing their songs. A light breeze was blowing, and it had a fine clean scent about it. It was just past midday. The sun, now high in the sky, was golden and fine, warm but not hot. It was one of the better days either man could remember in a long time, and very unlike the typical days in Hades, where it is always on the verge of raining and the skies are the color of a really nasty bruise.

The meadow was warm and pleasant, but there was still something uncanny about it, and so Odysseus was not surprised when he looked again and saw three ladies sitting on the grass having a picnic. They were quite elderly, and dressed in classical gowns. Odysseus knew he had seen them before, and a moment's thought brought them back to mind. These were none other than the Eumenides, those three Weird Sisters who used to travel around the ancient world giving hell to parricides. They were bad news wherever you encountered them, but the important thing was to talk to them in a friendly fashion and not give them any reason to get sore at you.

"It's my old friends, the Eumenides," Odysseus said, walking up to the ladies, with Achilles following him. "Hello, Tisiphone, Alecto, hi, Megaera. You girls are a long way from dear old Hellas."

"Hello, Odysseus," Alecto said. She was tall, with gray hair neatly marcelled. Her nose was a commanding beak, such as might have looked well on the prow of a man-of-war. "We expected you to come this way."

"How could you have foreseen that?" Odysseus asked. "None but the witches know we are here."

"We are sisters to the witches," Alecto said. "When we visited them in the Witches' Kitchen, they told us you'd be passing through here, which is the Meadow of the Interlude. In this place only good influences penetrate. That is why my sisters and I are not in our usual horrific form. That'll come later. Right now we can take a few minutes off and be nice."

"I've always thought you were nice," Odysseus said. "And

so has Achilles here. Come up here, Achilles. Do you know these ladies?"

Achilles came up somewhat bashfully. "I believe I made their acquaintance briefly, once when I visited Orestes. Tell me, ladies, why do you search for Odysseus?"

"It was our surest way of finding you!" Tisiphone cackled.

Achilles turned pale. "And why did you wish to find me?"

Alecto said, "It is our best way to find Faust and the stolen lady whom we seek. I refer, of course, to Helen, your wife."

"Why do you want Helen?" Achilles asked.

"We have nothing against her personally. She's booty, and she has to go back to Hades immediately. We are the enforcement arm of the Classical Construct Placement Division. Azzie Elbub, the demon who took her from Hades, had no right to do so. We do not approve of such things. We are going to return her to you. Are you not glad?"

"Very glad," Achilles said, though now he was beginning to have his doubts. "It's what I'm here for myself."

"Good," Alecto said. "We weren't entirely sure *what* you were up to. Too many heroes manage at last to get out of Hades and then spend all their time lollygagging around the Earth, forgetting their duty and just enjoying having a body again."

A little more time was spent in conversation. And then it was time for the heroes to pursue their quest for Helen.

MARLOWE

Chapter
1

It was a big day in London on that overcast but mild September 30, 1588 when the Rose Theater in Southwark reopened with the play *Doctor Faustus*, starring Edward Alleyn. Not only was this an important play, in view of its advance notices, but it was also the first play since the recent bout of plague had abated. This gave it a special panache, and ensured a full house. The people came early, before dawn even, long lines of them crawling from places even beyond the city, from Graveslines and Swiss Cottage and Hampton Court, from Shepherd's Mill and Reindeer's Head, from Baxby and Weltenshire, moving steadily in the steady rain. By ferry and by foot they crossed the Thames and London Bridge to await the trumpet that announced the beginning of the play.

Early in the day before the performance, Mack and Mephistopheles met in London at the Tavern of the Drowned Man.

"Gentlemen!" the publican said. "I did not see you arrive!"

"That is because you were fooling with the serving wench," Mephistopheles said.

"Not so, sir! I was behind the bar all this time, polishing the brass and chatting with Mistress Henley, who provides our daily repast."

"Well, so what if you didn't see us arrive?" Mephistopheles demanded. "Do you believe that my friend and I conjured ourselves into your low abode?"

"Not at all, my lord!" the publican declared. "It takes no witchcraft to come into this place! The door is always open and

I am always ready for business! What may I bring Your Worships?"

"A bottle of your best Malmsey should do nicely," Mephistopheles said. "What do you think, Doctor?"

Mack had been gathering his wits about him, for the transition from Florence to London had been swift enough, and his clothing, which Mephistopheles had changed for him in midflight, was still unsettled. But with Mephistopheles elbowing him into the booth and the publican looking at him openmouthed, he soon recovered his native alacrity.

"Malmsey will be fine," Mack said. "And was that orlotan pie I noticed on the shelf?"

"Indeed it is, sir," the publican said.

"Then bring us a couple of slices of that," Mack said, glancing to Mephistopheles, because he wasn't entirely sure that food was included in his traveling allowance.

"Yes, and half a loaf of your best wheaten bread," Mephistopheles said. He smiled ingratiatingly. "Has Dr. John Dee been in this morning, perchance?"

"Not yet, my lord," the publican said. "But he will arrive soon, no doubt, because we have today his favorite, eel pie and mashed potatoes, and he'll not pass up on that delicacy, especially since he is leaving soon for the court of the king of Bohemia, or so Dame Rumor tells us."

"Perhaps Dame Rumor will also tell you that my friend and I are quick to chastise if we do not receive our provender promptly."

"I will see to it that the provender is brought forthwith!" the publican declared. "Polly! Get the lead out of it and serve these gentlemen their fare!" And so saying, he hurried off, the bar rag flapping from the back pocket of his broad-backed pantaloons.

"What is this place?" Mack asked, as soon as they were alone. "And what did you do with Marguerite?"

"I've left her in my waiting room in Limbo," Mephistopheles said. "You need no woman along for the task that lies before you this day. As for the where of it, this is London, my dear Faust, and the year is 1588, an eventful year for England, and for you."

"For me?" Mack said. "Wherefore sayest thou?"

"It is the year and day of the premiere of the first showing of that famous play based upon your life. I refer, of course, to the *Tragicall History of Doctor Faustus* as enacted by the players of the Earl of Nottingham and with the nonpareil Edward Alleyn in the title role. But you must have known of this in Cracow through your necromantic musings."

"Oh, yes, of course," said Mack, ever eager to take upon his shoulders the mantle of learning. "The famous play about me! And you've brought me here to see it! It is good of you, my dear Mephistopheles."

Mephistopheles frowned. "I haven't brought you all this way to sit in an audience and suck an orange and applaud the lies a poet tells. There's work for you to do here."

"Well, of course," Mack said. "I thought not otherwise. What would you have me do?"

"Hearken," Mephistopheles said, and then desisted, for Polly, the serving girl, had arrived with the orlotan pies, which were actually made of sparrows, the wheaten bread, which turned out to be oaten, and the Malmsey, which was no more than vin ordinaire from Bordeaux. Still, it was as good as you could expect from a riverside pub in the momentous year of the Spanish Armada, with plague raging in the city and the duke of Guise with his thirty thousand Spanish veterans penned up in Scheveningen and snarling across the Channel. Mephistopheles and Mack fell to with good appetite. Presently Mephistopheles pushed his plate aside and said, "Now hearken to me, Faust, for you have work to do upon this day."

"I am all ears," Mack said, "and eager to do your bidding."

"Christopher Marlowe is the author of this play," Mephistopheles said, "and he will be in the audience tonight. After the performance—which will have notable success—he will meet with a certain man, and have a conversation with him."

"Aha!" said Mack, though he wasn't sure where this was leading.

"That man," Mephistopheles said, "is Thomas Walsingham, an old friend of Marlowe's. Thomas' father, Sir Francis, is secretary of state to Elizabeth, queen of England, and he also commands her secret service, by means of which the intentions of the various factions in this war-torn year of Europe's woe will be known."

"Walsingham. All right, I've got it," Mack said, grabbing for anything out of Mephistopheles' proliferant peroration. "What do you want me to do to this guy? Mugging happens to be a sideline of mine, and I can promise you—"

"No, no," Mephistopheles said, "you are not to touch Walsingham. Just listen."

"All right, I'm listening," Mack said.

"Walsingham will ask Marlowe to serve once again in his father's Secret Service, as he did in bygone years. Marlowe will agree. That's the fact of it. It leads to Marlowe's premature death. But in this case, immediately after Marlowe and Walsingham talk, you will seek out Marlowe and convince him to do no such thing."

"I'll convince him, all right," Mack said. "Is this Marlowe skilled at arms? I guess I'd better have some weapons for this. Do you know where I can pick up a good cudgel?"

"Forget the cudgel," Mephistopheles said. "No man ever convinced Christopher Marlowe by force, and not much by persuasion, either. No, you will demonstrate to him what the consequences of his spying for Walsingham will be."

"And what will those consequences be?"

"Five years from now, on May 30, 1593, Marlowe will go to an inn with Ingram Frizer, Robert Poley, and Nicholas Skeres. He will remonstrate with them concerning evidence he has as to their traitorous actions on behalf of Henry the Third of France, asking them to turn King's evidence and throw themselves on the mercy of the Privy Council. Scorning such a course of action, these men will seize Marlowe and stab him to death, and then bruit it about that Marlowe irrationally attacked one of them, Frizer, who, hard-pressed, killed him accidentally and in self-defense. Thus England and the world will lose its foremost poet, dead at the age of twenty-nine, whereas, had he lived, he might have been expected to write many more fine plays exposing the pretensions of standard piety."

"I get it," Mack said. "You want this Marlowe to live, is that it?"

"Oh, I wouldn't go so far as to say *I* want it," Mephistopheles said. "It is but a suggestion, a choice for you."

"But you have laid out the course I am to follow."

"Certainly. But only if you want to. You could also steal the magic mirror of Dr. Dee. You have heard of the famous Dr. Dee, no doubt?"

"Of course," Mack said. "But just at this moment the name 'scapes my ken."

"Dr. Dee is the foremost necromancer and magician in England, a name to be spoken in hushed tones along with those of Albertus Magnus and Cornelius Agrippa. He has been asked by no less a personage than Elizabeth of England to cast her horoscope, and the queen is noted for her hardheadedness. Dee leaves presently to take up residence at the court of Rudolph the Second of Bohemia. And he will take his magic mirror with him. You must somehow get that mirror."

"What do I need this magic mirror for?"

"Oh, you might use it to convince Marlowe to avoid working as a spy for Walsingham. When he gazes into it, the mirror will show the bloody result if he should persist in that course. Seeing his death before his very eyes should change his mind. Do you understand all that I have told you?"

"I think so," Mack said. "But how am I to get this mirror away from Dr. Dee?"

"My dear fellow," Mephistopheles said, "I can't be expected to do *all* your work for you. Ask him. Should he prove obdurate, give him this." Mephistopheles took a small object out of an inside pocket in his cloak, wrapped it in a scarlet silk handkerchief, and handed it to Mack. Then he arose and gathered his long black cloak closely about him. "Farewell, then, Faust, I'll await your results."

He made as if to go. But Mack plucked him by the sleeve. "What is it?"

"If you would be so kind as to settle the bill, if it please Your Demonship."

"Have you no money of your own?"

"I may need it. You can't tell what might come up on an assignment like this."

Mephistopheles contemptuously threw a handful of coins on the table and made as if to disappear. Then, remembering appearances, he stalked out of the tavern and found nearby a little cul-de-sac where his vanishment would not be remarked.

Mack put the handkerchief-wrapped object into his pouch without looking at it, then counted out the exact change from what Mephistopheles had left, pocketed the rest, made enquiry as to the location of Dr. Dee's house, and departed.

In the next booth, concealed from Mack and Mephistopheles by its high back, a muffled figure stirred. He was a fox-faced fellow dressed in crimson and green finery, complete with large starched ruff. Azzie, for such it was, tapped his fingers thoughtfully on the oak table, and his long upper lip lifted in a humorless grin.

He had followed Mephistopheles here in a surreptitious manner, eager to get to the bottom of the mystery of the demon's behavior. So *that* was what Mephistopheles was up to! Cheating! And there had to be a way that Azzie could make use of that knowledge. He considered for a moment, then thought he found a way to go about it.

He conjured himself out of the tavern upon the instant, before the astonished publican could present the bill. Let the superstitious lout blame it on Marlowe's Faust. Azzie had devilish work to do. Swiftly he mounted to the starry firmament, bound for the spiritual regions, where he had something of interest to say to a certain former witch of his acquaintance.

Chapter
2

"We shouldn't be meeting this way," Ylith said, looking around with worried glance. But it seemed she had nothing to worry about. This cocktail lounge, The Mixed Spirit, just inside the blue-black walls of Babylon, and just around the corner from the temple to Baal, was well known as a neutral place where the operatives from Good and Bad got together from time to time, exchanged information, and tried to suborn each other. Since each side thought it had the advantage in the suborning business, neither had gotten around to proscribing meetings. Babylon in those days, before the Hittites moved in and trashed the neighborhood, and before Alexander ruined the place for good as he did Thebes, was a fun place to spend some time. The city was famous for its musical revues, its great zoo where animals of all varieties wandered in a paradisaical setting, its hanging gardens, which were like a frozen Niagaras of vegetation tumbling down from the heights of the upper city. Although this information was later suppressed by the jealous Athenians, Babylon was the intellectual capital of the world in those days, a place where Phoenician and Jew, Bedouin and Egyptian, Persian and Indian, could meet in cheerful confab in one of the city's many coffee houses — for Babylon had learned the great secret of coffee, espresso style, the steamed water pushed through the fragrant brew by great bellows operated by the Nubians and Ethiopians who had a monopoly on the trade. Babylon was also a food capital, whose shish kebabs were second to none, and whose baby buns were famous as far as Asmara and beyond. And above all, Babylon was splendid with color and pageantry, a place given to public festivals and to kingly revels.

"Relax, there's no harm in it," Azzie said. "Just because we're on different sides doesn't mean we can't have a date now and then and get caught up on the latest gossip."

Ylith looked at him fondly but with dubiety in her gaze. Azzie *was* a handsome demon, there could be no doubt about that. His orange-red fur was close-cropped and lustrous, his long, thin-bladed nose had a great elegance about it, and his lips, twisted and smiling, had touched hers too often for her to be able to gaze upon them with complete indifference. Yes, she still cared for him. But that was not the reason she had accepted his invitation. She knew that resisting him was good for her soul; and besides, it gave her a frisson to feel the pangs of a love that never could be, a love that she had transferred recently to the angel Babriel. Yes, Babriel was very good indeed, and that was good, as far as goodness went. But of late Ylith had begun to feel immortal yearnings, which she hoped were not also immoral.

Snap out of it, girl, she admonished herself. And then, to Azzie: "So what's new?"

"Nothing much," Azzie said with an elaborate shrug. "Just the same old skulduggery and double-dealing. You know what a demon's life is like."

"Who have you been double-crossing recently?" Ylith asked.

"Me? No one. It's been a quiet time for me, since the Powers That Be in all their wisdom decided not to employ me on the current Millennial contest."

"Mephistopheles is a competent demon, so I hear," Ylith said. "No doubt he'll do a good job for Your Side."

"No doubt. Especially since he improves on chance with guile."

"That's to be expected. He's a demon, after all."

"I know. Guile's fine. But outright cheating is not, according to the agreement."

"Cheating?" she echoed. "I'm sure Mephistopheles wouldn't cheat. He's an upright devil, from all I've heard."

"Perhaps it wasn't cheating, then," Azzie said. "Perhaps I misunderstood."

She sat up, her back stiffening. "What did you misunderstand?"

"It was the merest nothing," Azzie said, breathing on his fingernails and buffing them on his flaring red velvet jacket.

"Azzie, stop teasing me! What did you see?"

"Nothing at all. But I overheard . . ."

"What?"

"I overheard the redoubtable Mephistopheles giving instructions to Johann Faust, the contestant in our game of Light and Dark."

"Well, of course he gave him instructions! Otherwise Faust wouldn't know what to do."

"Now he knows all too well," Azzie said.

"Stop these vague presentimentalistic mutterings! Tell me what you are hinting at."

"Mephistopheles is supposed to offer Faust a choice, correct?"

"That is well known."

"I heard him tell Faust exactly what choice he should make, and how he should go about accomplishing it."

"You mean he coached the contestant?"

"That's exactly what I mean. Forget about free will in this contest, my dear. It is Mephistopheles' will that is being served."

She stared at him openmouthed. And Azzie told her of the conversation he had overheard between Mephistopheles and Mack in the inn in London, and how Mephistopheles had directed the famous magician to save Marlowe, and had even suggested to him how to go about it.

"Azzie, if you're just trying to stir up trouble . . ."

"I'm always ready for that," Azzie said. "But what I have told you is absolute stone truth, without elaboration or embellishment."

Ylith was silent for a time, taking it in. She took two sips of her nectar frappe, an ambrosial beverage that disappeared from the world when Alexander the Great leveled the walls of Babylon and destroyed the frappe parlors in an act of misplaced Macedonian piety. Then she said, "If you say true, this is very serious."

"I never thought otherwise," Azzie said. "But you see, I am at a disadvantage here. Mephistopheles is on my side, and it wouldn't look right for me to go to the High Council with word of his misdoings. And yet, within me, Ylith, there beats a heart dedicated to truth and justice, just as your own does."

"How can you say that?" Ylith demanded. "You and your kind willingly serve lies and Badness!"

"Yes. But we do so in the cause of truth," Azzie said, employing paradox when the simple truth would never do. "We Darksiders just have our own way of going about it."

She shook her head at him, but her smile was fond. "You always were a silver-tongued devil!"

"A demon who would not lie in the service of beauty deserves not the name of Evil. But what I have told you about Mephistopheles is the simple truth unvarnished."

Ylith didn't understand Mephistopheles' motives. "If he rescues Marlowe," she asked, "won't that be a Good Thing, since it will give the world more of his plays?"

"That's one way of looking at it," Azzie said. "But since Marlowe is a mighty blasphemer against all things good, his unwritten plays are more likely to subvert the cause of piousness than to promote it."

"Azzie," Ylith said, "you have given me much to think about here. I shall have to consider what to do with this information."

"Use it as you please," Azzie said. "My conscience at least

is clear. Now, shall we drink up and be about our divers pursuits?"

Ylith nodded, and finished her frappe. The two of them left.

In the next booth, a small figure stirred. He was clad in thigh-high boots, a stout leather jerkin, and he wore a long yellow beard.

"Ha, ha, my fine fox-faced demon," said Rognir — for such it was. "So that's how the land lies, eh? I see through your little scheme, though, and I see through the damnable self-interest that brings you to forswear your own side in order to gain temporary advantage."

Since his stint of cleaning up at the Witches' Sabbat under the foremanship of Azzie, nothing had gone well for Rognir. He had hurried along to Montpellier. He had arrived too late for the jamboree. The various dwarverias had been there and gone. There were many empty kegs of beer lying around, that was all. He had gone home, tough burrowing all the way, and found when he got there that someone had broken into his buried treasure, stealing it all. It was not Rognir's only trove, of course. No self-respecting dwarf keeps all his loot in one trove. But still, the loss was not inconsiderable, and the bad luck rankled.

Rognir was still angry at the way Azzie had treated him at the Witches' Sabbat. He had been harboring a grudge against the demon ever since, hoping to find something to use against him; for dwarves have long memories and can hold a grudge longer than mountains can hold their shapes. Now he rubbed his chubby hands together, thinking how best to use this knowledge so recently come upon. And then a course of action occurred to him, and he left the tavern and went to the outskirts of Babylon, there finding one of the underground dwarf tunnels that leads to anywhere and anywhen. A ready-made dwarf hole was just what he needed. Suddenly he was in a hurry.

Chapter 3

Charon had quite an interesting load of dead that day. He had picked up three fishermen drowned off the coast of Sparta, brought to the underworld in a sudden squall that had blown up from the north. The fishermen were penniless but had promised payment through a cousin, one Adelphius of Corinth, who maintained a fund in the Dead Souls' Ferrying Society Relief Scheme. They explained that an obol for each of them had been deposited into a bank account in the Greater Hellenic Savings & Loan with offices in upper Corinth. All Charon had to do was call at any time, or send his representative with proper documentation, and he could collect his money for their passage.

Charon didn't like it. He was old-fashioned. Cash on the barrelhead was what he wanted; or, since it was a boat, cash on the fiddlehead. He suspected that the fishermen were trying to defraud him and ride free. At first he refused to take them. But a honey-tongued banker among the dead crew of Charon's boat, named Ozymandias, though he was not a king of kings, who had been killed in Corfu during a riot there fomented by Hellenic secret agents, and so had fallen under Charon's purview rather than under the customs of his own native country, insisted that the scheme was entirely sound. Charon couldn't find an argument to use against it but he still didn't like it. Of course, even he had to stay up with the times. In strange ports that he called at when he needed repairs for his boat, the people didn't take obols. Funny money, they called it.

In any event, it was all academic now. Here he was,

wrecked on a reef in the Styx, at a place where there shouldn't have been any rocks at all.

It was a noisome spot, dark and marshy, with lowering skies and a constant little wind that smelled of dead fish. Small, scum-covered waves lapped at the lapstraked sides of the boat. There were low misshapen trees near the bank, and from several of them hung dead men. The dead men waved their arms and begged to be taken down. Coals to Newcastle, Charon had all the dead he could handle. He had twenty or thirty of them packed onto his little boat. They sat on the forecastle and played cards with a tattered Tarot deck. They lounged on the deck, their loathy shirts open to their scabrous waists, paddling their feet in the water under a gibbous moon. Leaving the becalmed vessel they splashed around in the marsh, playing water polo with a moldy old head that had floated by.

Charon walked up to Faust and said, "This is your fault, you know. What are you going to do about it?"

"There's nothing I can do," Faust said. "It's the fault of that damned demon, Azzie. He doctored my good luck charm."

"Why don't you throw it overboard, then?" Charon asked.

Faust shook his head. "That's the worst thing you can do. No, we simply must ride it out."

"That's what you keep on telling us," Charon said. "But time goes by and we're still sitting here. You better do something pretty quick or it's over the side you go."

Faust looked at the noisome waters. It would almost be a relief. Down below he could see vast shapes swimming sluggishly. He knew that beneath the Styx there was a vast kingdom that men know nothing of. It almost tempted him. Why not give up this ceaseless travail which availeth naught? Let them throw him over — what did he care? What a pleasure it might be to drown forever, and to join the slimy swimmers of these dark waters!

But he roused himself. He was Faust! And Faust would

not give way to despair! That was for lesser men, not him. He would find a way out of this situation.

And then there was a faint brightening in the air. Could there be lightness even on the Styx? He looked into the distance. Yes, there was something moving on the waters. As it came out of the mists he saw that it was a little rowboat. And there was a little man rowing, bending to the oars with a lusty stroke.

Charon looked and said, "Who in hell could that be?"

"Thought you had the Styx all to yourself, eh, Charon?" Faust said.

The rowboat came up to the side of Charon's bark. Aboard was Rognir, dressed in a yellow sou'wester, with a big flappy rubber raincap on his large shaggy head. "What ho!" he cried. "Do you happen to have Faust aboard?"

"Why, yes, as a matter of fact we do," Charon said. "But who are you?"

"I'm Rognir," said Rognir. "I come from an entirely different realm of discourse. But I know who you are. Hail, Charon! Why are you parked here in the doldrums? On my way I passed docks and loading stages packed with dead souls. They were crying out for you, Charon, and they had coins in their hands."

"Damn it," Charon said, "I knew I was missing out on business. I am here, Rognir, because some baleful person has put a curse on my boat, a rudder curse I believe it is called, and my goodly little ship will only go in circles, and so has run itself on a sandbar, the only sandbar within a hundred miles of here, and here my boat hangs and refuses to get off. And what are you doing here?"

Rognir explained that he had come to speak to Faust, because he had important news for him.

"I have been listening in to the demons," Rognir said. "You are acquainted perhaps with one Azzie Elbub, demon, and a bad lot even by the standards of Hell?"

"I have met him," Faust said. "He sought to turn me aside from my purpose, which is to take my place in the contest of Dark and Light and so win redemption for mankind and undying glory for myself. Not only that, he gave me a defective Motive Spell, one infected with Jinx, as I see now, which has brought Charon's boat to a standstill."

"I think I can do something about that," Rognir said. "Here. Try this." He handed over a tangled cord.

"What is this?" Faust asked.

"A Spell of Unloosening. Untie the knot, and you will be free."

Chapter 4

Mack approached the London house of Dr. Dee. Mack said, "Are you sure you've got it straight now?"

"I think so," Marguerite said. "But I don't like it."

"Forget about that. Just do what I told you. It'll work out, believe me."

Marguerite looked unhappy, but quite pretty. Her chestnut hair was shining. She had had a chance to freshen up after Mephistopheles had brought her to join Mack. Even her gown, of green with panels of spotted dimity, was fresh and shining. Mack had seen to it that she looked her best.

He approached the door of a queer, humpbacked old house with shuttered windows that made it look like a cat sleeping. It was in a noxious part of London. On either side were the shadowed headquarters of dubious business enterprises, because this was the notorious Tortingham district, only later to be gentrified to the confusion of cutpurses, lollygaggers, yokels, and assorted cony-catchers. Here was where the famous Dr. Dee now made his home.

In his sitting room, Dr. Dee, tall and angular, clad in his doctor's gown, was regarding an ancient volume of curious and forgotten lore. He paused and looked up.

"Kelly!" he cried.

At the other end of the room, a short, broad-shouldered man looked away from a ball of yarn he was untangling. Edward Kelly, medium extraordinary — a fey-eyed Irishman from

County Limerick, with a fur cap pulled down over the sides of his head — quirked an eyebrow.

"Yes?" he asked.

"I've a premonition of someone on the stair," Dee said.

"Shall I go and see who it is?" Kelly asked.

"Prognosticate first, for I've also a foreboding or two."

Kelly reached across the table and put a glass of water in front of him. With a moistened forefinger he roiled the surface, then stared into it intently. In its swirling depth he saw strange shapes uncoil, glimpsed the forms and visages of drowned things and the many-colored windings and unwindings of spirits no more palpable than so many twists of smoke. He heard sounds as well, for that was how the gift took him. And he looked into the water and saw a man and a maid. Around them, visible only to his eyes, hovered a nimbus of mysterious events.

"There are two people approaching the door," he told Dee. "They are a strange pair, though it is not easy to say wherein their strangeness resides. The man is tall and yellow-haired, and the woman brown-haired and beautiful. They look decent enough."

"If they look good to you, then we'll see them," Dee said. "It was just a matter of certain feelings that came over me."

"So why ask me?" Kelly said. "Why didn't you look into your magic mirror and learn all about them?"

"The magic mirror is in the other room," Dee said. "And I don't see what you're so cross about."

"Me, cross?" Kelly said, scowling. "What makes you think I'm cross?"

"Well, you look cross."

"Why should I look cross," Kelly asked, "when I have nothing to complain about? Didn't I follow you and your psychic circus across Europe? Am I not the star act in your dog-and-pony show? Do I not do all the work, the better to give you the energy to enjoy all the credit?"

"Now, Edward," Dee said. "We've been over this ground before. Go see to the arrivals."

Thus grumbling, Kelly went to the door. The servant was never around when you wanted him to do something like this. It didn't take much prognostication to know that the servant was in his room under the eaves, nursing the old war wound he'd got under the Black Prince, or so he told the tale. Kelly thought about Ireland as he walked to the door, Ireland green and boggy, with the young girls who used to walk by him on their way to sheep flocks they tended on the downs beside the cold and glittering sea. He shook his head irritably. Stop speaking, Memory.

He opened the door.

"Hi," Mack said. "We'd like to speak to Dr. Dee, if you don't mind."

"What do you want to see the doctor about?"

"That's for his ears."

"Give it to my ears or his ears will never hear."

"It's for his ears alone," Mack said.

Kelly shrugged and led them to the sitting room.

"Something secret and important, so he says," Kelly told Dee.

Mack nodded to the doctor and smiled.

"We are interested in buying your magic mirror," he told him.

Dee raised his heavy eyebrows.

"Sell you my magic mirror? Sir, you must be daft! A mirror with the power and foresightedness of mine is not sold like a bag of horse feed. This mirror of mine, my dear sir, has been the object of covetousness in royal circles throughout Europe. The king of Poland offered me an estate for it on the Wladiwil, complete with servile peasants and wild boars, and the title of duke to go along with it, and to sweeten the deal he threw in the favors of the beautiful young countess of Radzivill whose callipygian accomplishments have caused restlessness and social upset as far west as the Weser. I turned him down with a laugh, a laugh of scorn, my dear sir, for to offer mere worldly goods for my mirror, which presents a view into the unseen kingdom, and can prognosticate future events, is to offer dross for gold."

"I realize that," Mack said. "But I come to you with an offer you can't refuse."

"Can I not, now? Let's hear your offer."

Mack produced the scarlet silk handkerchief Mephistopheles had given him, still enfolding its mysterious prize. History fails to tell us what was involved, or its precise effect on the vain and supercilious Dr. Dee. Only one thing is certain. Some ten minutes later, Mack and Marguerite left Dee's house and were on their way to Southwark, the magic mirror under Mack's arm, nestled in a form-fitting case of chamois.

Chapter 5

At the theater, the crowd was coming in slowly. Although the theater held somewhat less than three hundred persons, thousands were seeking entry, drawn from all parts of the kingdom. These theatergoers were dressed in all their finery. Men and women alike wore long cloaks, since there was a chill in the air even on this fine May afternoon. The audience was a motley bunch. There were many nobles from the court, among them Lord Salisbury, Lord Dunkirk, Lord Cornwallis, the Lord High Executioner, and Lord Faversham. Some had come with their wives, others with their mistresses, pert in their paste diamonds, and still others, the very young ones, like Lord Dover, who was only eight, with their parents, or tutors, or, as in the case of Viscount Delville, seven years old and sickly, with their bodyguard-doctors. These were the notables; but most of the audience was made up of common people: heavyset cloth merchants from Meaching Row, tall, thin apothecaries from Pall Mall and Cheapside, angular feed merchants from Piccadilly, and the even commoner sort, sturdy vagabonds who had cadged a ticket and called no man master, soldiers on leave from the Netherlandish wars with their fantastical plumed caps and deep-cut sleeves. There were more than a few clerics in the crowd, who had come not to amuse themselves but out of a serious purpose, because *Faustus* was supposed to be a sacrilegious play, and they expected to get good material out of it for their Sunday sermons. They all trooped in, jostling and hawking and spitting and buying oranges and little bags of candy from the wenches who provided such things, and they gawked around at the theater, which was small and oval-shaped with a row of boxes to either side, and a raised stage that extended out over the foremost ranks of the audience. Flambeaux flickered in the din of loud English voices calling to one another. "I say, Harry!" "Oh, there's Saffron!" "Look, here come Mélisande and Cuddles!" And the like.

The admission at the door for those without passes was threepence ha'penny, for the Earl of Nottingham's men didn't do this for free. But they paid anyway and no demurs were raised in that free-spending, easy-thinking crowd, for this was a day of celebration, and the future was uncertain, for if the Spanish Armada landed, as some predicted, and prevailed over the naval forces of the red-haired queen, your money wouldn't be worth boo anyway. Down near the candled floodlights, the groundlings had assembled in their best piebald hose and multicolored jerkins to talk and carouse and make japes at the actors.

To a flourish of trumpets, Edward Alleyn came out upon the stage. Young Will Shakespeare, already balding, noted for his future use how the chattering young fops and their loud-laughing ladies quieted for a moment. The houselights of magnesia and naphtha were set alight in pewter bowls set on top of three-legged standards. They had recently replaced the adamantage, the old rush stage lighting in a copper pot that had served well enough in pretheater days. Sparks were applied to them and they flared up, calling the audience to attention. The hautboys in the small ensemble took up the *Faustus* theme.

The setting on the stage represented the town of Wittenberg in the previous century. It was quite realistic except for the fact that the Draken watchtower where Faustus would later meet the Spirit of Earth was leaning somewhat precariously to the left, for stage design was still in its infancy and proper bracing for the sets would only be achieved in the early eighteenth century. As the curtain went up there was a prolonged clearing of throats, this being the height of the phlegm season, and a rustling of feet covered in many different substances, but most of them consisting of an irregular and scratchy surface, the only sort you'd expect in this day of preindustrial handicrafts. Their roughness accounted for the annoying sounds they made when dragged back and forth through the eggshells and orange peels and the peanut hulls covering the floor in that year of plague when the populace was mad for amusements and willing to pay any price for them.

Just as the performance was beginning Mack hurried in late, and slid along a row of seats with murmured sorrys and oh-excuse-mes and took his seat somewhat breathlessly, the magic mirror, safe in the chamois case, clutched to his side. Marguerite followed, and took her seat beside him with a giggle of girlish anticipation.

"I've never seen a play before," she confided. "Is it like sitting around telling stories?"

"Very similar," Mack said. "Except that people act out the story instead of someone telling it."

"Or sometimes both," a man sitting beside him remarked.

Mack turned. A man of middle years was sitting beside him, robust of form and ruddy of face, with piercing dark eyes and a look of hawklike intelligence.

"Faust!" he said.

"Yes," the personage said. "And you are a stinking impostor."

"Shush," said a surly voice in a row in front of them. "Can't you see the performance has begun?"

On stage, Edward Alleyn stepped forward, swept off his cap with a flourish, and struck a pose.

"I'll discuss this with you later," Mack said.

"*Shush!*" the man in front of them said.

On the stage, the chorus had finished its opening speech. Edward Alleyn, resplendent in a crimson surplice, with a gilded cross upon his chest, was saying, "Now that the gloomy shadow of the Earth, longing to view Orion's drizzling look . . ."

"There's nothing to discuss," Faust said. "Simply begone at once. I'll take over from here."

"Not a chance," Mack said.

Their exchange was interrupted at this point by the audience, who was not interested in hearing the rude argument of a pair of jackanapes.

"Shut up!"

"Stick a boot in it!"

"Stuff it!"

And similar exclamations.

Faust and Mack were forced to desist, for neither of them wanted the truth of the matter to be known. So they glared at each other out of the corners of their eyes while Marguerite and Helen, on either side of them, patted their hands and whispered to them to remain calm. On stage, the actors had gotten beyond Faustus' dialogue with the Seven Deadly Sins, who remained onstage with colored costumes and lugubrious faces, and proceeded to the entrance of several devils.

Mack's mind was working with lightning speed, both defining the game he was involved in and planning out his next move. It was obvious to him that he had more to gain here, and therefore more to lose, than he had thought at first, back in Cracow when he had broken into Faust's studio and accepted Mephistopheles' offer. It was true that the real Faust was here trying to claim his own; but what did that matter to Mack? Mack's reality was more important to him than Faust's, and his reality seemed to have led him to *become* Faust. Therefore this other Faust, whom he had taken over from, had no real claim to the Faust persona.

Still, it was going to be quite a problem. He needed a way to handle this, get Faust off his back, give him a chance to do his thing. If he let Faust oust him now, what would he be?

An advantage! He needed an advantage! Surely that was

the point of all military strategy — to realize when you are in a spot and to seek — the Equalizer.

It was at that moment that he bethought himself of Dr. Dee's magic mirror, pressing against his side in its chamois case.

He realized that by peeking into Dee's magic mirror he might get a glimpse of the future, and thus he could know what to do in this encounter between him and Faust.

He slipped the mirror out of its case, disguising the noise by grinding his feet in the peanut shells on the floor, and remarking to Marguerite, "It's disgusting, how they keep these places." Now the mirror was in his lap.

Just as he was about to look into it there was an explosion on stage, and a bright flash as of hellish lightning. Mack had seen that light before. It was Mephistopheles, conjuring himself.

The tall and handsome demon stepped out of the smoke, adjusted his evening clothes, advanced to stage center, and, peering around at the audience, spotted Mack. "The mirror!" he shouted.

"Yes, I've got it!" Mack shouted back. "Don't worry, it's here!"

"You must destroy it!" Mephistopheles shouted.

"Beg pardon?"

"Get rid of it at once! They've just passed a ruling! By looking into it you'll invalidate the whole contest, since contestants must not be granted foreknowledge of events. It would skew the result, you see."

The audience was mumbling to themselves uncertainly at this point, and sniffing often at the perfume-sprayed nosegays that they held in their dirty, lace-gloved hands. Feet clad in various materials shuffled noisily in the peanut shells, and there was something ominous about the sound, some strange over- or undertone, or both, some unbelievable bass note of madness about to erupt that had an effect on the ear as a tremendous and perhaps bloody happening waiting in the figurative wings that is Everyman's heart from which it would soon be born.

Time to get out of this crowd. Mack got to his feet and edged his way out into the aisle, the better to get the hell out of the place if something happened — because the feeling that theaters are places where sinister things may happen is a notion that sprang into existence contemporaneous with the first theater itself, and it may be that this selfsame first performance of this play of *Doctor Faustus* gave rise to the legend that it is easy in the theater for something weird and frightening to happen. Marguerite followed along behind him, hanging on to his coattails so as not to get lost in the crowd that had begun to roil and tumble around them.

There was a reason for their panic. One member of the audience, not as simpleminded as he looked, had counted the number of actors onstage and seen that this was not the number given in the playbill. When he relayed this information to others — "There are supposed to be seven devils onstage, but I count eight" — a wave of uncertainty came over those watching. Wooden-framed spectacles were hastily clapped on the long noses that were prevalent in that day as all the spectators consulted their playbills. If there were too many devils on the stage, at least one of them had to be real. It didn't take any Thomas Aquinas to figure that out. Any rightminded person who viewed the matter without prejudice could see beyond a doubt that the tall, thin guy who had suddenly appeared bore more resemblance to the devil of their dreams than the other guy, the actor in the shabby red cotton suit and ill-fitting slippers. And seeing that, a sudden let's-get-the-hell-out-of-here mood swept over the audience, and they began to rise and scrape their feet in the peanut shells, prefactory to stampeding into the exits.

Eight devils. And then a ninth appeared. For it was then that a dapper-looking fox-faced demon made his own appearance onstage, in a bone white lounge suit with white penny loafers and a turquoise scarf with a Tibetan mandala painted on it draped around his shoulders. Seeing this, the crowd went a little wild.

"Hang on to that mirror!" Azzie shouted to Mack. "You can never tell when an item like that will prove useful. Anyhow, you need it for the contest!"

"No, he doesn't!" Mephistopheles cried. "It's only one of his possible choices."

"Then who are you to tell him he can't make that choice?"

"I'm not saying anything of the kind," Mephistopheles said. "I'm merely advising him not to look into it himself, since foreknowledge would compromise the contest, to the mutual embarrassment of Dark and Light."

The audience, driven into a superstitious mania by the triphammer succession of downright weird events with sinister overtones, began to panic. Grown men flung ladies' hampers filled with the most delicate hams, roast beefs, sides of pork, and the like out of their way to get to the nearest exit. In vain the band struck up a galliard. The rest was triple time.

Chapter
6

While this was going on, Rognir the dwarf sat in a dwarf public area and planned mischief. He was trying to decide on the most mischief he could do to Azzie. This was only in part because he hated the fox-faced demon. It was also because Rognir took a keen intellectual pleasure in bringing any proud demon down a step or two. Rognir didn't like demons, and he especially disliked fox-faced demons, and he liked this one least of all.

To discomfit a demon! Rognir was merely doing what any ichor-blooded dwarf would have done once he saw the opportunity. Anything that would put a demon into disgrace was to be welcomed. If it could also turn a profit for the dwarf, so much the better.

Trouble was, he hadn't been too sure what the information he'd overheard meant. It was obvious to him that Azzie was working behind the back of another demon, Mephistopheles. But how? What was he doing? What were the two of them up to? What was this Millennial contest, anyway? (For dwarves rarely are informed on the great events of their day.) Rognir, having told Mephistopheles of what was going on, now came up with a new scheme. He was sitting on a toadstool when this thought came to him, a very large orange toadstool with bright yellow spots, the sort that only a dwarf can eat without instantly perishing. Rognir was not eating, however, even though his jaws were working continually. A witness leaning close could have noticed that the dwarf's back teeth were grinding and he was evidently in the throes of inspiration.

"Having told Faust about matters, and then Mephistopheles, I have been genuinely mischievous. But it seems to me that I can think of yet another contrivance. So I'll hie me away to those regions in or near the Empyrean where the spirits of light are said to dwell. . . ."

But before he had finished his speech, his dwarvish conjure power kicked in and he was on his way.

PARIS

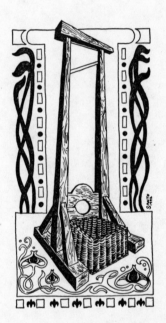

Chapter
1

W here are we now?" Mack asked.

"This is a tavern in the Latin Quarter of Paris," Mephistopheles said. "I feel at home with students. They have always had a lively regard for the devil. And Paris, of course, is the devil's own city. I thought it would be an appropriate place to begin the last act in our contest."

Mack looked around. He and Mephistopheles were seated at a long rough-hewn wooden table. There were others at the table, all young men, students by the look of them. They were immersed in their own conversations, which were carried on in loud voices and with elaborate gestures and much shrugging. The tavern was dark, extensive, and low-ceilinged. Waiters hurried back and forth carrying trays crowded with tumblers of wine, with plates of mussels in a red sauce, and with wedges of bread on the side. There were loud guffaws of laughter, catcalls, bursts of song. These students were young and had the whole world ahead of them, and they were studying in Paris, already the most notable city in Europe and therefore in the world.

"What's happening this time?" Mack asked.

"This is the year 1789," Mephistopheles said. "Paris, indeed, all France, is in an uproar. Spurred on by the recent American Revolution, the common people are ready to rise and throw out the ineffective royal court and the corrupt nobles. It is the dawn of a new age for the masses, and sunset for the privileged few. In the palace of the Tuileries, the desperate

Louis the Sixteenth and his wife, Marie Antoinette, frightened by the threats and insults heaped on them by an increasingly unmanageable populace, are preparing to flee this very night, taking a coach to Belgium, where they will meet up with royalist armies burning to avenge the insult to the royal family."

"Sounds exciting," Mack said. "Do they make it?"

"Alas, it is not to be. History tells us that at crucial moments, things go wrong. At the end, the royal family is brought back to Paris by the Republican Guard. Soon after, they will lose their heads to the guillotine."

"Are they very evil, this king and queen?" Mack asked.

Mephistopheles smiled sadly. "Not evil at all. Merely creatures of their time and place. Their deaths will solve nothing, and the act of destroying them will revolt the world. There will be battles and massacres, and France will stand alone with the armies of Europe against her."

"I suppose you want me to save the king and queen."

"What you do is entirely up to you, of course," Mephistopheles said. "But it *would* be a notable deed."

"What should I do?"

"The escape is set for tonight. One by one, the royal family will come out of the palace and get into coaches driven by loyalists. But right at the beginning there will be a fatal delay. Marie Antoinette will take so long at her preparations that the escape will be set back some hours. Because of this delay, the duc de Choiseul, waiting in a wood outside Paris with a force of hussars loyal to the king, will conclude the escape is off and abandon his post. It is a key point."

"There are other key points?"

"Several others," Mephistopheles said. "Once the flight is underway, a certain Drouet will recognize the king as his coach passes through the village of Saint-Menehould. Drouet gives the alarm that leads to His Majesty's capture. His seeing the king is a matter of pure luck. If Drouet could be diverted . . ."

"I'm beginning to get the idea," Mack said.

"Or, failing that, the king and queen might still be saved if the bridge at Varennes were open rather than blocked. The blocked bridge prevents the royal coach from crossing to the Belgian frontier and safety. So there are three chances; Marie Antoinette's delay, Drouet's recognition, and the blocked bridge at Varennes. Change any of these and you change history. Are you ready, Faust?"

"I think so," Mack said. "As ready as I'll ever be."

"Excellent. And please, Johann, try to make this a good one. It *is* the last, you know. I'll look in on you from time to time and see how you're getting on. Maybe even lend a hand." He winked. "Till later!" And with that, Mephistopheles vanished.

By asking a passing fishwife, Mack learned that Marie Antoinette was at Versailles, some leagues outside of Paris. In the Place Saint-Michel he found a public coach and paid a centime for a place on it. The streetcar, as it was called, drawn by four horses, clanged through Paris, stopping here and there to take on and discharge passengers, until it passed beyond the city limits into a country lane that meandered through green fields and tasteful clumps of trees.

Mack got off at the palace of Versailles and walked up to the main entrance. The armed guard at the door, resplendent in the crimson and white of the queen's livery, raised his pike to the ready. "You, there! What do you want?"

"I crave an audience with the queen," Mack said.

"She's not seeing anyone today," the guard said.

"Yes, I know. But this is urgent."

"I told you, she's not seeing anyone."

"Tell her Dr. Faust is here," Mack said. "She'll reward you. And I have something for you myself." He handed the guard a gold piece.

"Thanks, citizen," the guard said, pocketing the coin. "Now get out of here or I'll have you arrested for bribery."

Chapter
2

The Archangel Michael's house was set on an elevated half-acre lot in an exclusive suburb of Heaven. Michael was in the front yard working on his roses. He looked up to see Ylith, the student angel and former witch, coming up the marble steps.

"Ah, there, Ylith, how nice to see you." He put down his trowel and wiped his hands. "Can I get you some lemonade? It's quite a hot day, though dry, a typical heavenly or good sort of day."

"No, thanks," Ylith said. "I came because there's something I'm perplexed about."

"Well then," Michael said, "you must tell me all about it. What seems to be the matter?"

Ylith said, "I've found evidence that Mephistopheles is cheating."

"Aha!" said Michael, but rather mildly. "But that's only to be expected, considering who he is."

"What is more disconcerting," Ylith said, "I have also found evidence of *you* cheating."

"Me?" Michael said.

"Yes, you," Ylith said.

Michael was silent for a moment, thinking. Then he said, "You are new to our circles, aren't you?"

"Yes, I am," Ylith said. "But what difference—"

Michael held up a hand.

"And therefore you are inexperienced, and lacking in knowledge of the great harmony that holds Good and Bad together in a single unity and dictates the rules of their behavior."

"I never even heard of this great harmony," Ylith said. "Does it really make a difference? I'm talking out-and-out cheating."

"All the difference in the world, my dear. For consider: If Light and Dark are to contest at all, they must do so as equals in an ongoing contest, and with the knowledge that to struggle does not mean to win once and for all. Both Good and Bad are interdependent. For the one must exist for there to be the other. Do you understand?"

"I think so," Ylith said doubtfully. "But what difference—"

"So there is a sense," Michael went on, "in which Good and Bad are equal outcomes. On the level of interaction, we espouse one cause or the other. We play to win, and we try to put down our foe forever; even though, on a higher level, we know that true victory is neither possible nor practicable, nor even desirable. Are you following?"

"I'm not sure," Ylith said. "But please go on."

"It follows that, as equals in the game of Good and Bad, each of us must have access to the same techniques. Good must not be handicapped by being forbidden 'bad' alternatives that are available to Dark. Since Bad from time to time uses 'good' means for its own Bad ends, it follows that Good can use 'bad' for *its* own purposes. The final issue, my dear Ylith, is not what is good and what is bad, but what is in here." And Michael touched himself in the region of the heart.

"Does that mean it's all right for you to cheat?" Ylith asked.

Michael smiled and looked away. "It means that we have as much right to cheat as Bad does."

"And you think it's *right* to cheat in order to win?"

"I would say instead, it's not wrong," Michael said.

"Well, now I've heard everything. I must go think this over."

Chapter
3

It was evening in the Tuileries. The windows were ablaze with a thousand candles. People hurried in and out the high carved front doors. They were wearing republican blue and gray rather than royalist white and crimson. On a little bench across the street from the ceaseless crowds, Mack sat and considered the situation.

Breezes stirred the small, carefully trimmed trees that bordered the palace. And then Mack felt something, something more palpable than a breeze. It was a thin, disembodied voice that quested up and down the tree-lined avenue, saying, "Faust! Faust! Where are you, Faust?"

Mack looked around. "Did someone call me?"

Ylith materialized beside him. She was wearing magnificent riding attire of black velvet and sueded leather. Her riding boots had a deep shine, and her long dark hair was caught up in a white chiffon scarf. "Remember me?"

"Indeed I do," Mack said. "You locked me in a mirror maze in Peking when you thought I was cheating."

"I've learned a thing or two since then," Ylith said. "What are you planning now?"

It was in Mack's mind to turn away and sulk and not tell this good-looking but impetuous and very judgmental spirit-woman anything at all. If she was so smart, let her figure it out for herself! But, sensing advantage, he conquered his pique and said, "I'm trying to rescue the king and queen of France."

"Why do you want to save them?" Ylith asked.

"I scarcely know. I haven't met them, you understand. But it seems I have to do something in this contest, and that looks like quite a good thing. I mean, what the hell, they are rather silly people whose main crime was to be born noble. And anyway, Mephistopheles thought it would be a good thing for me to do."

"I see," Ylith said. "So of course, since Mephistopheles wants it, Michael is opposed to it."

"I suppose that follows," Mack said. "And since you are on Michael's side —"

"I don't know what side I'm on anymore," Ylith said. "But I did you a wrong before and I'm here to make up for it now. What can I do to help?"

"I need to get the queen to hurry up. It's eight o'clock already, time to go, but she hasn't come out."

"I'll see what I can do," Ylith said. With a graceful double gesture of her long hands she faded out of Mack's sight.

Chapter
4

Ylith reappeared in a corridor leading to the royal chambers on the second floor of the Tuileries. She saw at once that it was just as well she had stayed invisible. Soldiers of the National Guard lurched drunkenly up and down the gorgeously wallpapered corridors, pawing at frightened ladies-in-waiting, guzzling vin ordinaire from long-neck bottles, messily eating croissants and getting crumbs all over the carpet. Ylith passed invisibly through the Guard, found the queen's chambers, and darted inside. There she beheld Marie Antoinette asleep fully dressed on a chaise lounge. Even in sleep the queen's fingers clenched and unclenched, as though trying to hold on to something that escaped them, life itself perhaps.

Then Marie Antoinette became aware that someone was in the room with her. Her blue eyes opened wide.

"Who are you?"

"Just a friendly spirit, Your Highness," Ylith said. "I've come to help you get out of this mess."

"Oh! Pray tell me!" cried Marie Antoinette.

"To put it to you straight, Marie, if I may, your escape is scheduled for eight o'clock this evening. At that hour you are to come downstairs disguised as a governess and hurry past the guards and into a certain carriage. The driver will convey you to the larger carriage outside of Paris where you will join the king and continue your escape toward Belgium."

"Yes, that is the plan," Marie said, wide-eyed. "How did you know? And is there anything wrong with it?"

"The plan is fine," Ylith said, "but history tells us that you were some hours late getting to the carriage, and that this delay upset the carefully contrived timetable that was to make it all possible."

"Me, some hours late?" Marie said indignantly. "Impossible! Oh, it might be true if this were some mere love-tryst I were keeping, of the sort that history will no doubt insist on connecting my name to, as if I were a shameless whore and common slut like that du Barry. If that were the case I might dawdle, in order to increase my piquancy and the anticipation of the dark and handsome stranger waiting for me. I'd pretend to have forgotten my muff, my jewel box, or my spaniel, and he would stamp and twist his moustaches, standing there beside his coach, and his excitement would grow as he contrasted my apparent light-mindedness with the severity of the occasion. But this is not a flirtation, my dear spirit, and I am not so light-minded as to arrive late for the appointment that is meant to save my life."

"I'm glad Your Highness is not as frivolous as history makes you out to be," Ylith said. "We only need to leave this place at eight sharp and the thing should be child's play."

"Yes, I agree. But you have made an error. The time set for the departure was eleven o'clock."

Ylith considered and shook her head. "Your Majesty, you must be wrong. My source is history itself."

"I hate to fly in the face of history," Marie said, "but I spoke to the coachman but an hour ago. He was very clear that it was eleven."

"I was told eight," Ylith said.

"They must have told you wrong," Marie said.

"I'll just go check," Ylith said.

She conjured herself out of there and into the multicolored realms that exist between the discrete layers of being, and sped through them all the way to the Library of Important Earth

Dates and Times situated in Spiritual West 12 11, where the history of everything is recorded with exact times given.

Ylith went to the big, recently installed computer that kept track of facts about Earth for the Spiritual Kingdom. The computer was an innovation that many spirits both Good and Bad had fought against, for computers were considered newfangled inventions that time had not yet softened into acceptable custom. But many considered this a frivolous view. The consensus among the creatures of Dark and Light was that the appropriate rule here was, *as below, so above,* and that even the spirits had to keep up with the changing times on Earth.

Ylith went to an open terminal on the computer and introduced herself.

The computer said, "I assume you have a problem. Tell me what I need to know."

Ylith wasted no time. "I need to find the correct hour of departure in an important historical situation. Marie Antoinette thinks the time to leave to meet the coachman who is going to take her out of Paris and away from the guillotine is eleven P.M. I have been told it is eight P.M. Which is correct?"

"I'm sorry," the computer said, after no more than a nanosecond's hesitation. "That's classified information."

"It's a simple fact and it's got to be on record! It can't be classified!"

"It's not, really," the computer said. "I was told to say it was if anyone asked for a fact of a certain class of facts."

"What class is that?"

"The class of simple and apparently easily ascertainable facts, which are, in fact, almost impossible to pin down."

"Well, what's so difficult about looking it up for me or whatever it is you do?"

"The fact itself is not the problem," the computer said. "It's the routine for looking up facts that's disabled just now."

"Why?"

"Because the technicians are introducing a new packing order for the facts already on file. To be able to use it, they'll have to invent a new locating order that can make sense out of the new packing order."

"And meanwhile no one can find out anything? That's ridiculous! Why don't you do something about it?"

"Me?"

"Yes, you!"

"I'm not supposed to," the computer said. "They told me they'd let me know when they had it worked out."

"So you're saying you don't know the fact I'm asking about?" Ylith said.

"I'm not saying that at all!" The computer's tone was hurt. "I know all the facts. It's just that my retrieval system is disabled. That makes it technically impossible for me to tell you."

"Technically! But not virtually!"

"No, of course not virtually."

"So give me a virtual answer. Or can't you even do that?"

"I could if I wanted to. But I don't want to."

Ylith heard hurt pride in the computer's voice. She decided to take a different tack. "Wouldn't you do it for me?"

"Sure, babe. Just a moment." Lights flashed. Then the computer said, "I make it three A.M."

"Impossible," Ylith said.

"Not what you expected? I told you, the retrieval system is down."

"I know, but you said you could bypass it."

"I did. It came up three A.M.!"

"Is that really the best you can do? All right, I'll have to make do with that. Thank you."

Chapter
5

Ylith hurried back to Marie Antoinette. "What time have you got now?"

Marie consulted her hourglass. "Just going on eleven."

Ylith looked at her water watch. "I make it almost eight o'clock. Well, what the hell. All right, let's get going."

"I'm ready," Marie said. "Let me just get my purse."

Outside, a tall coachman stamped his feet to keep up the circulation, and looked inside his coach from time to time at the tall hourglass which rested upright in a rosewood cradle. "Damn, damn, damn," he muttered to himself in Swedish.

At last a door in the Tuileries opened and two women hurried out, one blond, the other dark.

"Your Majesty!" the tall coachman said. "Where the devil have you been?"

"What do you mean, where have I been?" Marie asked. "I am here at the appointed hour."

"I hate to contradict you, but you're four hours late. It's going to make it difficult."

"Me? Late? Impossible!" She turned to Ylith. "What time do you have?"

Ylith consulted her small traveling hourglass. "Eight o'clock."

Marie consulted hers. "I make it just eleven."

"And I," said the coachman, "have three in the morning!"

The three looked at each other in consternation, simultaneously bemoaning the lack of a unified time-keeping system in the world at that time. To Ylith it was now painfully obvious that Marie Antoinette was figuring in French Royalist Time, the coachman in Swedish Reformed Time, and she herself in Spiritual Standard Time, and that in each of these times and many others, Marie Antoinette was late for a vital appointment.

The coachman said, "No help for it, let's go. But we're late, very late."

Chapter
6

Mack was having a bit of a doze at the Hôtel de Ville when someone shook him roughly by the shoulder.

"What is it?" He awoke with a start and peered into a small, bearded face.

"I'm Rognir, the dwarf."

"Oh, yes." Mack sat up and rubbed his eyes. "I guess you are. What can I do for you?"

"Nothing at all. But I bring news. Ylith asked me to come by and tell you she wasn't successful in hurrying up the queen. Something about uncertainty as applied to time, but I can't remember that part."

"Damn!" Mack said. "So the royal carriage has left late on its ill-fated run to Varennes!"

"If you say so," Rognir said. "No one bothered to fill *me* in on what's going on."

Mack said, "I'm trying to prevent the royal family from capture. But I don't know what to do now unless I can get a horse."

"A horse? What do you need a horse for?"

"So I can get to Saint-Menehould where I'll get my next chance to change the fate of Louis the Sixteenth and Marie Antoinette."

"Why don't you get there by magic?" Rognir said, pouring out a mugful of wine for Mack.

"I don't know the right words," Mack confessed.

"That other fellow would."

"What other fellow?"

"The one I helped on the Styx."

"You mean Faust?"

"That's who they tell me he was."

"I'm also Faust."

"If you say so."

"But he's trying to get rid of me!"

"Tough on you, then," Rognir said. "Nothing personal. I figured that helping him would put out of joint the nose of a certain demon of my acquaintance. He shortchanged me on a recent work contract. Dwarves have long memories."

"And short, bristly beards," Mack said. "Damn! How am I to get to Saint-Menehould before the royal carriage?"

"You need to get out there and get a horse," Rognir said.

Mack stared at him. "You think it's as simple as that?"

"It'd better be," Rognir said, "or you're really in a lot of trouble."

Mack nodded. "You're right. All right, I'm going."

Some time later, Mack was galloping through a dark forest upon a spirited black charger. He had seized it from a groom Rognir had located for him in front of the Tuileries, in the name of the Committee for Public Safety. No one had wanted to argue with him.

And so he galloped along the dimly lit forest path congratulating himself on the fine mount he had chosen. Then he heard something behind him, turned and looked, then turned back and hunched over the horse's neck. Yes, he had a fast horse, but it wasn't fast enough to keep the rider behind him from gaining steadily.

There was nothing he could do about it. The pursuer drew up even with him, and he saw it was Faust, the black tails of his long coat flapping wildly, stovepipe hat pasted flat against his forehead by the wind, grinning maliciously.

"So, impostor, we meet again!" Faust cried.

They galloped side by side for a time. Mack was having a lot of trouble just hanging on to his horse, since galloping at top speed through a forest at night with another rider neck and neck and screaming insults was not his usual practice. Nor was it Faust's, presumably. But the magician of Wittenberg was doing fine, riding like a Magyar, as they say, and he was also managing to keep Helen on the back of his horse, too, her scrumptious arms wrapped around his waist. Mack of course was carrying Marguerite, who had been silent so far, entranced by the flickering play of moonlight and shadow. The horsemen were evenly matched as to weight. But Faust had by far the edge in aplomb.

"Give up your pretension to my great name!" Faust thundered. "For if the issue be joined 't will soon be clear that Faust alone is fit to write the notes of destiny that bear his psychic scriblature, and other poor wights like you just better get the hell out of my way before I do some major star-level ass-kicking around here, you know what I mean, boy?"

Faust's words were garbled and his imitation of slang of the future was unfortunate, but the intent of his words was clear: Get out of my face, or else.

"I can't go away now!" Mack howled back. "This is my story!"

"Like hell it is. I am the only and the maximum Faust!" Faust cried, and the glow in his lambent werewolf's eyes was disquieting. Edging his horse closer to Mack's, he took from an inner pocket of his waistcoat an object about three feet long and studded with jewels, and with a glow about it that proclaimed it not just a mere scepter, as it might have appeared, but a magical one, stolen, in this case, from Kublai Khan by Mack. But the magical scepter was now in Faust's hands, and those hands knew no mercy. By the way Faust held this scepter, Mack could tell that the magician of Wittenberg had somehow divined its efficacy; *viz.*, that when you pointed at a person and said, "Bang!" that person was annihilated in a manner that anticipated the death-beams of a later age.

Faced with that much occult firepower, Mack almost gave up hope. Then he saw at hand a desperate expedient for avoiding the power-thrust of the magical scepter. The expedient was looming up in the form of a great oak. Mack timed his move carefully, then swung his horse into Faust's path. Faust checked to the other side, the instinctive move in such a circumstance, and Mack swung to the right, around the tree, while Faust crashed head-on into it with such force that the stars he saw became visible to Mack's eyes for a little while even though they were imaginary. From his rear, Mack heard Marguerite utter a small whimper of sympathy. The doctor crashed to the ground, dazed, while his maddened horse ran off in one direction and Mack galloped off in another, the way that led to Saint-Menehould. Helen, consort of warriors, leaped to the ground before the moment of impact, rolled several times, rose to her feet, and adjusted her coiffure. The launching of one sorcerer or a thousand ships — it was all the same to her. One should be at one's best whatever the occasion.

Chapter
7

After galloping alone for a considerable distance, Mack came to a clearing in the forest. Here he saw a country inn with a curl of smoke coming from its chimney. It seemed a good place to take a badly needed break. And so he stopped, helped Marguerite to dismount, tied his horse to a post provided for that purpose, and drew water for him from a nearby hogshead. Then he and Marguerite went inside.

There was the usual tavern keeper polishing brass behind the bar, and at the end of the room there was a fire nicely burning. Another traveler sat near it, face turned away from Mack, warming his hands at the fire.

"Good day to you, travelers," the tavern keeper said. "Will you have a cup of brandy to cheer the appetite?"

"It's too early for a drink," Mack said. "Just a noggin of fir-knot tea to keep us awake."

"Take a seat at the fire and warm yourselves," the tavern keeper said. "I've got the fir knots mulling nicely and I'll bring mugs of it right over."

Mack went over and sat down beside the fire, nodding politely to the man who sat there already, wrapped in a long cloak, his face concealed in a hood, with a bow leaning on the wall beside him.

"Good evening," the man said, and threw back his hood.

Mack stared. "You know, I think I've seen you somewhere before."

"You might have seen my bust at some museum," the stranger said. "I am Odysseus, and how I got here from my house in the suburbs of Tartaros would make a pretty tale, had we but time. But we don't. You wouldn't happen to be Faust, would you?"

Odysseus spoke in Homeric Greek, with a slight Ithacan accent, which Mack was able to understand since Mephistopheles had never taken away his Language Spell.

"Well, yes," Mack said. "That is, I know him after a fashion. That is to say, I have been doing Faust's job for him, but now I am of two minds about the whole proposition."

"Are you that Faust who travels with Helen of Troy?" Odysseus enquired.

"No, that's the other one," Mack said. "I travel with Marguerite." He turned to introduce Marguerite to Odysseus but found that the girl had already fallen asleep in a corner of the booth.

"But you claim that you are Faust, too?" Odysseus asked.

"Right now, I play the part of Faust in this contest between Dark and Light. But the real Faust is trying to force me out."

"And what do you intend to do?" Odysseus asked.

"I'm not at all sure," Mack said. "It's starting to weigh on my conscience, this matter of my taking his part. Maybe I just ought to drop out and leave the Faust role to him."

Odysseus said, "You seem to be doing well enough at the job. Why should you give it up? What does Faust have that you do not?"

"Well, this other Faust, you see, is a great magician, so he's got the right to represent mankind . . . ."

"Not a bit of it!" Odysseus hitched his cloak more closely about himself. "Why should mankind be represented by a magician? They're about the same as politicians, only worse. Don't you know the truth yet? Magic always works against mankind."

"I never thought of it that way," Mack confessed.

"Magic is power, and only a few people are good at it. Do you think it's right to have a bunch of magicians leading the people? Would you really want Faust to rule you?"

"I just assumed magicians knew more than ordinary men."

"What they know is not necessarily useful to the rest of us. I've had some experience with magicians. In my time we had Tiresias. He was really preeminent. But do you think we'd let him lead us in politics or war? Never! Our leader, Agamemnon, was flawed in many ways, but he was a man, and he didn't claim any special dispensation from the gods or spirits. Beware of men who claim to speak for the gods!"

"But he's the real Faust!"

"Maybe so. But that doesn't make him the real possessor of the Faustian spirit. That is you, my dear Mack, a man standing up just as he is, without special knowledge or abilities, without magical powers, and nevertheless trying to rule himself."

Mack took heart from these brave words. He finished the tankard of fir-knot tea that the tavern keeper had brought him and stood up, getting the sleepy Marguerite to finish hers and rise with him. "I'd better be getting on."

"And Faust?"

"He follows behind me."

"Ah, good," Odysseus said. "Do you hear, Achilles?"

Achilles, who had been slumbering in a dark corner of the booth, gave a start and sat up. "Did you call me, Odysseus?"

"Get ready, my friend! Faust comes!"

Odysseus and Achilles! Mack hoped these two would hold up Faust for quite a while.

"Come, Marguerite," he said.

"Coming," she agreed, stifling a yawn.

They left the tavern, remounted, and rode off again in the direction of Saint-Menehould.

Chapter 8

Faust arrived at the inn in the forest twenty minutes later. He had a yellowish bruise on his temple from his headlong contact with the oak tree, but other than that seemed perfectly all right. Helen was windblown, but lovelier than ever.

Faust entered the tavern and came face-to-face with Odysseus, who said, "I know who you are. You are named Faust."

"There's no secret about that," Faust replied.

"And you have Helen of Troy in your possession."

"Well, of course I have her!" Faust said. "She is the most beautiful woman in the world, and therefore the only suitable consort for me. Who are you and what do you want?"

Odysseus introduced himself and Achilles. If Faust was impressed, he did not show it.

"The fact is," Odysseus said, "we want Helen back. Your demon had no right to kidnap her from her husband's home in Tartaros."

"Don't take it up with me," Faust said. "She was given to me, and I'm going to keep her."

"It seems to me I've heard all this before," Odysseus said, alluding to the events that began the *Iliad*, when Achilles objected to giving up the girl Briseis to Agamemnon, and, when Agamemnon wouldn't give her back, sulked in his tent until the Greeks almost lost the Trojan war.

"Maybe you have heard it," Achilles said. "It matters not. Give her to us."

"Not a chance. Are you going to try to take her from me?" From an inner pocket of his cloak he drew a flintlock.

"If we wanted to, believe me, we could," Odysseus said. "And yon weapon would not stop us. But hold your sword, Achilles. There is a better way."

Odysseus put two fingers in his mouth and whistled, a long, low, mournful whistle that was answered almost at once by a screaming and shrieking noise that at first seemed like wind and then resolved itself into old ladies' voices.

The door of the tavern was suddenly blown open by a blast of ill-smelling air. The Furies flew in. They came as three big crows with dusty black feathers, screaming and squawking and bombarding everyone with smelly excrement. Then they transformed themselves into their human shape—three old women, longnosed and red eyed, wearing ragged, dusty black garments. Alecto was fat, and Tisiphone was skinny, and the third, Megaera, was both fat and skinny, but in all the wrong places. All the sisters had eyes like fried eggs after the yolk has run. They danced around Faust, screeching and cackling, laughing and hooting, leaping and capering, and Faust tried to maintain a dignified silence, but it was difficult with these ancient harridans carrying on so.

At length Faust said, "This behavior will do you no good, my dear ladies, because I am not of your time and construct and so it is unlikely that your presence will fill me with pious horror."

"Pious, schmious," Tisiphone said. "Maybe we can't coerce you physically. But you will find it difficult to carry on a conversation with us screaming in your ear all the time."

"This is ridiculous," Faust said.

"But that's the way it is," Tisiphone said. "Maybe you'd like to hear us sing a particularly irritating folk song with several hundred choruses? All together, girls."

Faust reeled back in alarm as the Furies burst into an early Hellenic version of "Roll out the Barrel." It somewhat resembled the sound of a pack of hyenas in heat, but was worse, far worse. Faust bore up under it for a moment, but found he couldn't think, could barely breathe, and finally in desperation he held up his hand.

"I crave a moment's silence, ladies, while I consider my situation."

With precious silence reigning again in his head, Faust retired to the other end of the room to have a little conversation with the tavern keeper. But the Furies didn't trust him, because immediately they began to converse among themselves, in voices that seemed to emanate from his own mind. The voices were pretending to be his own interior consciousness, saying, "Well, hell, I don't know how I got myself into this fix. I can't even hear myself think with this din going on in my head. And if I *were* to think, what would I think about? Helen? But how can I think of Helen when these old hags have my mind filled with the horror and repulsion of themselves?"

And although it was the old ladies who were putting these thoughts in his head, it seemed to Faust that the thoughts were his own, and so he said, "What use is it to have Helen when all I can hear in my head is a recipe for blood pudding and some instructions for how to cheat at mah-jongg? Well, I see that these old ladies have the better of me." And then aloud he said, "All right, since you want her back so badly, take her!"

The old ladies were gone as suddenly as they had come. Helen was gone with them. Odysseus and Achilles had also left, and Faust ate a pannikin of bread and washed it down with a draught of wine. He was annoyed at having lost Helen, but then he hadn't wanted her much in the first place. Being rid of her freed him to devote all of his powers to the main chance, becoming the Faust of record in the great contest of Dark and Light.

There was no time to waste. He went outside and took to his horse again, and soon he was riding hard on Mack's trail.

Chapter 9

Mack came at last to a clearing, and beyond it was the village of Sommevesle where Mack hoped to find the duc de Choiseul, the great white hope of the royalists. He discovered him sitting outside an inn at the edge of town and reading the used horses ads in the Paris newspaper.

"You are the duc de Choiseul?" he asked.

The man looked up from his newspaper and peered at Mack over wire-rimmed spectacles. "I am he."

"I have news of the king!"

"Well, about time," the duc de Choiseul said. He folded the newspaper to the front page and pointed to a dispatch from the *Paris Revolutionary Journal.*

"Have you seen this? Danton and Saint-Just are calling for the king's blood, and for Marie Antoinette's, too. We used to call that libel in the old days, and punish it severely. But nowadays people can publish what they please. And they call that progress! Where is the king, sir?"

"He is coming here," Mack said.

"When?"

"I'm not really sure," said Mack.

"Oh, that's great," the duc de Choiseul said sarcastically, screwing a monocle into his left eye and peering at Mack disapprovingly. "Hours late already, the villagers ready to mob us because they think we're here to collect taxes, and you tell me he's coming. And just exactly *when* is he coming?"

"It's hard to be precise about the arrival of kings," Mack said. "He's moving as fast as he can. The queen had certain preparations to make. So don't go away yet. The royal pair is on their way."

"The royal peasants are on their way, too," the duc de Choiseul said, gesturing. Mack looked and saw a mob of peasants armed with pitchforks gathered in a compact crowd at the foot of the street.

"Well, what of it?" Mack asked. "They're only peasants. If they cause you any trouble, shoot them down."

"Easy for you to say, young fellow. You're obviously a foreigner. You don't live around here. But I have estates filled with these fellows. I need to get along with them next year when I exercise the droit du seigneur. This is France, where sex is important! And anyhow, these peasants are only the visible few. There are thousands more just beyond town, and more gathering every hour. They could peel us like a peach. And you advise me to shoot them down!"

"It was only a suggestion," Mack said.

"Hello," the duc de Choiseul said, turning away. "Who's this?"

A rider in black was galloping up the road, coattails flying. It was Faust. He clattered into the courtyard, vaulted off his horse, and approached the duke.

"Your orders have been canceled," Faust said. "Sir, get your troops out of here at once."

"Hoity-toity," said the duc de Choiseul, who was addicted to humorous English expressions. "And who might you be?"

"Dr. Johann Faust, at your service."

"No," Mack said, "actually, I'm Johann Faust."

"Two Fausts bearing contradictory messages," the duc de Choiseul mused. "Well, tell you what. I think you fellows had better stay here with me until we find out what's up. Soldiers!"

The men seized Faust's horse and his person. The magician struggled in vain against their iron hands. Mack, seeing which way matters were going, bolted away before they could grasp him, bounded across the leaf-blown little square, and vaulted onto his own horse. He set spur to flank and galloped off at a good clip, with Faust, seized by the soldiers, shouting curses at him from behind.

Chapter 10

Emile Drouet, postmaster of Saint-Menehould, sat in his chair in the window of his bedroom, late at night, still awaiting messengers from Paris. The night was cool and quiet, a welcome relief from the exciting day. There had been such news from the Paris Committees! And all day, flights of nobility had passed through the village en route to the frontier! Drouet's thoughts were practical, though. He was wondering how the coming revolution would affect the postal service. He had told his wife earlier in the day, "Governments may come and governments will go, but no matter who runs them, they will need a reliable postal service." But was that true? Drouet and his fellows had worked hard to make it so. They had complicated the existing postal system in many ingenious ways, so that no new staff could understand it. "They'll need us to straighten it out for them." But still he wasn't entirely sure. Revolutions were queer things. . . .

Below his windows, the square was moonlit. Even at this late hour, a few people passed back and forth. Then he heard a clippity-clop sound, as of horses' hooves, resound from the dark hillsides that lay beyond the wet and dripping forest. And a highwayman came riding, riding, out of the gloom of the woods into the gloom of civilization.

Citizen Mack, for so it was, swung down from the saddle and set his revolutionary cap firmly on his head. He looked around keenly, expecting to see nothing much but surprised all the same. Behind him another horse came into town, more slowly. Marguerite sat on this one.

Mack brought the horse to a halt under M. Drouet's window. He said, "M. Drouet, I have something to show you that you may find of interest."

"And who, sir, are you?" Drouet demanded.

"I," Mack said, "am a special envoy from the Council in Paris. I need you to come with me at once."

Drouet slipped on wooden sabots, wrapped himself in a long dark raincoat, and came downstairs.

"Where are we going?"

"I'll show you. Marguerite, stay here with the horses."

Mack led him through the village and out the back side, past the livery stable, the public latrine, and the maypole, coming at last to a little-used road in the woods.

"What is this?" Drouet asked.

"This is the back way through Saint-Menehould," Mack told him.

"But my dear sir, no one comes this way."

Mack was well aware of that. He also knew that just about now the great yellow coach with the king and queen should be passing through Saint-Menehould by the main road. By taking Drouet to this little-used detour, he expected to forestall any possibility of Drouet's even getting near the king, much less recognizing him.

"Sir, this is madness," Drouet said. "Nobody comes this way!"

"Not usually," Mack said. "But soft! Hear you not hoof-beats coming as from a distance and riding hard?"

Drouet listened, and Mack listened with him. It was odd how the imagination worked. Standing in this quiet place, with no sound but the gentle susurrus of the wind passing overhead through the soft boughs of chestnut and oak, he could swear he was hearing the distant sound of hooves. It was only his imagination, of course.

"Yes, I hear it," Drouet said excitedly.

"Of course you do," Mack said, congratulating himself on his scheme.

Prematurely, as it turned out, for now the sound became louder, and it was accompanied by a telltale squeak that could only be the springs on the royal carriage protesting as they jounced along the deeply rutted and high-crowned bypass road.

The little leaves shimmered in indistinct moonlight. Drouet stared, transfixed, as the sounds grew louder. And then the coach came rolling up, glimmering faintly in the moonlight. It drew up to them, moving slowly now because of the curvy schematics of the road. Glancing inside as it went by, Drouet gave a violent start of amazement at what he saw.

"Your Majesty!" he exclaimed.

"What the hell?" Mack said under his breath.

And then the coach had gone by.

"Did you see him?" Drouet asked. "It was King Louis, plain as day. I remember seeing him at the royal levee held for postmasters from all over France last year. And the queen was there, too!"

"It must have been someone else," Mack said. "There are a lot of people in France today who look like those two."

"This was them, I tell you!" Drouet cried. "Thanks, citizen, for leading me to this seldom-used byway. I must return to the village and give the alarm!"

He turned to go. Mack didn't know what had happened, but he knew that this turn of events needed instant action. He had a sandbag in his pocket, something no experienced mugger is ever without. As Drouet turned to go, Mack pulled out the sandbag and swung it, catching Drouet on the back of the skull. Drouet dropped noiselessly onto the mossy forest floor.

Moments later, a lone horseman came galloping up, his crimson cape billowing behind him. It was Mephistopheles, looking every inch the fiend from Hell on a tall black horse with fiery eyes. "Did you see the royal coach go past?" he cried.

"I did," Mack said. "What were they doing here?"

"I rerouted them," Mephistopheles said proudly. "Got them off the main road entirely so they wouldn't be seen by Drouet. I told you I'd help."

"All you've done is mess everything up," Mack said. "I told you I could handle it myself."

"I was merely trying to help," Mephistopheles said sulkily, and vanished, horse and all.

Mack turned to the unconscious Drouet. He looked as if he'd stay unconscious for quite a while. Mack dragged his body into the shrubbery and covered it with ferns. Then he hurried back to Marguerite and the horses. He still had one chance left to save the royal party. The bridge at Varennes! And with Drouet unconscious here in Saint-Menehould, he should be able to keep the bridge open, letting them escape into Belgium!

Chapter
11

The pale light of false dawn revealed the tall stone houses and narrow lanes of Varennes. Here and there, on street corners, drowsy National Guardsmen leaned on their muskets, keeping guard over the sleeping nation. Then the early morning silence was broken by the hoofbeats of Mack's horse ringing out from the cobblestones and reverberating from the stone-fronted houses.

Mack rode through town at a smart trot, and came to the bridge over the Aire. It was not a large bridge. It had a stone bed and it was buttressed from beneath by timber balks cut in the nearby Ardennes. Below it, the Aire river flowed placidly by on its journey to the sea.

The bridge was crowded, for even at this hour there were a number of carts upon it, filled with produce and driven by snappy-tempered fellows with sharp whips. It was obvious at once that nothing could get through; certainly nothing as big and cumbersome as the king's yellow coach. Drouet or not, the bridge was blocked. Unless . . . Mack decided to take a high hand.

"Clear the way!" he cried. "Hot stuff coming through!"

There was a chorus of protesting cries. Mack assumed the role of traffic policeman, waving this one to go forward and that one to back up, all of the time shouting, "In the name of the Committee on Public Safety." Cursing, hooting, drinking, whistling, but also deeply impressed, the cartmen tried to obey his orders. But as fast as Mack got a cart off, more carts piled onto the bridge. They seemed to be coming from all over, carts of all sizes and shapes, carts filled with manure, apples, corn, wheat, and other products of the ingenious French and their Belgian neighbors. Cursing and sweating, Mack stood in the center of them and tried to direct traffic. But where in hell *were* all these carts coming from? He kicked up his horse and, with Marguerite following, pressed through the cart traffic jam and crossed the river.

On the other side, he went around a little bend and came across a tall white-clad figure with an unearthly light glowing around him even in broad daylight. This figure was directing cart traffic toward the bridge.

"Who are you?" Mack demanded. "And what do you think you're doing?"

"Oops," the white-clad figure said. "You weren't supposed to see me."

At that moment Mephistopheles materialized, horse and all, beside Mack. He looked at the white-clad figure and exclaimed, "Michael! What are you doing?"

"I was just sending some carts into Varennes," Michael said, his expression somewhat sulky.

"And causing a traffic jam," Mephistopheles said, "and thereby impeding our contestant. You are interfering with the contest, Michael, and this is not permitted even of an archangel."

"Nor is it allowed to a fiend," Michael said. "I'm doing no more than you've done."

Mephistopheles glared at him. "I think we had better discuss this in private."

Michael glanced at Mack and pursed his lips. "Yes. There are matters that no human should hear." The two spirits dematerialized.

Chapter 12

Mack rushed back to the bridge. It was jammed, packed, loaded, overburdened, and suffused throughout its length and width with carts and their attendant horses and drivers. There were carts to the right and carts to the left and low, lean carts between. Mack raged among them, trying to get some order. But more and more carts came piling onto the bridge, drawn there by Michael's promise of early morning price reductions at the big market in Varennes.

The pilings groaned ominously. Then one last cart piled high with dried herring from the Baltic shouldered itself onto the bridge. There was a creak of tortured timbers, and then the whole thing gave way.

Mack scrambled off the bridge just in time to save himself a dunking. The bridge collapsed in slow motion, and carts fell dreamily into the limpid waters of the Aire. A many-throated cry of chagrin could be heard, and a great bellowing of oxen. Then there was silence. And then, from the distance, could be heard a jingling sound — the harness of the king's horses as the royal coach came up the road and pulled to a halt before the ruined bridge.

Losing no time, Mack hurried over to the royal coach. "Your Majesty!" he said. "There is still time."

"What are you talking about?" Marie Antoinette asked. "The bridge is blocked. We are undone."

"Yet there is still a way," Mack said.

"What is that, pray tell?"

"Get out of the coach at once, Your Majesties. We will purchase horses from the yokels about here and ride, back at first toward Paris, that will throw them off the trail, then we will take another branching and get across the frontier to safety. There is still time to effect your escape."

Louis turned to his wife. "What do you think?"

"Sounds too risky to me," Marie Antoinette said.

The king demurred, and Marie didn't think much of the scheme, but finally they agreed. Mack coaxed them out of the coach. They stood in the early morning light looking more than a little stupid, and as if unused to standing on their own feet on the ground. Mack hurried away and hired horses. He had calculated that they could still get out of this. After all, no one knew the king was here. No one except Drouet, and he had left him securely trussed back in Saint-Menehould.

The king approached the horse Mack had gotten for him, and somewhat hesitantly got up on it. Then Marie Antoinette climbed up on the other horse. At last, all was in readiness.

But then, just before they could ride off, a cloud of dust appeared down the road and grew larger and separated into separate riders. It was Drouet, and he was at the head of a thousand armed men.

Spotting the big yellow coach he cried, "The king and queen! Put them under arrest! They must return to Paris immediately!"

Guardsmen did as he bid. Drouet rode up to Mack.

"So, we meet again. You did me a poor service back there, citizen. I think I'll do the same for you."

Gesturing to two guards, he said, "This man is a counter-revolutionary. Seize him!"

Mack said, "Just tell me one thing. How did you get here so quickly?"

"Not through *your* help," Drouet said. "Luckily for me, this gentleman came along and rendered assistance."

Another rider trotted up and Mack saw that it was Faust. "You again!" he breathed.

Faust smiled smugly. "I got away from the soldiers easily enough, and then I found this fellow and helped him, and so put paid to your scheme."

Then Mephistopheles appeared. "Let that man go," he said to Drouet.

Drouet was badly frightened by the demon, but he blustered, "We're holding this man for the tribunal."

Mephistopheles said, "Sorry. Supernatural matters take precedence. This is the end of the contest."

He reached out and put his hand on Mack's shoulder. They vanished together. A moment later, Marguerite vanished, too.

JUDGMENT

Chapter 1

After Mephistopheles conjured him away from Varennes, there was a break in the continuity of Mack's consciousness. He fell into dreams of a strange sort, but the details swam out of his grasp. Then there was a period of sleep, and finally, Mack awoke.

He found himself lying on a green couch in a hazy, indistinct sort of place. He tried to make out details, but they fuzzed before his eyes. Still, he knew of only one place that had this sort of green couch. He had to be in Mephistopheles' office in Limbo!

He got up and looked around. Through a low archway there was another room, and in it was the storage locker with the salvaged Botticelli.

There was the sound of a door opening and Mack turned, ready for trouble. Ylith came in. She was wearing a beige sheath dress that came down to midcalf on her fine legs. Her long dark hair was worn in a soft upsweep and pinned in place by imitation tortoiseshell combs. Her face was customarily pale, but a quick dab of rouge had put dots of color in her cheeks.

"It's all over," she said. "That was the last sequence where you needed to make a choice."

"I thought that's what Mephistopheles said! What happens now?"

"Now the judging begins. That's where I'm going. I just stopped by to see how you were."

"That was good of you. I don't suppose I was invited to the judging?"

"Not that I know of," Ylith said.

"That's very like them," Mack said with some bitterness. "Mephistopheles was all smiles and attention when there was something he wanted me to do, but now that it's over I don't even get asked to the celebration."

"Humans are rarely asked to these matters," Ylith said. "But of course I see what you mean."

"And when do I get my reward?"

"I don't know anything about that," Ylith said. "You'll just have to wait. This is Limbo, and in Limbo, people wait."

Ylith conjured herself away with an elegant move of her slim hands. Mack paced around for a while, then saw a pile of books on a little table and sat down in a chair beside them. He picked up *The Road to Hell and How to Find It*, a product of the Satanic Press. He read, "Do you really want to get into Hell? Don't be surprised. A lot of people do! You're not alone. Hell is characterized by the importance of the appetites. Unlike the stories told, you can feed these appetites perfectly well in Hell. Trouble is, they never stay fed. But they never did when you were alive, either. Let us consider. . . ."

Suddenly there was a flash of light and a puff of smoke. When the smoke cleared away Faust was standing there. He was looking good, dressed in a fine scholar's gown with an ermine collar.

"Hi, there!" Mack said, happy to see a familiar face, even if it was Faust's, and even if it was frowning.

Faust said, "Look, I'm in a hurry. Did you see a tall, very skinny man with yellowish eyes and long, lank dark hair and a somewhat weird expression go by here?"

Mack shook his head. "Nobody's passed this way since I've been here except for a female spirit named Ylith."

"No, she's not the one I'm looking for. The count of Saint-

Germain said he'd meet me here. I hope he's not going to be late."

"Who's he?"

Faust gave him a superior look. "Only one of the world's greatest magicians, that's who. He came along after your time."

"But your time is also my time. How do *you* know about him?"

"Oh, well," Faust said, "I am a great magician myself, the greatest who ever lived, and it is to be expected that I would know the important men in my line of work past and future. Living or dead, or yet unborn, we magicians stay in touch."

"Why did you call up this Saint-Germain guy?"

"I'm afraid it would be premature for me to tell you," Faust said. "Let's just say I have a little surprise in store."

"A surprise? But the contest is over."

"The contest is indeed over, though it will be interesting to hear what Ananke will make of your clumsy and uninformed efforts to influence history. But despite this being the end, the last word has not yet been spoken. To put it to you succinctly, my dear Mack, Faust himself has not yet been heard from."

"Faust? You mean you?"

"Of course I mean me! I am Faust, am I not?"

"In a way. But in a way I'm Faust, too."

Faust looked at Mack long and hard, and then threw back his head and laughed.

"You, Faust? My dear fellow, you are the very opposite of the Faustian ideal, an abject sort of creature, mean-spirited, docile to your masters, treacherous to your friends, vulgar, uninformed as to history, philosophy, politics, chemistry, optics, alchemy, ethics, and, above all, the master science, magic." Faust smiled cruelly. "Now, Mack, you may have filled Faust's shoes for a time, as a child can step into an adult's boots, and perhaps even take a step or two. But now, thankfully, your clownlike moment on the stage of human history is over. My friend, there is nothing Faustian about you, or, indeed, anything even interesting about you. You are one of the lowest common denominators of humanity, and we don't need you here any longer."

"Oh, is that so?" Mack said, his mind boiling with incoherent retorts. But he spoke to the empty air because with a single intricate gesture of his left hand, Faust had conjured himself away.

"I wish I could do that," Mack said aloud, alone again in the Waiting Room in Limbo, rage leaking out of him and being replaced by self-pity. He said aloud, "It isn't fair, putting me up against all these famous people, to say nothing of spirits who can conjure themselves where they please in the twinkling of an eye, whereas I, a common, earthy sort of man, must proceed on foot, and make effort, and take every step that lies between here and there."

"What dreary self-pitying do I hear?" a deep and sarcastic voice behind him said.

Mack turned quickly, startled, because he had thought himself entirely alone. There was Odysseus, tall and splendid, magnificent in a freshly pressed white tunic. Thrown over it was a cloak with the many folds beloved by sculptors. Odysseus had a face so noble that it could make a common man like Mack, with his common features and snub nose and freckles, consider himself no comelier than an ape. Odysseus stood a head taller than Mack, his skin bronzed, muscles rippling in his well-formed arms.

"Hello, Odysseus," Mack said. "What are you up to?"

"I'm on my way to the great assembly hall to listen to Ananke's judgment and perhaps offer a few ideas of my own. And you?"

"I'm waiting for Mephistopheles to come with the reward he promised me."

Odysseus shrugged. "Do you think it's wise to take it? Personally, I wouldn't accept an obol from these present-day devils. They seek to enslave you by making you dependent on them. But to each his own. Farewell, Mack."

And with that, Odysseus released a Traveling Spell from his leather sack of spells and vanished from sight.

"These old Greeks think they're such big deals," Mack said peevishly when Odysseus had gone. "They've got all those old gods working for them, that's why they can get so much done. And they stick together, the ancient gods and classical men. Whereas someone like myself, a modern man, has only the feebleness of his own intellect to steer him through the complexities of the various worlds, and only the faltering strength of his own two legs to carry him where he might wish to go. But there are journeys too far for human legs."

"Say you so?" said a voice behind him.

Mack had a moment to wonder if there was some special mechanism in the universe that enabled people always to conjure themselves into existence behind his back. He turned and beheld Rognir the dwarf, who had just come up through a hole in the floor that he had cut with his mattock.

"Of course I say so," Mack said. "Everyone else around here gets about by magic. They just have to say the word and they're where they want to be. But I am forced to walk, and I don't even know where I'm going."

"That's really tough," Rognir said with heavy sarcasm. "What do you think I do, buster?"

"You? I never thought about it. How *do* you get around?"

"Dwarves travel in the old-fashioned way. On foot. Dwarves don't *just* walk, however. They first dig tunnels to wherever they want to go, and *then* walk. You think it's easy to build a tunnel?"

"I suppose it's not," Mack said. He thought about it for a moment. "I suppose sometimes you encounter rock."

"The places we tunnel through are made up more of rock than of dirt," Rognir said. "We dwarves get positively cheerful when there's nothing but *dirt* to tunnel through. Rocks and boulders are bad enough, but the worst is tunneling under a swamp. You have to shore up the tunnel as you go along, and that means you have to cut balks of wood and drag them to where you need them. Balks of wood don't come ready-cut, and forests are usually far away from where you want the wood. Sometimes we use shaggy little ponies to help us, but most of the time it's just muscle power and grit."

"I guess you don't have it very good."

"Wrong again," Rognir said. "We dwarves feel that we have it very good indeed. We are not humans, remember. We are a class of supernatural being, though we don't make a big deal of it. We could have petitioned the high powers for special abilities. But that's not our way. We are the one and only race in the cosmos that isn't asking anybody for anything."

"Aren't you concerned about who wins the contest between Light and Dark?"

"Not in the slightest. The outcome doesn't affect us dwarves. Concerns about Good and Evil leave us cold. Dwarves know no good except digging, and no bad except digging, either. Our destiny is mapped out from birth to death: we dig till we drop, and when we're not digging we walk our tunnels and find jewels and attend jamborees. We don't expect spirits to come along and do our work for us."

"Well, I suppose I should feel properly ashamed of myself," Mack said, feeling, in fact, a little abashed. "But what do you expect me to do?"

"Tell me if I'm wrong," Rognir said, "but isn't it true that all these spirits and demigods and Faust himself are fighting for the right to rule mankind for the next thousand years?"

"That's my understanding of it," Mack said.

"Fine. So what are you going to do about it?"

"Me? You mean me personally?"

"That's who I'm referring to," Rognir said.

"Why . . . Nothing, I suppose. There's nothing I *can* do. And if there were, why should I?"

"Because it's *your destiny* they're talking about, dummy," Rognir said. "Don't you want a say in it?"

"Of course I do! But who am I to tell people how I should be ruled?"

"Who *is* the one to speak for mankind? Is it Faust?"

Mack shook his head. "Faust thinks he's Mr. Universal, but he's really just a loudmouth magician with a couple of good tricks. People like that are different from the rest of us. I know some of their tricks, but when they talk about the higher aspects of the alchemist's art it leaves me cold."

"Quite properly so," Rognir said. "It's all a lot of hot air. There's only digging. That's for us, the dwarves, of course. As for you, why should you let a mug like Faust tell you how you are to be ruled?"

Mack stared at him. "But what can I do?"

"For one thing," Rognir said, "you can get angry."

"But I'm not mad at anyone," Mack said. But even as he denied it, he felt the stirrings of a long-suppressed rage. At first he thought he was faking it, as he had faked so many things in his life, and he told himself to calm down, it would go away. But this feeling of rage didn't go away. Instead it grew and spread through his head, until he could feel black anger inflaming his eyeballs, engorging the veins of his neck, threatening to burst out the top of his head.

"Well, damn it, it's not right!" he burst out at last. "Nobody should decide the fate of the common man but the common man himself. It's been too long that we've let spirits, and so-called great men like Faust, decide our destinies for us. Now is the time to do something about it!"

"Now you're talking," Rognir said.

Mack's shoulders sagged. "But what can I do?"

"It's an interesting question," Rognir said, and turned to the tunnel he had just excavated and walked into it.

Mack stood still in the room and stared for a while at the hole Rognir had disappeared through. He had a great desire to dive into it himself. But of course men don't dive into tunnels like dwarves. Mack crossed the room and opened the door. Outside, the vast, indistinct landscape of Limbo spread out before him. There were hills ahead, but they were nebulous, and seemed to disappear into the clouds, unless those were mist-veiled mountains behind them.

Looking more closely, Mack saw there was the indication of a path. He followed it through swirling white and yellow mists. Presently he came to a crossroads. There was a sign that read ROAD TO EARTH and pointed one way, ROAD TO HELL another way, THE WAY YOU'VE COME pointing back the way he had come, and ROAD TO HEAVEN as the last direction. Mack made up his mind and started walking.

Chapter 2

It was a clear day in the part of Limbo reserved for the judgment of mankind's destiny. The sky was fishbelly white, but that was not unusual for the time of year. A few snowflakes had fallen earlier, but no real accumulation was expected. In the distance, the hills of Nothingness were a low blue line on the horizon. It was literally true that on a clear day you could see forever.

Mephistopheles and the Archangel Michael were sitting side by side on a tall pillar recently vacated by Simon Stylites, who had found a better way to mortify his spirit by picking a punishment from the future and forcing himself to watch televised reruns of every game the Tampa Bay Buccaneers had ever played.

Michael hadn't visited Limbo in quite a while, not since he had met with Mephistopheles to set the contest. He was happy to see that nothing much had changed. There was still the same dear old vagueness about where the sky ended and where the land began, the same pleasing ambiguity over the colors of things, the same uncertainty as to shapes. Vagueness! And its concomitant, moral uncertainty! After a long life of absolutes, there was something refreshing about it.

"Limbo is just the same as it ever was!" Michael said.

"My dear archangel," Mephistopheles said, "if you rein in your passion for paradox for a moment, you can see that there's been a lot of change around here. Don't you notice all the building that's going on?"

"Oh, that, of course," Michael said. "But that's quite ephemeral. Underneath it's the same dear old Limbo." He peered in a westerly direction. "What *are* they putting up there?"

Mephistopheles looked in the indicated direction. "Didn't you know? That's the new Palace of Justice, where the judgment will be announced."

Michael peered at it. "It seems to be a most noble structure."

"It's certainly large enough," Mephistopheles said. "I understand quite a few guests have been invited from both sides. Even some humans, though that's quite unusual."

"Well, it seems only right," Michael said. "After all, it *is* their destiny being decided."

"So what?" Mephistopheles snorted. "The forces of Light and Dark never consulted mankind back in the good old days. We just told them the way it was going to be, and they had to like it or lump it."

"Science and rationalism have changed all that," Michael said. "It's what is called progress. A good thing on balance, I believe."

"Of course you believe that," Mephistopheles said. "What else could you say, given your predisposition to affirm?"

"And what else could you say but the contrary?" Michael asked.

"You've got a point there," Mephistopheles admitted. "We're both restricted in our viewpoints."

"Exactly. That's why we have Ananke to do the judging."

"Where *is* Ananke, by the way?"

"No one has seen her latest incarnation. Necessity has strange ways of conducting herself. And there's no use complaining about it. She just says it's Necessary, and never explains why."

"Who's that coming?" Mephistopheles asked.

Michael looked out across Limbo. Even with perfect vision, it took him a moment to bring into focus something as small as a man on the vast landscape of zilch.

"That's Mack the Club!" Michael said.

Mephistopheles looked. "Are you quite sure? That is the man I've been dealing with during this contest."

"Oh, it's definitely Mack," Michael said. "Is it possible that you made a mistake in Cracow, my dear demon? Has the wrong Faust been performing in your contest?"

Mephistopheles looked again, and his lips thinned. His dark eyes seemed to smolder. Glaring at Michael, he said, "I seem to see a fine spiritual hand in all this!"

"You give me too much credit," Michael said.

Mephistopheles looked again. "That's definitely the fellow who's been doing the contest. Are you sure he's not Faust?"

"Afraid not. His name is Mack, and he is a common criminal. I'm afraid you picked the wrong man to decide human destiny, my dear Mephistopheles."

"And you have picked the wrong devil if you think you can get away with this!"

Michael smiled but did not reply.

Mephistopheles said, "We'll settle this later. I must get down to the banquet hall. Darkside is catering the refreshments this time." He peered out across Limbo again. "Where *is* that fellow going?"

"Read the signpost. He is on the road to Heaven," Michael said.

"Really? I didn't know *that* was the direction to it!"

"It changes from time to time," Michael said.

"But why?"

"We of the forces of Good," Michael said with dignity, "try not to spend too much time asking why."

Mephistopheles shrugged. Together the two great spirits proceeded to the Palace of Justice.

Chapter 3

Azzie was strolling through the outer courts of the Palace of Justice when he came across Michelangelo himself. He recognized the painter from pictures he'd seen of him in art books at Demon U. Michelangelo was just putting the finishing touches on a gigantic fresco.

"Looks good," Azzie said, moving behind the painter.

"Would you mind getting out of my light?" Michelangelo said. "The working conditions are bad enough here without you making them worse."

Azzie moved. "It must be wonderful to create art."

Michelangelo sneered and wiped his sweaty forehead with a paint rag. "This isn't art. I'm just doing some touch-up on an old piece of mine."

"But you could do original painting if you wanted to, couldn't you?" Azzie asked.

"Sure. But in order to paint, a man must aspire, and what is there to aspire to after you've reached Heaven?"

Azzie had no answer because he'd never thought about it. Michelangelo returned to his work, and, watching him for a moment, Azzie thought he looked perfectly content.

Outside the great auditorium, in the circular corridors that surrounded the circular building, innumerable spirits were standing around, drinks in hand, eating hors d'oeuvres and talking. There were more spirits here than the place could hold, in fact, because every aethereal, indeed, the greater part of all sentient beings, had wanted to attend. The front office had come up with some new packing orders in an attempt to accommodate all. Even so, the concept of virtual space had had to be invoked, to the distaste of the purists who felt that either you're there or you're not there.

This was the big day, Judgment Day, the biggest event of the Millennium, the super Mardi Gras of the universe. It was time for everyone to get together with everyone else. Groups of spirits kept on arriving, looking around with awe at the Palace of Justice, then exclaiming, "Gee, so this is the place!" And then going on to somewhere else, usually the cafeteria, where for the most part they ordered light salads, because they didn't want to lose their appetite for the orgy that was promised if Bad won, or the feast that would be presented if the victor was Good.

All this noise and excitement was a change for Limbo. Limbo was usually a quiet place without anything much happening in the way of entertainment. The inhabitants of Limbo didn't expect much and were willing to live and let live. They tended not to make value judgments, since that was the sole stock in trade of the two adjoining principalities of Dark and Light. The Limboans sauntered along in their strange vague milieu, eating occasional absent-minded meals, making love in their inadequate way, having mediocre poetry readings and folk dance festivals of no great merit. Time was so eventless here that nobody bothered to keep it. The lack of seasons also contributed to the monotony. And now all of a sudden they were hosting the contest of the Millennium. It just went to show you could never tell.

Chapter
4

In the great assembly hall, the central point of the Palace of Justice, all was in readiness for the great event. The audience sat in long curving rows chatting to each other, but for the most part sitting quietly, except in the sections marked for virtual reality, where myriads of onlookers were shuffled in and out at close to the speed of light, so that everyone who wanted to could see the performance without appreciable delay.

And yet, one thing wasn't right. Ananke hadn't shown up.

No one had any doubt that the great goddess Necessity would reveal herself when she was ready, and that she would choose what she considered a suitable vehicle in which to do so. But who would it be? Expectations in the audience ran high, and people kept on craning their necks around hoping to catch the transformation. But even these knowledgeable ones were surprised when Marguerite, sitting by herself in a back row, suddenly arose as two friars, one blind, the other mute, came down the aisle with their staves tapping, walking directly toward her.

The mute one stared. The blind one turned his face upwards, and, with an expression of ecstasy, said, "She is come to us at last!"

Marguerite, her eyes wide and glowing like opals, came out of her seat and into the aisle. People made way for her as, accompanied by her friars, who fell into step behind her, she made her way to the stage. Her face was ivory white, her lips were pale, and her glowing eyes were like tiny flames in a dark mirror. She seemed far more than a mortal woman at that point.

There was not a sound from the audience as she moved to the throne that had been prepared for her. She sat down lightly, and turned to face the audience.

"The time of Judgment is at hand. But first, I believe there is one who would speak."

Odysseus stood up, made a deep bow, walked forward, stopped, and turned to address his first remarks to Ananke.

"My greetings to you, Great Goddess. I know, as well as all of us, that you rule everything and everyone. Yet since this is to be a contest to settle the self-determination you have graciously allowed for mankind, I would take it as an honor if you would let me put forth a claim that has not been heard here."

"Come up to the stage and speak, Odysseus," Ananke said. "Great is your fame in the annals of mankind. A viewpoint such as yours must be heard."

Odysseus mounted to the stage, arranged his cloak, and began in a low, rumbling voice.

"I should like to propose," Odysseus said, "that all assembled here consider a proposition I am about to put before you. My idea is simple, and even though it may seem revolutionary, I beg you to consider it. So here it is: I propose that you bring the old Hellenic gods back to Earth and leave human destiny in their hands."

There was a scattered murmur of voices in the audience, but Ananke held up her hand for silence. Odysseus continued.

"Consider: You already use a Greek concept, Ananke, Necessity, as your final arbiter of what is to be. Your concepts of good and evil, which began as absolutist statements in the early days of the Church, have been ameliorated to the point where they make no difference at all. The gains you have made in truth have been accompanied by a loss in veracity. In place of the old free dialectic of Socrates and the Sophists, you have the didacticism of the various leaders of religions, churches, and covens. You will permit me to say to you that this is all rather crude, intellectually unsound, and unworthy of human beings with a capacity for reason. Why let yourselves be swayed by emotional statements? Why preach salvation when you don't believe in it yourselves? I beg of you, bring forth the reign of the old gods again, the irrational old gods with human qualities. Let Ares rage on the battlefield as he has never stopped doing. Let Athene stand for what is good and pure, and put Zeus back as divine arbiter, all-powerful but not all-wise. Our contribution, the Greek contribution, was to propose gods who were very powerful but not very smart. We cut the cloth of the supernatural to cover the frailties of our own inner beings. Now let's have an end of hypocrisy, admit that the new gods and spirits didn't work, and return to the old ways. If nothing else it will be an aesthetic gain."

When Odysseus had finished and returned to his place in the audience, there was much buzzing of conversation among the myriad sitting spirits. But Ananke called for order and said, "Excellent are the words of Odysseus, and they will be considered. But we have another speaker who wishes to put forth a claim, and he is as famous in his way as Odysseus in his. I refer to none other than Dr. Johann Faust, who has gone to considerable difficulty to be with us today. I give you Dr. Faust."

Faust walked up to the stage, whispered, "Thank you, Marguerite, I'll make it up to you somehow," then turned to the assembled spirits.

"My right honorable friend, Odysseus, has been known throughout history for his ability to charm through words. I myself am no charmer. I'll tell you some blunt truths, however, and you can make of them what you will. First, as to Odysseus' argument: A classical construct has great charm, no doubt, but no force of rightness about it. Those Hellenic fellows and their gods have had their day. The world forgot their religious views with very little regret. We don't need that lot back again. Not them or any other gods. I say, let's put down all the gods, both ancient and modern. We men don't need gods. We are like workers voting for a class of superior beings with which to oppress themselves. What do we need with these airy concoctions? Why should gods or devils or anything else rule our fate? I am Faust and I stand for man triumphant, man in all his frailties ruling his own destiny, without recourse to the supernatural. With but a single decision we could dissolve the whole thing—the entire airy parliament of devils and angels who plague us with their cross talk and their endless arguments. Man will do his best, and needs no supernaturalism to exhort him to greater efforts. But if a go-between is needed, if a council of wise men is required, I have brought forth a group of people with more right to rule mankind than all these deities with their conniving qualities. I say, let the magicians rule us! They have always done so; we have just not admitted it to ourselves."

Faust clapped his hands. A line of men walked slowly out onto the stage.

Faust said, "Here are Cagliostro, Paracelsus, Saint-Germain, and many others. This is the council that should advise the world."

Michael stood up and said, "You can't do this, Faust."

"The hell you say. I'm here and I'm doing it. You have discounted man's ability to call up magic. I have here the greatest seers that ever lived. They have plumbed Nature's secrets. Their gifts belong to them as right of conquest, not the gift of some masquerading spirit. We humans can take care of ourselves, led by these geniuses, who are the precursors of the scientists who will come later."

"This is quite out of line," Michael said. "Your gathering all these magicians is illegal, impossible, and outside the rules. Time and space can't be manipulated in this way. Am I right, Mephistopheles?"

"Exactly what I was going to say."

"I defy you!" Faust said. "We magicians repudiate devil and God! Get away from us with your incomprehensible rules! We will rule ourselves."

Both Michael and Mephistopheles bellowed, "Begone!"

Faust and his magicians stood firm.

Michael said, "Let Ananke decide, for Necessity rules us all."

Faust said, "Ananke, you can see that I am right."

Marguerite wavered. "Yes, Faust, you are right."

"Then you must decide in our favor."

"No, Faust, I cannot."

"Why? Why?"

"Because, in the conjectures of Necessity, being right is only one quality to select for. There are others, and they are equally important in the makeup of what will be."

"What are they?"

"There is warmth, Faust, and you have none. There is the ability to love, Faust, and you do not have it. There is the ability to rule yourself, and you, Faust, do not have it. There is compassion, Faust, and you do not have that, either. What Odysseus proposed was nostalgic, but your ideas are anathema. Therefore, Faust, despite a valiant effort, you have lost and the world will continue without you telling it what to do."

There were cries from the audience. "But who has won, Dark or Light?"

Ananke held the audience in her gaze. "Now, as to the results. Let's start from the top and work down. But first, as to the ancient gods and the old religion, that is mere sentimentality, because the old never returns, never comes back into favor. The old gods are gone, and they will not return. As for Faust, he will put himself to be your new leader. But there are a few things to be said about Faust, too, notably, he is cold, indifferent, doesn't really care to lead you. These are the various claims, and we leave them where we found them.

"Now comes the judgment of what is and what will be.

Each of the acts which Mack performed may of course be judged in a variety of ways, in terms of results, in terms of intent, in terms of the urban or rural influences — in short, they provide a dialectical mess which Good and Bad could argue about for another Millennium. Here are the results:

"First, Constantinople. The icon that Mack saved is later destroyed. The city gets sacked by those who came to preserve it. Bad wins a point here.

"Second, Kublai Khan loses his scepter. The loss of the scepter deprives the Mongol horde of part of its luck and driving energy. Threat to Western civilization eased. Good wins a point thereby.

"Third, in Florence, a priceless work of art is saved. De' Medici and Savonarola, both potential influences for Evil, die untimely deaths, sparing the world much woe. A point for Good.

"Fourth, Dr. Dee's mirror was not really important. But Marlowe was. Had he lived he would have written more edifying and, ultimately, morally beneficial works. A second point for Bad.

"Fifth, saving or not saving the French royal family wouldn't have made that much difference in the long run, in averting the democratic reforms of the nineteenth century. But evil was done to the king and queen. A tie here.

"Finally, there was cheating on both sides. This, too, cancels out. This contest is hereby declared no contest!"

Chapter 5

Mephistopheles didn't find out at this time. But later he got the news from an angel who had been traveling down from Heaven to Limbo to be present at the announcing of the contest winner. This angel had chosen to go by her own wing power, because she felt she needed the exercise and because it was a long time since she had seen the sights along the way. As she made her way down from the heavenly mansions, leaving behind one of the very desirable suburbs of Heaven, whom should she see but Mack, trudging along up the rocky road that led to the supernal heights of the divine palace above. He was moving slowly, the angel noted, but he was on his own two feet and he was moving. That was all the angel knew.

"But where can he be headed?" Mephistopheles asked.

"He looked like he was going to see You Know Who," the angel said.

"Not You Know Who!" cried Michael.

"That's how it looked. Of course, it's possible he was just sightseeing."

"But how can he presume to seek out God? How dare he? Without a pass? Without a recommendation? Without an escort of spiritual dignitaries of proven piety? It is unheard-of."

"It's what's happening," the angel said.

"I wish I could see what's going on," Michael said, and Mephistopheles nodded in agreement.

Chapter
6

When Mack reached the topmost cloud mountain, he beheld, directly in front of him, the great pearly gates, which opened slowly on their valves of gold as he approached. He entered, and found himself in a bounteous garden in which every tree and bush bore good things, and there was not a slug or weevil in sight. And then a man came hurrying up to Mack, a tall, bearded man in a white robe before whom Mack bowed low, saying, "Hello, God." The man hastened to help him to his feet, saying, "No, no, don't bow to me, I'm not God. I'm afraid He can't come talk with you right now, as He'd love to do, but He sent me, His servant, to tell you that He has decided to overrule Ananke and proclaim you the true victor in the contest."

"Me?" cried Mack. "But what have I done to deserve that?"

"I'm not clear on the details," the bearded man said. "And anyhow, it's nothing personal. It's just that a decision has been made to turn the workings of the world over to common rogues and people no better than they ought to be. The old gods have tried to lead mankind and failed, God and the devil have tried and failed, Law has tried and failed, Reason has been insufficient, and even Chaos has proven insufficient. This is the era of the common man. Your simple, self-serving actions, Mack, done for your own good but with a vague hope that they would serve nobler purposes, must be declared the winner of this contest, for even that hint of idealism has in it more conviction than all those greater and more complicated ideas."

Mack was dumbfounded. "Me run things? No, it's impossible, I won't hear of it. Frankly, it sounds like blasphemy."

"God exists in the blasphemy, the devil in the piety."

"Look," Mack said, "I think I'd better discuss this with God Himself."

"If only that could be!" the man said sadly. "But the One God is not to be seen or talked to, not even here in Heaven. We have searched for Him and He simply isn't here. He seems to have absented Himself. There are even those who say He never existed, and of course we have no photographs to prove that He did. But our legends say that at one time He did exist, and that the angels visited Him often and basked in His countenance. He used to tell them that Heaven and Hell were in the details. No one understood that. He told them that as below, so above. No one understood what that meant until slums began to appear in Heaven, and then crime."

"Crime in Heaven?" Mack said. "I can't believe that."

"You'd be surprised what goes on here. It was along about that time that He suddenly told everyone that He wasn't God at all, not the big one, the immanent, the indwelling, no, He was standing in for God because God had had something else to do. But everyone wondered what that could be. Some suspected that He was starting things all over again in another space and time, and this time simplifying them so that they worked. It was felt by general consent that God was disappointed with how things had turned out in this universe, though of course, being a gentleman, He'd never breathed a word about it. Perhaps 'intimated' would be a better word."

Mack stared at the bearded man in the white robe, then said, "You really are God, aren't you?"

"Well, yes, in a manner of speaking. What's the matter?"

"Oh, nothing," Mack said.

"You're disappointed, aren't you?" said God. "You expected Someone Else."

"No, no, not at all."

"I know that's what you're thinking. Remember, I'm omniscient. That's one of my attributes."

"I know. Omnipotence, too."

"Well, yes, that. But that's a power best left in abeyance. God's real task is resisting His own omnipotence and refusing to be bound by it."

"Bound by omnipotence? How can that be?"

"Omnipotence is a strong hindrance when combined with omniscience and compassion. There's always such a temptation to interfere on the side of gentleness, to right a wrong."

"So why not do that?"

"If I put my omnipotence in the service of my omniscience, the result would be a clockwork universe. There'd be no free will. No one would suffer the consequences of their actions. I'd always have to be there to see that no sparrow fell from the sky, that no person died in a traffic accident, that no doe was ever taken by a leopard, that no human went hungry, naked, cold, that no one died before their time, or, indeed, why not go all the way and make it so they don't die at all?"

"That sounds good to me," Mack said.

"That's because you haven't thought it through. Suppose everything that ever had been continued to exist. All of them with their claims, their priorities, their desires. All of which must be met. And of course some other arrangements must be made. If the leopard isn't allowed to eat the doe, then we have to provide other food for him. Turn him into a vegetarian? But what makes you think that plants don't know they're being eaten, and don't resent it as much as you would if someone were eating you? You see the ramifications. It would leave me doing everything, interfering constantly. People's lives would be unutterably boring if I did all the important stuff for them."

"I see there's quite a lot for You to think about," Mack said. "But then, You're omniscient. That must help."

"My omniscience tells me to limit my omnipotence."

"And what about Good and Evil?"

"Well, I realized, of course, that it was absolutely important, but I could never quite figure out which was which. It was all very complicated. I had deliberately projected this less-than-godlike image of myself. Even though I am a god, and the only God at that, I still had a right to be humble. And I had the right to give myself something to be humble about. Even though I was omniscient and omnipotent, I refused to use those powers. I felt it was an unnecessary restriction, trying to make Good right all the time. It seemed very partisan and one-sided to have to support Good constantly. Anyhow, since I was omniscient in those days, I knew that in some ultimate analysis, Good and Evil were complementary, equal. Not that that solved anything. I refused to be checked by it. I said the trouble with knowing everything was that you never learned anything. I preferred to go on learning. Maybe I *did* know the secret reason behind everything. I never let myself know what that secret was. I have said that even God is entitled to His secrets, and had the right and duty not to know everything."

"But what am I supposed to learn from all this?" Mack said.

"That you're as free as I am. It may not be much, but it's *something*, isn't it?"

Chapter 7

There's always a letdown after something as big as a Millennial contest. Soon after it was over, Azzie found himself at loose ends again. He decided to see what had happened to Faust and the others.

He found Faust in a tavern outside of Cracow. Amazingly enough, the angel Babriel was also there, sitting with him in a booth and drinking a beer. They welcomed Azzie when he came in and offered him a drink.

Faust continued his conversation, saying, "Did you hear that dame, Ananke? That was Marguerite, who earlier did everything she could to win me!"

"It was nothing personal, old boy," Babriel said. "She was speaking as Necessity."

"Yes, but why did Ananke choose her?" He thought about it a moment, then said, "I suppose it's because she had the qualities that Necessity required in its blind direction of human destiny."

Babriel blinked, sipped his ichor, put it down. "You see that, do you? You've learned something, Faust!"

"Not enough," Faust said. "We could have done it, Babriel! We humans, I mean. We could have thrown off all the yokes. If only I'd . . ."

"Not you alone," Babriel said. "I hate to sound smug, but it was the failings of all mankind that were judged, not just yours."

"There's something unsound about it," Faust said. "It's

rigged against us from the beginning. They find what qualities we're lacking, then say that those are the ones they want, and that we lose because we don't have them. When we get those qualities, they have something else in mind. But where would they even get the idea of how we should behave if not from us?"

"True enough," Babriel said. "Come now, let's not talk politics. The game is over. Let's have a drink, talk over the good times we had, and be on our way."

Just then Mack came in, singing a student's song. Since the contest he had pulled himself together remarkably. He was a merchant now, and on his way to becoming wealthy. He had a beautiful girlfriend who looked a lot like Marguerite. Since his visit to Heaven, he had taken up his life on Earth again with good cheer.

The others gathered around him. Azzie asked, "So what did He say?"

"Who?"

"God, of course. We watched from the Palace of Justice as you mounted into Heaven. What did you learn?"

Mack blinked and looked uncomfortable. "I can't say that I learned anything. Anyhow, it wasn't God I saw. It was just a friend of His."

"But he told you you won the contest, didn't he?"

"Not exactly. My understanding was, I got to do whatever I wanted with my own life. And that's what I'm doing."

"Is that all you can tell us?" Azzie asked.

Mack frowned and didn't answer. Then he smiled again.

"Come, friends," he said, "I've reserved a table for us at the Wounded Duck. They have a roast goose ready for us. We'll eat and toast our accomplishments and laugh at our failures."

That seemed a good idea to everyone. But Faust said he'd be along later. He left the tavern and walked down Little Casimir Street, and came to the elegant little tea shop where he'd arranged to meet Helen. He went in.

Helen was seated at a little table, sipping orange pekoe. She smiled coldly when he entered and sat down.

"So, my dear," Faust said, "you gave those old ladies the slip. And you've come back to me!"

"Only to say good-bye, Johann," Helen said.

"Oh? That is your decision?"

"I've decided to return to Achilles," Helen said, nodding. "That's a necessary part of the Helen archetype. I returned finally to Menelaus when he was my husband, you know."

"Well, I suppose it's for the best," Faust said, not really sorry to see her go, because she was entirely too much of a good thing. "Our archetypes aren't well suited to each other. We are both dominant, unique. But imagine the fun we could have had!"

"More fun for you than for me," Helen said. "And besides, you prefer the little goosegirl type. Why don't you take up again with your Marguerite?"

"How did you know about her?" Faust demanded. "Never mind, I know you won't tell me. Anyhow, Marguerite is out. The fact of the matter is, I don't really respect her, even if she was Ananke, however briefly."

There came a hammering at the tea shop door. Then there was a chewing sound, as of three old crones gnawing on the wood. Green slime ran under the door.

"We mustn't keep the Weird Sisters waiting," Helen said, arising and walking to the door.

Alone in the tavern, Faust stared out into space, seeing nothing but his own shattered dreams. No one pleased him. Men, women, spirits, all seemed entirely too light-minded. Even Ananke had been a lightweight, intellectually. He remembered how good it had felt, standing at the head of the greatest legion of magicians ever assembled. They could have ushered in a new age. Under their rule, mankind would finally have amounted to something. . . . Or died trying! Though it was not yet to be. But someday . . . Someday, mankind would be worthy of Faust. *Then* let them look out!

He rose to leave the tea shop. And then there was a brightening in the air and Ylith stood before him, looking quite fetching. Faust gazed at her without change of expression. He supposed she had come bearing another announcement from Good or from Bad, and he didn't want to hear it.

"Yes," he said, "what is it?"

"I've been thinking," Ylith said. Then she hesitated. She was wearing a long gown, emerald green, gathered in front in the Empire fashion. A single strand of glowing pearls set off her slender neck. Her hair was pulled back, emphasizing the long oval of her face.

She continued, "I used to be a witch who served the forces of Dark. Then I converted to Light. But I have found that the two are very much alike in certain important aspects."

"No doubt," Faust said. "But why are you telling me all this?"

"Because I want to begin again," Ylith said. "I want a new life, beyond Good and Evil. I thought of you, Faust. Right or wrong, you go your own way. And so I thought I'd ask you — do you by any chance need an assistant?"

Faust looked at her. She was comely, she was intelligent, and she was smiling. He straightened his back and squared his shoulders. He could feel the Faustian spirit returning to him.

"Yes," he said. "I think this is a matter we might pursue to our mutual satisfaction. Sit down, dear lady. Stay. This may be the beginning of a beautiful moment."

About the Author

ROGER ZELAZNY is the author of the Hugo-winning *Lord of Light* and the bestselling *Amber* series, including the classic *Nine Princes in Amber*. He is a six-time Hugo winner and has won three Nebula Awards.

ROBERT SHECKLEY is a novelist and scriptwriter whose short fiction has appeared in *Playboy, Atlantic Monthly,* and *The Magazine of Fantasy and Science Fiction*. One of his short stories was adapted to film as *The Tenth Victim*.